ACCURSED

THE REALM TRILOGY
BOOK THREE

L. MARIE WOOD

Mocha Memoirs Press

COPYRIGHT NOTICE

PRAISE FOR L. MARIE WOOD

"There's a wicked atmosphere which grows page after page right until the end..." —Buried.com

"...at times [Crescendo] actually made me shiver." —Danielle Naibert, editor, *Horror Haven*

"A chilling debut and a must-read for lovers of Horror and Mystery." —C. Highsmith-Hooks, author, *The Soul of a Black Woman*

"Wood fearlessly allows all her characters to be exactly who they are, whether they're noble or petty, weak or strong." —RJ Joseph, author, *Hell Hath No Sorrow like a Woman Haunted*

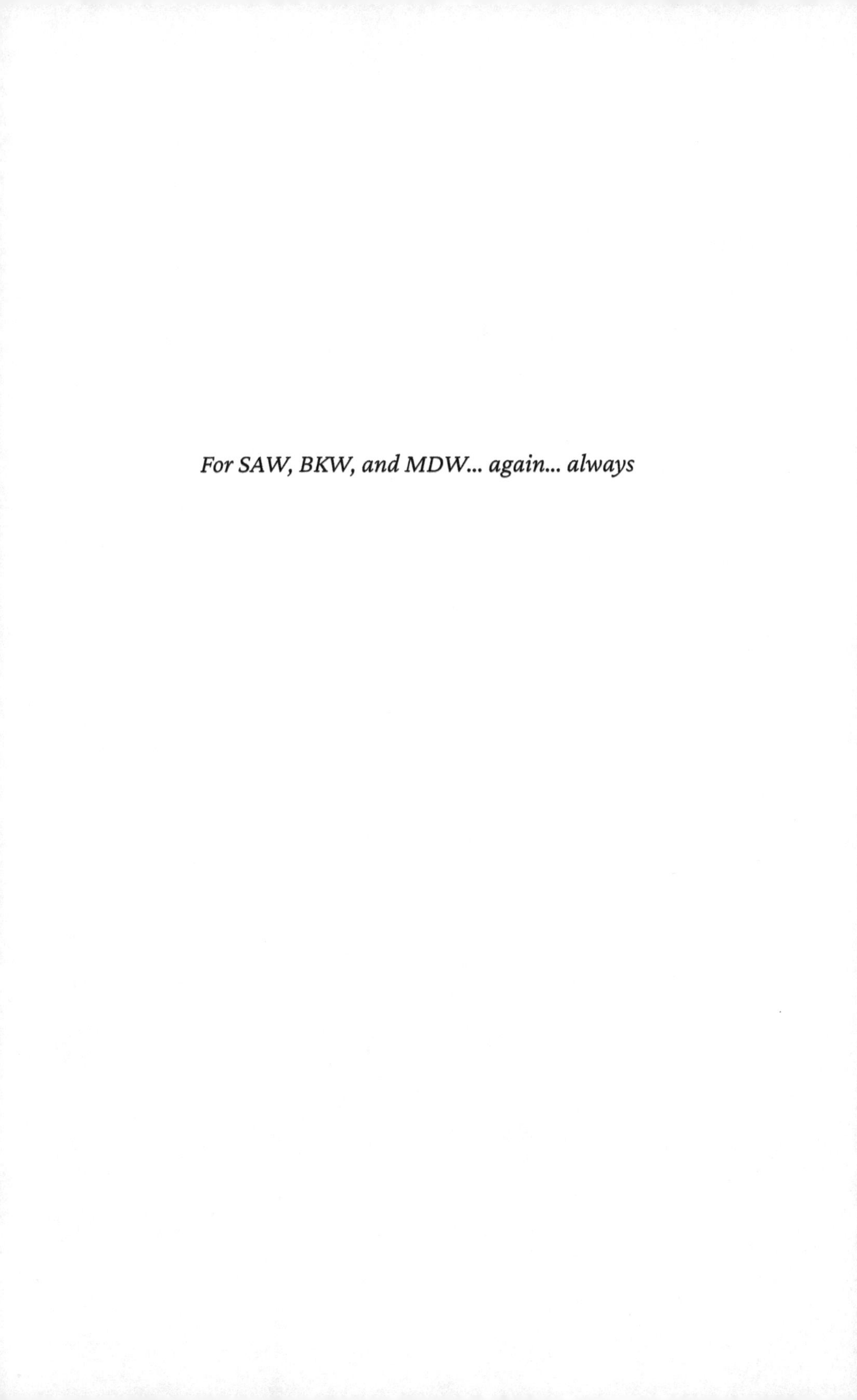

For SAW, BKW, and MDW... again... always

Acknowledgments

Thank you, people in my house, who endured me as I finished this one. I must have written and/or edited in every room. It had to be done.

Thank you, Laura Fasching. You are a walking book bible for this series. I am grateful for your vice-like memory

Thank you, reader, for consuming these words and letting them do what they do.

CHAPTER I

"Don't worry, sister. Not since Djet has there been such a call for retainer sacrifice, and never one of royal blood. More than a thousand years, my love."

"Are you not dead? Obliterated from sight, stricken from the world as if no breath came forth from your lungs?" She laughed ruefully, her chest filling with emotion that threatened to choke the life out of her faster than any ailment ever could. "Am I not Merneith?" Hatshepsut continued as she raised her hand to caress her sister's cheek, feeling the tears there. "You must take care, sister, before Thutmose makes fantasy so."

Nefrubity thought of the story their mother reluctantly spoke into the air as she lay dying, words from long ago telling why she must always stay out of sight and knew what her sister said was true. Yet still, Hatshepsut was dying and Nefrubity knew a part of her soul would die with her there, hidden away in the shadows.

"Djeser-Djeseru —" Hatshepsut rasped and Nefrubity simply

nodded. She could not tell her sister that Thutmose had already begun defacing her tomb, wiping her from history, before she had even drawn her last breath. It was for that reason that Hatshepsut was being cared for there, between the palace and her would-be tomb, instead of in the gathering place she had designed for her final hours. The door that was to lead to the mastaba where she would be held until the final preparations to the tomb at Djeser-Djeseru were made didn't open to that space at all; it didn't open to anywhere. But that wasn't a conversation one would have with Pharoah as she took her final breath – not unless one wanted to greet that afterlife ahead of her. Still, Nefrubity wondered if Hatshepsut knew it was a false door, wondered how much about this final deception her sister was aware of. Did she understand the threat she was under – the threat to her kingdom? Were circumstances different Nefrubity was certain that Hatshepsut would have been keenly aware, but she did not detect that level of perception in her sister anymore. Her body was breaking down faster than her mind was, but there was an undeniable toll being taken. She was slower, quieter as she died. It made Nefrubity fear her sister's next breath as much as she wished for it to come steady and strong. Was Hatshepsut aware of what was happening but just too far gone to argue? The deception had been hastily constructed, would have crumbled under close scrutiny in such rudimentary form, but Pharoah had said nothing... her sister who never held her tongue as a child and found no reason to as an adult, had said nothing at all.

Nefrubity couldn't allow her thoughts to linger there. There was too much to do.

She would say nothing about Djeser-Djeseru, nothing about what Thutmose was doing. nothing, nothing. Better to let Hatshepsut believe she would enter her mortuary temple and be buried there as a pharaoh should, rather than be whisked away and hidden in obscurity when the moment of her death came to be, even if her concealment was in an effort to secure safe passage in the afterlife. Nefrubity thought it better to make sure her plans were kept secret, even from the one who had protected *her* her whole life.

Hatshepsut nodded, satisfied. She swallowed with great effort before whispering,

"With Senenmut."

Nefrubity bit back her tears. Yes, Senenmut waited for her sister there in that grand tomb, the palace they could not share in life built in large form for them in the seclusion of the earth, but he would have to wait longer. If Nefrubity had anything to do with it, Senenmut would have to wait a little while longer.

Hatshepsut winced as she shifted her legs. She tried to press her thighs with her useless hands, the skin so inflamed the epidermis appeared to be flayed exposing raw, chaffed flesh to the elements.

"Be still, Hatshepsut," Nefrubity tried, her voice threatening to break under the strain as she tried to console her dying sister. "A'aru awaits Osiris's call."

Hatshepsut nodded with some difficulty. The smile she tried to give her sister cost much more.

"Bastet embodied," Hatshepsut said finally, causing Nefrubity's tears to flow as they had not before. She shook her head vehemently and stroked her cheek.

"It is you, Ma'at-ka-re," Nefrubity breathed but Hatshepsut frowned. Nefrubity rarely spoke her sister's royal name and Hatshepsut wasn't sure she liked the formality of it there in the room that would witness her death. "It is you who protects me."

"For you only, *okhti*," Hatshepsut said, her voice sounding weathered and abraded as the irritation that the surface of her body was suffering made its way inside.

Hatshepsut's wan smile made Nefrubity look away, overcome with emotion. Even as she took her final breaths, Hatshepsut would not let formality separate them. Not birthright, not marriage, not even the throne. Nefrubity cast her eyes around the room furtively to make sure there were no prying eyes witnessing the pharaoh allowing what looked like a peasant to address her by anything other than her royal name. But there was no one. They were alone.

"Find him, sister," Hatshepsut continued, her eyes boring into Nefrubity's with an intensity that would have frightened anyone else. "Do not allow him to rule."

Nefrubity nodded. She dipped a corner of cloth into the bowl of myrrh and rose water and delicately wiped Hatshepsut's face with it. Hatshepsut inhaled deeply, letting her eyes close. She smiled weakly but contentedly as she inhaled the fragrance again.

"From the merchant in Ta Netjer that you like so much," Nefrubity supplied. "I made it for you myself today."

Hatshepsut nodded and opened her eyes to look upon her sister. Her eyes thanked her for the last mortal pleasure she would experience, for her unwavering dedication, for her love. But when she spoke it was to reiterate that final order.

"You must destroy him, Nefrubity. Neferure's blood stains his hands from all those years ago as much as mine discolors them now."

Nefrubity looked at Hatshepsut, the twists that adorned her head threaded with slivers of gold filament jostling as she turned to regard her closer.

"Sister! What would cause you to say such a thing at the hour of—"

"Should I not speak the truth, of all times, now? If spoken now, words might be believed, hearts might be opened, and—"

"And lies forgiven?"

Nefrubity took her in; her sister, pharaoh of Egypt, dying on the floor of a room she had never seen before, speaking words of poison. She found that she could not meet Hatshepsut's eyes.

"My precious child... she was of your flesh and blood," Hatshepsut hissed as she thought of Neferure, her voice taking on the coldness that her subjects had come to know once again, perhaps for the last time. "And he cut her down to clear his path."

"Not of royal birth, she," Nefrubity said quietly. "Senenmut's lineage would not have let her ascend, unless she were to marry..." her voice trailed off as a possibility she had never allowed herself to consider barged in, taking over her mind, clouding it.

Hatshepsut let the silence sit between them for a moment, allowing Nefrubity to gather meaning in the turn of the conversation. Finally, she whispered, "She said no."

"You do not know that Thutmose asked her to join him nor what she may have said in return. You do not know that any of this occurred behind the chamber door," Nefrubity said, her chest heaving with emotion that she had not intended to show. But it didn't matter, not anymore, not between them. Hatshepsut already knew all of her secrets.

Hatshepsut remained silent.

Nefrubity hated her for it.

"You do not know, Hatshepsut," Nefrubity said sternly, hoping that the pause she had taken before speaking again had given her words more weight.

"Know I that Thutmose was all too happy to turn away from his duty so that he could sail the Nile in his youth, entering the far corners of the kingdom and doing... whatever he pleased." Hatshepsut's voice dipped as she spoke, showing her sister a level of respect, she would never have shown anyone else.

"Know I that Thutmose bid me continue to rule, begged pharaoh be my title rather than regent even after he was fit. A life of wonder, of travel and conquest is what he craved and, because father had named me successor to the throne before his death, the child who would be king thought to leave it to its rightful heir. But something changed."

Nefrubity shook her head and looked away, unable to be a party to the deceit but not having the heart to contradict her dying sister. She squeezed her eyes shut against the memory of Thutmose defacing the relief depicting their father crowning Hatshepsut king in Amun-Ra's regalia just the day before, chipping away at it on the walls of Hatshepsut's funerary temple himself instead of tasking a slave with the job. 'Lord of All,' he had sneered as he worked, the voice Nefrubity had come to love so much, smooth and earthy, like whispers in the night, turned hard. He cut away at the stone in short, deliberate strokes, perhaps oblivious to Nefrubity's tears, perhaps ignoring them.

As much as she hated to acknowledge it, she knew very well who Thutmose had become.

"Something made him desire more. Desire it all."

Hatshepsut's breathing was labored, and it pained Nefrubity to hear the gentle wheeze beginning to form in the back of her throat.

"Did he ask you, sister, to betray me? To wed him and help him take the throne by force, if that is what was required?"

He had not but Nefrubity squirmed under Hatshepsut's gaze anyway. She hated the implication her sister was making; the smirk on her face set Nefrubity's teeth on edge. She had done nothing to make Hatshepsut question her, yet there they were.

Nefrubity wished she had the internal fortitude to say something, to stand up for herself even if it was against a woman with not many breaths left in her body, but she did not. Hatshepsut was pharaoh after all, and even then Nefrubity knew her place.

But what exactly did Hatshepsut know? Nefrubity couldn't help but wonder how much Hatshepsut knew about her and Thutmose. They had been careful – always careful. That Nefrubity rarely showed herself beyond the tunnels and hidden passages in the royal palace, that she never ventured outside the perimeter gates no doubt helped them to keep their relationship quiet, but even with those precautions in place, they kept to the shadows. Thutmose had seemed to understand the arrangement well enough, and he should have: as part of the royal family, he knew how much danger Nefrubity had been in when the elder Thutmose died and then again when Hatshepsut assumed singular reign. The court might have called for blood for the gods so that the new reign might prosper – they might have sacrificed her first before bringing it up as an option to the pharaoh. It would have been a tribute to the old ways, a nod to a time when Egypt's might was unchallenged and they would have begged forgiveness if the pharaoh disproved, but by then it would have been too late, at least for her. Nefrubity knew that Hatshepsut would have gutted the court, killing everyone connected to the sacrifice and their families too, but Nefrubity herself would still be dead. So, she hid herself away, slinking around in the tunnels and hidden chambers, making a life in the dark as her mother had instructed.

Thutmose had joined her there, loved her there, said he wanted to make a life with her, in private if that is what she willed, but a life together, nonetheless. They had worked it out. Thutmose would take a lesser wife among the children of his court, perhaps of the nurse or vizier. Either she would produce a male heir, or he would find another to do so. Thutmose would parade them around and reliefs and statues would be made in their image, but they would never have his heart. That would belong to Nefrubity alone. Aunt and elder by a few years, forgotten and hidden away; these are the arguments she made against him tethering himself to her, but he kissed the opposition away until there was nothing left but their love. That there could be any other reality had never entered Nefrubity's mind.

Hatshepsut's stare warmed the side of Nefrubity's face, and she wanted to scream. She wanted to yell, to rail against her, to tell her that she was wrong about Thutmose, son of her husband, the boy she had trained to be a scribe, a priest, a scientist, a soldier... the boy she had loved as a son. Nefrubity wanted to remind Hatshepsut of all of those truths, help her remember the boy she now accused, but she was afraid of what she saw in Hatshepsut's eyes. She was afraid of the seed of doubt that those eyes had planted in herself.

"Neferure's son reflects his father's countenance as though he were standing before a looking glass," Hatshepsut said unprompted. Her voice was low so that it could not be overheard, but it wasn't unkind. Even at her end she was never unkind to the sister who had not had the chance to live.

Nefrubity shook her head sharply and pulled her arms around herself. The words Hatshepsut spoke cut deep. The children Thutmose had sired had been brought into the shadows to be rocked in her arms, baby girls let loose to play with her hair which she let grow long and thick. Indeed, many of the children in the palace were brought to sit at Nefrubity's knee: her, a seemingly lowly but wise servant, educating them in the history of the royal family had become a sort of unspoken tradition. But not Neferure's child. Nefrubity had never thought to ask why—

had assumed that Hatshepsut would bring the child herself when she could get away and they could ooh and aah over the baby together as sisters without the throne between them. But that had not happened. Now Nefrubity understood. Neferure's son Amenemhat had not been brought to her because she would see Thutmose's lie in the child's face.

"Sister," Hatshepsut started, seeing the pain in Nefrubity's eyes, "I do not tell you this to hurt you. Only to make clear why it must be done. Thutmose's deceit is boundless."

Wise. Hatshepsut's eyes reflected her wisdom, her vision as she spoke and for the first time her strength did not warm Nefrubity, did not make her feel as if she was safe. Nefrubity found herself wondering how much Hatshepsut knew again, and what she thought of it all; her sister in love with her step-son-turned-nemesis, if only in her mind. Had Hatshepsut ever been happy for her? Maybe back in the days when Thutmose seemed less interested in the throne and more in frivolous things? Did she think it novel that her sister had found love even when she'd had to hide herself away from the world?

Did Nefrubity amuse her?

Nefrubity and Hatshepsut weren't all that different when she thought about it. Hatshepsut had also found love and had to hide it. The birth of her only daughter had almost exposed it all and would have, if not for a slave girl's sacrifice for Hatshepsut's cause. The payment of 500 Deben in exchange for the lie about the elder Thutmose's virility even as he lay dying in his private chambers was worth more than that family would ever know. That it cost the girl's life was a consequence that Hatshepsut had been willing to assume.

Yes, Hatshepsut knew more than Nefrubity had ever imagined. Now, as her eyes remained trained on Nefrubity, it seemed she knew everything there was to know.

Wise, yes. But also, cunning.

"What would you have me do, dear sister? What would quench Pharaoh's thirst?" Nefrubity wished she could have bitten back the anger in her voice, but it was there.

Hatshepsut looked as if she had been slapped.

"'Tis not what *Pharaoh* would have you do," Hatshepsut started, straining to make her words heard. She touched Nefrubity's hand and Nefrubity did not pull away. Nefrubity allowed Hatshepsut to draw her gaze with stricken eyes. "'Tis what your *sister* begs of you. Nefrubity,"

Hatshepsut's hand shook as she brought Nefrubity's own to her dry, colorless lips and kissed it.

"Everything that we are depends upon it."

CHAPTER 2

Heavy.

Ornamented with gold and beads of carnelian, turquoise, and lapis lazuli.

Heavy.

As dead as she was.

Nefrubity clutched the wig in her hands, plunging her fingers into the strands knowing that if she was seen with it, she would be dispensed with before she could draw another breath. Beheaded, likely, her blood left to spill upon the floor of the hidden passage where she stood in tribute to the mighty Pharaoh's transitioning soul.

Tears burned Nefrubity's eyes as she caressed the wig, the hair still as shiny and supple as when it adorned the slave girl's head, remembering the production getting it on Hatshepsut's head one last time had been— the very last elaborate task of her sister's life. She had been so weak, so fragile in those moments that Nefrubity was afraid the dressers might break her neck.

Hatshepsut insisted on being prepared while she was still

alive; she wanted to feel the royal garb she had worked so hard for around her once more before the end. That meant Nefrubity had to be relegated to the shadows as the dressers worked to position the headpiece, fit the false beard. She had to listen in silence from the darkened corner of the room as Hatshepsut moaned and cursed the gods for such pain at the hour of her death. But then they were gone and Nefrubity and Hatshepsut were alone at last... for the last time.

After ushering the three women who had served her since the day, she had become pharaoh out of the room, wishing them good health for the rest of their days and claiming she wanted to die alone as her father had, Hatshepsut reached for Nefrubity, desperation showing in her actions if not in her words. She was close to her final moment. And she needed her sister.

And Nefrubity had gone to her. Without hesitation, she had raced across the room, the fear of being discovered momentarily abated. Nefrubity had taken in her dear sister's last words, words that spoke not of exploration or trade, of discourse, or law but of being a child and playing Mehen with their mother in their living quarters as the breeze found its way from the Nile to caress her cheek. As the kohl that darkened her eyes ran, staining her cheeks with the flow of her tears, Hatshepsut talked of making *fetir meshaltet* filled with chocolate and rejoicing when the folded pie was ready to drizzle honey over and eat. Knowing her sister the way she did, Nefrubity handed her the thing that she knew would give Hatshepsut the most joy as she departed the life they shared and moved on to A'aru: In Hatshepsut's hand Nefrubity pressed an ivory lion's piece, part of the Mehen set they played with their family as children. Nefrubity would weave the board and the ivory games pieces - the hand-carved lions and smooth marbles - into Hatshepsut's wrappings herself after her mummy was taken from Djeser-Djeseru. Because her body *would* be mummified like the royalty that came before her and her mummy would be placed in Wādī Al-Mulūk, the necropolis hidden in the mountains that Amenhotep I prepared not only for his family, but for all pharaohs to come. Nefrubity would wait until Hatshepsut was interred there, in her grandfather's safe haven from thieves, would wait until all the fanfare and funerary commitments were done, until the inner chamber was sealed, and the entryway closed, and then she would remove her sister's body from the elaborate tomb she had built for herself. She had to. If she didn't, her sister would be in danger forever. As she wound the hair from Hatshepsut's wig around her fingers so tightly that she cut off her circulation, she felt herself begin to tremble. The weight of Nefrubity's mistake threatened to consume her.

Waiting now.

Waiting for her transition to be complete, for her eyes to prepare themselves to see dynasties beyond their own, for her legs to walk lands that don't yet exist: Nefrubity pressed her nose into Hatshepsut's wig. She hoped the message she had placed on the inner wall of Djeser-Djeseru would warn people away... would warn Thutmose away. She had seen the look in his eyes, knew that he intended to remove Hatshepsut from the royal scrolls as soon as possible—that he had likely already begun to do that very thing. Nefrubity also knew that there were some in the royal court who agreed with his claim that the throne had been taken from him and that he, dutiful son that he was, had allowed his stepmother her way. There were not many - most had been there to see Hatshepsut offer the throne back to Thutmose when he came of age and knew he turned it down. The more progressive members of the court believed that since Hatshepsut was born a princess, claim to the throne was inherent in her as much as in Thutmose. But now the throne was empty and Nefrubity knew Thutmose would make a spectacle of assuming the mantel. Would he go as far as to deface all of her statues, destroy her cartouches, remove her name from the scrolls and erase her reign? Even though Nefrubity wanted to deny what she saw in his eyes, she felt the truth in her heart. He would do that and would feel justified doing so. It would pale in comparison to what he thought Hatshepsut had already done to him.

But the rest?

Nefrubity thought of her dear niece on the floor of her chamber, her mouth filled with bile.

She thought of Hatshepsut's skin, inflamed and raw after the poisoned cream she used had seeped into her pores.

She thought of the sneer Thutmose thought he had hidden from her whenever Nefrubity spoke Hatshepsut's name.

Yes, Thutmose would erase Hatshepsut from history and put his name in its place, claiming her conquests, her partnerships, her empire as his own. He would do everything he could to make the world forget her sister ever existed—Nefrubity was sure of it. But was he capable of the accusations that spewed from Pharoah's lips in her last moments? Images of Thutmose himself chipping away at Hatshepsut's legacy invaded her mind, twisting there, contorting, becoming something else. A man, older, heavier, crazed, throwing wrapped mummies into the Nile to be consumed by crocodiles under the guise of tribute to Sobek. A man, sagging and hunched, smiling at a relief depicting a queen engaged in sexual intercourse with a servant. These were visions; Nefrubity had never been more certain of anything in her life. Thutmose would seek to destroy her sister in the years to come.

But murder?

Hatshepsut bid he be killed but Nefrubity had not the stomach for it. Instead, she warned him—warned them all, using the last of Heka's magic to place an indelible proclamation for all eyes to see. She also spoke the words into Thutmose's heart hoping he would hear her, feel the love in her voice, and listen. It would be the last thing she would ever say to him:

He who shall do her homage shall live; he who shall speak evil in blasphemy of her Majesty shall die.

Nefrubity hoped it would be enough, that the gnats that would greet trespassers at the gates of Djeser-Djeseru, the locusts and spiders after, would be enough to drive the wicked away. She didn't want them to encounter what lay waiting for them if they breached the inner sanctum. She didn't want Thutmose to suffer the depths of Hatshepsut's wrath.

"Nefrubity," a voice called from inside the room—a voice that was unfamiliar to her, yet the only one she knew by heart. Nefrubity entered the room slowly, head bowed hoping to avoid what she could not. The body of her sister Hatshepsut lay prone before her, her thin hair fanned out atop the delicate rose silk of her final bedding. Her mouth was agape; her eyes, lids lowered, though not entirely closed, allowing just enough of the whites to be visible... to make Nefrubity's stomach turn. She was dressed in a garment she might have worn to a celebration. Indeed, that is the way Hatshepsut had wanted it. She would die as she had lived—regally and against the grain, going to greet the afterlife with all the pomp and circumstance due a leader with such a magnificent reign. Only Hatshepsut wouldn't be ushered into the afterlife wearing gold shiny enough to blind the gods. She wouldn't be going to the afterlife at all.

Nefrubity had made a mistake.

It had taken too long, navigating the tunnels in her grief,

desperate to hide herself from sight. It had all been so clandestine from the start: finding the old woman in the far reaches of Kush who would tell a nameless peasant girl pretending she wasn't from the empire the secrets of the god Heka, learning how to invoke the powers. Nefrubity had been afraid that she wouldn't be able to remember the incantation or maybe she would get back to the chamber too late to save Hatshepsut. In the end, that is what almost happened. In the end, that might have been better.

Henna on her nails, turned dark as rot.

"Sister," the voice called from behind her and then Hatshepsut was there, standing next to her, staring at her own inanimate form beneath the folds of linen. She grasped the hand of the body that lay dead before her, the body that had been hers as long as she had air in her lungs, with her new one, the smooth skin she now possessed engulfing that of the worn husk she had inhabited only hours before. A tear wet her cheek as she looked upon herself. The blotchy red rash that had raised on the inside of her arm moments after putting the poisoned cream on her skin was still there, bluish in death... angrier. Hatshepsut hadn't wanted to die; she hadn't wanted to leave the life she had worked so hard to create for herself behind: she hadn't wanted to be right. Thutmose had taken everything from her, used her infirmities against her and slain her, would assume her empire the moment he heard of her death... had tried to turn her sister against her. On that last score he would never have been successful. Nefrubity had always stood by her side, had always loved her, had been the only one to take action when there seemed to be nothing left to be done.

"I am sorry, sister," Nefrubity said, and the words startled Hatshepsut with their sincerity. Nefrubity was crying again as she had before when Hatshepsut straddled the line between life and death. But now there was no reason for tears, no reason for the sadness that nearly caused her knees to buckle. Hatshepsut put her arms around her sister and hugged her in a way that she hadn't been free to in years, no longer caring about who might see them and what cost would need to be paid to ensure silence.

"What is it, Nebe?" Hatshepsut's new voice murmured into Nefrubity's hair. "What causes you to cry now, after everything you have given me?"

Nefrubity sank into the embrace even though it felt foreign to her, the arms that held her unfamiliar. She allowed herself to sob as her body willed, not bothering to temper her emotion because should someone walk in on them now, her biggest affront would be that she and the girl mourned their beloved pharaoh before the body had been properly dressed.

"It is not right. What happened... this was not my intention," Nefrubity replied once she felt certain she could speak without her voice breaking.

"The incantation— you died before I could complete it, and this..." She let her voice trail off, unsure how to finish. This, what? Mistake? Abomination? Neither word was suitable, yet both spoke the truth she felt. But Hatshepsut did not see it that way. Her eyes had opened to a new life with new possibilities. She looked upon her awakening as a blessing more than a curse.

"It is as Heka wills," Hatshepsut said, pulling Nefrubity out of the embrace to look at her sister. Nefrubity stared back into eyes that were larger than Hatshepsut's and a deeper brown. Her skin was golden now, so different from the warm ochre that Nefrubity had loved to gaze upon. The woman her sister would not become was taller, slimmer; her voice was higher, more melodic.

Different.

Everything about Hatshepsut was different. Except nothing

was. She had taken the body of the servant girl who had come in the room to leave fresh water and aloe at Nefrubity's behest, using her as a starting point to shift to and from as Heka promised.

"It is as you made it, dear sister." Hatshepsut touched her head to Nefrubity's and it felt so wrong and so right at the same time. "You saved my life."

Nefrubity wrenched herself away from Hatshepsut and stood before the body of the only sister she would ever envision. Instinctively, her arms came up to hug her elbows, to draw into herself.

"You walk and talk, you breathe and see, yes, but *you*... you, Hatshepsut, do not live. You dwell in the body of a girl who dedicated her life to serve you. Where is she now? Do you feel her inside with you or is she gone? Cast out of her own body? Erased because I..."

Nefrubity almost didn't have the strength to continue. She sank to her knees before her sister's dead body and grasped her cooling hand.

"Because I was too late."

Hatshepsut went to her sister. She took her hands in her own and rubbed them, pulled her down gently, guiding them both to kneel. When she spoke, her voice was filled with emotions she almost could not control.

"Nefrubity, you have given me what no one else could have. What you see—this face, this body, these hands—they represent life. The life you wished for me. You loved me so much that you invoked the God of the gods, the one who made the sun and the moon, hidden from most, diminished by time, known intimately only by those who lived before Hor-Aha, before King Narmer. You bid him come out of the background, to show himself for the first time since he strolled the banks of the Nile with the chosen to help your dying sister. You beseeched him to use his magic to make me whole and that is what he did."

Nefrubity's smile was bittersweet. She wanted to be happy but something in her sister's bright new eyes left her cold.

"I begged for his medicine to heal you and his magic to sustain you. I did not supplicate resurrection," she said finally, her voice cracking under the weight of her words.

Hatshepsut looked over at her body, already growing cold to the touch, seeming more like stone than a vessel that once brimmed with life.

"Yet here we are."

Hatshepsut closed her eyes, remembering her sister's words, spoken hastily over her body as her vision clouded and her breathing slowed.

... he who is the one prayed to even when other names are called out. All seeing, all knowing. Ride the wings of her ba *as it traverses the plains; protect Hatshepsut's immortal soul. Oh! Dual God of gods mark the Lady of the Two Lands yours and keep her breath, save her blood.*

Hatshepsut wanted to ask Nefrubity how she knew what to say, where she had learned of such magic. Heka had not been talked of openly in longer than Hatshepsut could remember, yet somehow her sister had been able to gather enough knowledge to try to save her life. She wanted to ask many questions, but she would wait until Nefrubity was ready... if she ever was.

"You died before I could ask Heka to spare you death. Hatshepsut, now you will never die," she sobbed, emotion taking over. "The magic... it's evil, it's—"

"No, sister," Hatshepsut said, stopping the flow of words that threatened to spill from Nefrubity without pause. "It is what was *meant* to be."

Soon the room would be filled with people readying her for

interment. No one would think twice about the servant girls removing the aloe and water from Hatshepsut's feet. In 90 days, Hatshepsut's mummy would be entombed at Djeser-Djeseru. Nefrubity would remove it from the sarcophagus before Thutmose could desecrate it, placing it in an unmarked grave in a necropolis that only she and now Hatshepsut knew about. And then they would leave. No one would find her mummy there, Hatshepsut felt sure of that: no one would suspect a woman of such stature to be buried in the dirt. Together she and Nefrubity would have to unwrap her mummy, strip it of most of the finer materials that would touch her skin and replace them with looser thread cloth, wrappings that were nothing more than rags, to mirror the patchwork preparation used by some Egyptian families. They had to destroy any clue as to who the mummy might have been... make it so that even if people tried to guess who she was they would never settle on the pharaoh herself. While Hatshepsut's arm would be draped across her chest, positioned commensurate with royalty, she would have none of the other accoutrements that would give her status away. Hatshepsut wanted to keep something of her royal burial —felt she deserved at least one thing to pay homage to her reign —but Nefrubity had argued against it and she was right. Her mild-mannered sister would even try to reposition the arm after the ceremony was over, would likely break it if it came to that... even if though it would hurt her to do so. But she had to. Leaving it in that position could lead to discovery and Hatshepsut knew that Nefrubity would be right to do everything she could to avoid that. Nefrubity would take Hatshepsut's *nemes*, wig, and false beard off and burn them to ashes and they would both shed tears in that moment, Hatshepsut knew. But again, her sister would be right to do it. Those acts would strip her identity away, make Hatshepsut a regular Egyptian woman. Anonymous. She could be anyone.

Hatshepsut turned away abruptly. She could not bear to look upon her mummified face for long. She asked her sister to rewrap her and lay her in the dirt without company, offering to help shovel in the dirt afterward, but Nefrubity declined, deigning to do it all alone. There was one last thing she needed to do, one last promise to keep before she and Hatshepsut could leave the only land they had ever known together.

Nefrubity kissed every Mehen game piece and the serpentine board that had been carved from nothing by their great-great grandfather's hand, before securing it in Hatshepsut's new wrappings.

CHAPTER 3

Strangers.

Yet... not.

She could see herself in their faces; the slope of her nose, the high cheekbones passed down many generations. Even the shape of their ears, a thing she had never paid attention to before then, was similar, especially when they smiled. They were the pictures on the wall, smiling at her from behind dusty glass, but instead of existing as anecdotes and memories, they were there, right in front of her. Yet they didn't know her any better than she knew them.

Her father knew the teenager, the girl who had only offered a glimpse of the woman she would become in a few years and nothing of who she would be on the day she died. When he looked at her, he saw that girl, that *child*, who to him, was not ready for the joys and pains of life, the struggles and successes. For him, it was a nightmare being able to look into his daughter's eyes in that place, devoid of life, somewhere on the other side of the moon. It was too soon.

Gabby didn't think she could argue with that.

She studied her father's face, pinched in consternation, his weight shifting as he stood on uncertain ground. She could imagine the questions running through his head: can I hug her? Or would that be too much? Does she remember me? And there was something else, something Gabby couldn't put her finger on. It hung over his eyes like a visor, shaded them, and didn't allow her to look directly into them.

She looked at her grandfather, at the pride on his face... at the sadness. How must it feel to see her, the grandchild he had never touched, like this? To meet her for the first time after death had stolen her breath? His chest heaved; he clasped and unclasped his hands. He was torn, unsure, happy, sad. She could almost feel his agony.

Her eyes made their way back to the one she had thought wistfully of at every milestone in her life and found comfort again. He looked the same, her dad. He looked the way he did in her memory. Tall, head full of hair, kind eyes. Gabby didn't understand why that made her feel so relieved, but it did.

"Dad," Gabby started and felt her resolve give way when her father's face crumbled in relief. He moved toward her, arms open, and she stepped into them as she had so many years before. He cried then; they both did, and it felt good to do so together as they stood in a place that they could only know in death.

"I was afraid..." Doug said as he lowered his cheek to her hair.

"Afraid of what?"

"Afraid that," Doug took a deep breath before continuing, "after all this time, that you wouldn't remember me."

Gabby pulled back to look at her father, to see the emotions there, the battle he waged keep them under the surface. That he would think she might have forgotten him upset her on so many levels. He had been her movie watching partner, enduring hours of what she now knew to be abject torture as he sat through cartoon movies, princess movies, and rom-coms. He had been her first piece of gymnastic equipment and then unofficial gymnastics coach. He had been her fellow marshmallow burner and her ice cream before dinner secret keeper. He was her dad. Her soul could never have forgotten who he was even if her mind did.

"I rubbed leaves onto paper with charcoal, kept a binder full of them, and went out to see them change color every fall," Gabby said almost reverently. "I would talk to you sometimes, mostly in the beginning, right after..."

She met his eyes but only for a second, tears threatening to spill onto her cheeks.

"But sometimes I went out to look at the leaves when I was all grown up with kids of my own. Sometimes I would imagine you were with me. It knew it wasn't actually you— it was more like a presence. A feeling. But still..."

Doug nodded because he couldn't speak—there were no words to express how he felt. Grateful. Surprised. Happy. Incredibly sad. He didn't trust his voice to properly express any of it.

Leaves. She still loved leaves. Doug remembered how they used to blaze trails in the leaves together, how they loved to hear them crunch beneath their feet; how they loved throwing them in the air and letting them rain down onto their heads. Fall meant hot chocolate, warm jackets, and hunting for unique leaf patterns to the two of them; it meant father-daughter time, chilly noses, and making memories that would endure.

And they *had* endured.

She hadn't forgotten.

"I could never remember what they were called, those patterns on the leaves. I used to love to trace them with my fingers," Gabby continued as Doug remembered her laughter as she buried him in the leaves, trying to call up the word her father had said so many times and still coming up empty.

"Venation," Doug supplied, smiling in that knowing way that he always had, calling back all of the emotions that time had healed in Gabby. "The veins."

"Right," Gabby said and smiled back, and it felt like home.

CHAPTER 4

"They put your father's grave marker in today," Asha started after pulling the chair that she sat in most days closer to Chris's bed. "I think he would have loved it—the bronze is really beautiful... regal."

She smiled absently as she settled into the groove she had worn into the cushion and scanned the numbers on the monitor, comparing his heart rate and blood pressure then to what it was when she left the night before as she did. It upset her that she understood what it all meant now but after three months of looking at the numbers going up and going down and watching the lines drawing their crazy patterns, she had learned quite a bit. At least they had removed the ICP monitor, though Asha wasn't sure if that was a good thing in the end. If they weren't concerned enough to monitor Chris's TBI—traumatic brain injury she recited silently, quizzing herself with the mental flash card stash she had been building along the way—that could either mean he was out of the woods or he would never come out of them again. At any rate, she was glad the probe had been removed... she didn't have to think about the hole they had drilled in his skull to put it in place every time she looked at him anymore.

As if she was just hearing what she was saying, Asha huffed, admonishing herself.

"I don't know why I said that baby. I'm sorry. There's nothing to like about a grave marker... nothing to like about any of this."

Asha rubbed his hand, noticed that the IV had been rotated. Good.

She listened to the sound of the ventilator as it pushed air through the tracheostomy tube and into Chris's airway to inflate his lungs. The click before what reminded her of the sound a vacuum cleaner hose made when it didn't have a tool attached to the end was one of the things that kept her grounded. That and the steady beeping from the ECG. Not the sound of Chris's breathing; definitely not that gagging sound that he made when the mucus filled his lungs, threatening to plug his airway... to choke him. Nothing that Chris did in that place gave Asha comfort or peace. Nothing indicated that Chris was even there.

Chris hadn't done anything at all for five months—not since their engagement party... not since their lives had changed forever. Asha had needed two months to heal; one month in the hospital and three weeks at a rehabilitation center. Her mother had whisked her away then, keeping Asha away from Chris's bedside for a week before relenting. She hadn't wanted her to see what was left of the love of her life, hadn't wanted her to sit through the beeps and groans of the equipment connected to wires and cords and drips and whatever else was keeping him alive, not yet. What she didn't realize was that Asha *needed* to see him, needed to replace the memory of the fire in the balloon haloing his head before he repositioned them, putting himself under her in the gondola, doing whatever he could to cushion the blow. *The envelope*, her mind trilled, reminding her of the bit of trivia she had learned before the magical ride that was supposed to celebrate her upcoming nuptials, but instead signaled the death of her future. The envelope... that's what was burning. Chris must have seen the worst of it, probably saw the burners explode, the sky seeming to rush away from them as they plummeted, the fear in her eyes as she saw the earth rise up to meet them.

And then there was nothing.

Asha had pieced together what happened from friends and family, news accounts, even the lawyer who would leave her in peace. It was a miracle that they were alive, they said. They fell from over 100 feet up. Thank God they stayed in the gondola, some said before realizing that Asha's aunt, Chris's father, and the pilot had not. Asha's aunt and Chris's father were thrown, their bodies, crumpled and broken, were found miles apart from each other and far away from where she and Chris ended up. The pilot jumped but didn't fare any better than his passengers. He was found in close proximity to where Asha and Chris lay in the remains of the gondola. She and Chris had stayed inside it, their arms around each other as they plummeted to what they thought would be their deaths. Someone told her the gondola hit a tree, which slowed them down enough to shatter one's bones on impact—bones that required metal to repair—and to partially eviscerate and mete out brain trauma for the other, but not enough to kill them. Asha remembered Chris's face from some point in the event, whether on the ground waiting to be rescued or after hitting the tree, she wasn't sure. What she did know was that it was intact and without much blood on it, but wholly and completely not him. It was a mask.

Dead, yet warm. She needed something else to replace that image, the one that rested behind her eyes when she closed them to sleep.

Asha wasn't sure if seeing him now was better or worse.

She smoothed the sheets around his waist, working out wrinkles that weren't there. She put petroleum jelly on her finger and rubbed it on his lips to keep them moist. She surveyed him to see what else might be needed; a haircut? No. Shave? Not really—she had done it yesterday and the stubble that had grown back wasn't that visible. Asha sometimes liked to let the hair grow in a bit. It gave her the chance to see what Chris would look like with a beard... sort of. The droopiness of his mouth, muscles relaxed, cheeks grown waxen, their shape distorted by the swelling that was almost imperceptible until noticed, and one could never unsee it—all of that changed his looks enough that Asha sometimes imagined that she had herself been in the hospital longer than she thought she had, that she had been in her own coma and woken up decades later to find him aged. She had told Chris that she loved men with goatees when they were dating but he never grew one out, preferring to be clean shaven. Asha never thought she'd see Chris with facial hair, never thought she'd be able to feel the coarse hair under her hands or against her cheek, but now...

When she thought that way, she shaved it off right then and there, even if it was late and she was tired. She didn't want him to wake up and see the goatee and hate it, hate her for letting the hair grow out, hate her...

Asha looked away feeling silly, feeling sad, feeling everything.

Five months had gone by and he hadn't woken up.

Five months had gone by and his father's grave, covered with lush grass now, had finally gotten its marker, one that was different in every way from the vertical granite tombstone that marked her aunt's grave except in the date of death.

Five months had gone by and Chris's sister hadn't come.

Autumn *still* hadn't come.

It hurt Asha to know that his sister had not relented, had not let go of whatever problem had driven them apart even when she found out that most of her family was dead and that her brother was locked in his own private hell. She had not made her way to any of the funerals either. Asha's mother had been watching out for her. At Asha's request, her mother had called the police to do a wellness check for her after leaving enough messages to fill up her voicemail and not getting a response. She had reached out to friends who lived in the vicinity of Autumn's last known address—somewhere in Los Angeles—and asked them to look around for her. No one turned up anything. The friends described the squalor they encountered when they went to the address and cautioned her about what calling the police again or putting in a Missing Person Report could do—said if she was alive and the police found her, she would surely go to jail with all the drug paraphernalia laying around. Asha didn't know what happened after that and her mother wouldn't tell her; she just said that the family had stepped in and they would take it from there. Asha had looked for Autumn herself a few times after getting her wits about her but couldn't find anything either. So, saying that Autumn had not relented, had not softened and returned home in light of everything going on, wasn't really fair. Asha wasn't entirely sure Autumn knew what happened at all.

Asha settled into her chair next to Chris, watched the shadows draw patterns on the wall behind his bed, and bit back tears. The room only had one chair. The second one that had been in there in the early days had been removed long ago. She had let someone from down the hall use it when there was standing room only at someone's birthday celebration, feeling that it was the least she could do considering such a terrible situation. She saw the sadness in the woman's face—the one who came to get the chair—saw the gratefulness. Asha saw something else there too, something she didn't want to acknowledge. The woman's eyes had flicked to where Chris lay immobile, had taken in all of the machines around him monitoring vitals—sustaining life—and the look in her eyes was one of connection, one of commiseration.

Asha looked at Chris, at the slope of his forehead, at the natural arch of his eyebrows and remembered how they always gave her pause. He used to raise one when something surprised him, furrow them both when something irritated him. Full and masculine; Asha had always marveled at how he could manipulate them to convey his emotions, could make someone fall in love with the tiniest of movements. She used to trace them when he slept, relished the feeling of them moving under her finger, arching as he awakened to kiss her. Asha found her hand on them now, wishing the same thing would happen, that maybe she had found the magic button and it wasn't medicine or time or synapses firing... she just had to touch him the right way, stimulate his senses, make him react.

Nothing.

She pulled a hair, would have yanked it out if her fingers weren't trembling.

Still nothing.

And even if there had been something, the doctors had already warned her not to get too excited. They said that Chris was now in a persistent vegetative state, though how that differed from a coma, Asha was still fuzzy on. They said that he might grimace if he felt pain, even yank his hand out of hers if she pinched it. They said he might open his eyes one day too but cautioned her about getting excited if that happened when her face lit up. They said that it was normal for comatose patients to do that from time to time after a few months, said it didn't mean he was getting better even though it seemed like it should. If she talked to him, asked him questions, called his name, he wouldn't respond. There were no signs of cognition they said, trying to get ahead of it before he opened his eyes and stared right through her, breaking her heart in the process. But Asha hadn't had the chance to find out for herself yet.

She hadn't seen his eyes in just over 150 days. She wondered how long it would be before she started forgetting what they looked like.

Asha sighed and sat back in the chair.

"Another day," she said, her voice affecting a singsong quality that just didn't fit in that room.

"What can I talk about today, hmmm? I can tell you how the sun is shining outside but there's a chill to the air. You know how if you swing your arms back and forth, it feels cold? It's like that. It's getting close to fall now. September's almost over."

She stopped herself there, bit back the words that had almost spilled out—the ones that spoke of how it was three weeks past the day they were supposed to get married and that she'd forgotten to call the pastor, forgot to tell him the wedding would have to be... She couldn't even let herself think it or else the tears would come and she wasn't sure she'd be able to stop them. Asha wanted to tell Chris that the pastor had shown up ready to go, decked out in his vestments, and with Bible in hand. When he got there, he thought he was too early, wondered if he had the right house, because there were no decorations, no people, nothing—nothing except her dressed in sweats and a t-shirt. He asked what happened and she had broken then, right there on their doorstep, because she hadn't been talking about the thing that had happened to them, not really, not enough. The pastor had been away—something about running a mission at a church in the Caribbean and that had been enough to push her over the edge because that's where they were going to spend their honeymoon—that's where they were supposed to be the very next day. But now she wondered if they would ever go anywhere together again or if Chris would be making his next trip alone.

Asha wanted to tell Chris that but there was no way to do it; no way to make the story funny or ironic, happy-go-lucky, or even normal. It was terrible, one of the worst stories ever told. And it was theirs.

So, she changed the subject.

"Remember how we were wondering what happened to Bruno Mars? How it seemed like he fell off the face of the earth after that last hit, the one he did with that jazz guy who turned out to be a big deal overseas? Well, he came out with something new the other day."

Asha spoke as if she were talking to Chris over dinner. That's what the nurses said she should do and she was trying to do exactly that. She kept trying to do what they said, hoping that he really was listening... hoping that he would want to wake up and chime in.

They told her not to think that way, said that while they thought Chris could hear her, nothing is certain... told her not to get her hopes up because the odds of waking up from a coma or whatever a persistent vegetative state was, after so many months, especially after sustaining so much damage... the odds were...

"I heard it this morning. It's so smooth," Asha nodded her head, remembering the beat, the rhythm, the vocal choices, all the while imagining her and Chris listening to it together. If one of them had heard it first they would have called the other to listen, rewinding it so they could start from the beginning together... that's if life were fair. Chris hadn't always been a fan, but Asha's enthusiasm forced him to listen to Bruno Mars more and he grew on him. She remembered an early date of theirs: a picnic at an outdoor concert venue featuring none other than Bruno Mars. There were some other performers on the ticket, people he hadn't heard of, so to say that he was underwhelmed by the prospect of enduring the summer heat to see the show was an understatement. But Asha was more than excited, more than elated... it was like someone had come to her house and left money in her mailbox. She was ecstatic that Bruno Mars— *her* Bruno, the one she never let anyone turn off, no matter what song was playing... the one she listened to at least once a day— was coming to town. So, Chris had gotten the tickets, preparing himself to suffer through a night of loud mediocrity because the girl he was in love with, and he was sure it was love by then even thought it had only been two months, wanted to see him. He wanted to see her smile; wanted to know that smile was because of him.

Bruno Mars changed everything.

That night Bruno Mars drove Asha into his arms, swaying and dancing to the music that seemed to enter her body and caress her soul. Chris enjoyed the press of her body against his, was mesmerized by the way her hair smelled, was enraptured by the sound of her voice as she sang along. He also loved every minute of the set; the slow tracks, the up-tempo ones that sounded like they were from another era, the energy—all of it. Bruno Mars made a believer out of him that night, working through his songs with added riffs and other vocal techniques he didn't know the names of, showing Chris that he could sing just as well, if not better, live and in person. That night, under the stars and surrounded by hundreds of people on a perfect early summer night, Bruno Mars made Asha look at Chris with eyes that said she would love him forever. He started looking for engagement rings the very next day.

They used to talk about how cool it might be to have Bruno Mars sing at their wedding. Asha would joke that he was the reason they had fallen in love, but she had felt the inkling of it long before the concert. There was something behind Chris's eyes that called to her, something that always made her feel like she was the only thing he could see. Even in the beginning when they were just two of likely 300 people at the National Mall taking in the first few days of mild weather, throwing them-selves into the sun to ride bikes, stroll, even just sit on the grass and read a book, they were drawn to each other, his eyes like a magnet. He saw her first; she had been reclining on her elbows in the grass, her legs outstretched in front of her and crossed at the ankle, eyes closed, engrossed in the music piping through her earbuds. She couldn't remember if she had been listening to Bruno Mars then, but it definitely fit the story, so she told it that way and no one that knew her even thought to challenge that as too much of a coincidence.

Chris had been looking at her when she opened her eyes— he openly admitted that—but he hadn't started out that way. He was looking at the Smithsonian castle initially, trying to figure out what was in there and why the architect had designed the building in a medieval style that wasn't even used in the United States, remembering something about an unexplained bequeathment from a rich British guy with no heirs. He was lost in thought, his mind following that track, making him wonder if the guy with the money had required that the building be a castle, which then made him guess at what in the world could be inside that it required a castle to house it. Then Chris's eyes fell onto the carousel that was also in his line of sight and he got lost in the memory of riding it when he was a kid. He had ridden the sea dragon every time they went to the nation's capital, which was pretty often, his history buff dad unable to stay away from the museums for long. Chris loved the iridescent paint, the scales, and its tail. It was a popular seat and because he wouldn't ride anything else, they spent an inordinate amount of time at the carousel riding it, waiting until he could get on the sea dragon, and riding again. Autumn grew tired of it all and, after riding many of the horses multiple times, sat next to their dad on one of the benches, looking bored. Chris couldn't understand how she could stand it. What was the point in being on a carousel if you didn't go up and down? She had asked him why he wouldn't just get on another horse because after all, they did the same thing. He had just looked at her like she had sprouted horns. It was a sea dragon. *A sea dragon.* In his mind, that was enough of an explanation: he had absolutely no problem making them wait because it only made sense.

Chris had been wondering if they still had the sea dragon, wondered if anyone would have a problem with a childless man staring at a carousel, was thinking that maybe he'd even pay for a ticket to get on, when she caught his eye.

She was stunning.

It wasn't just that she was pretty... pretty was easy. The way Chris made it seem when he told her what he was thinking that day, Asha's hair had been haloed by the golden sunlight of late afternoon, the light kissing her shoulders before illuminating the ground around her, her back casting a shapely shadow on the grass... or something like that. Chris always had a flair for the fantastic, a way with words that was almost lyrical. As she got to know him, learned more about the people she would call family, she came to believe that he had gotten that talent from his grandmother, the writer in the family whose unpublished manuscript was left in a box somewhere in his dad's dusty attic.

The house.

Who was taking care of the house?

Asha realized she hadn't looked into that at all since the accident, hadn't tried to help Chris's family—distant cousins twice removed, the closest—handle the house, pack up things, notify the bank of his death. It wasn't her place, she knew, but still Asha felt terrible in that instant, like she had let the man who was to be her father-in-law down... like she had let *Chris* down. The voice in her head, the one that liked to rub salt in her wounds and laugh at how she cried when it burned, reminded her that none of them had come to check on Chris either, not before she had been cleared to come to his bedside and not after. Why should she extend herself, involve herself in affairs that didn't pertain to her because she was not Chris's wife, not family yet... not yet. She muted the voice then, cut that bitch off before she could destroy her by talking about a future that wasn't to be, taking a deep breath and expelling it from her lips as though exorcising a demon.

Asha would try to reach out to the family or Chris's father's neighbors or someone, she resolved. They probably wouldn't talk to her but she would make the effort. All she could do was try. She owed the man she loved that much.

A tear threatened to spill over her eyelids to wet her cheeks and she sniffed it back. She said something to Chris again, speaking audibly to stop herself from going down that rabbit hole again, her voice sounding loud in the relative silence of the room.

"Too bad we couldn't get Bruno Mars to sing at our wedding." Asha tried, grasping at straws. "He probably wouldn't have done it for less than what we make in a year combined, and even that might have only bought us an hour."

She laughed, imagined Chris laughing with her. She did a lot of that.

Chris had sung her favorite Bruno Mars song on bended knee when he asked her to marry him, his voice quavering as he tried to stay on key. As he crooned about how perfect she was, his nerves threatened to get the best of him before he could finish the chorus. Chris was nervous; more than he had ever been. He told Asha later that he almost hadn't gone through with it, not the way he had planned to. He was worried about the fact that they would be outside in front of people when he asked her—people with cell phones—and that could have been a recipe for disaster. But he went through with it in the end because he knew Asha would like it.

No... Chris knew she would *love it.*

And she would say yes...

... at least he hoped.

And she *had* said yes. Even though they hadn't been together for a year yet, even though they hadn't met each other's parents by then, Asha said yes, and it wasn't because of the way his voice shook as he kneeled in the grass that was turning brown and was littered with fallen leaves as autumn set in, and it wasn't because he had brought her back to the very spot where they had met months before to ask her to be his wife. It was because Asha had known she was going to marry Chris for longer than she cared to admit. She had just been waiting for him to catch up.

Asha took a deep, shuddering breath that she resented.

She needed some air.

CHAPTER 5

"It's unnatural... unhealthy too," Rosa said, slipping her arms around herself, rocking on the edge of the splintered bench. "I know it's where we're supposed to be, but it's still... it's not right."

Asha sat silently, listening to the woman speak. They had met many times before out there in the employee break area behind the hospital. Both of them had been trying to hide from the other family members who might have ventured out of their loved one's rooms to get a breath of fresh air. They hid because unless the person they had come to see was dead, none of the other visitors were worse off than people like Rosa and Asha, the ones who perpetually waited. If they had broken a leg in a car accident, they would go home relatively quickly; if it had been a heart attack it might take more time, but they were likely to leave the hospital and not have to come back. But patients in comas—in persistent vegetative states... they hardly ever woke up and left. There was rarely a light at the end of the tunnel for people like them, and even if there was, it was as dim as the prospects of life after awakening offered.

It hurt people like Rosa and Asha to see the hopefulness in other people's eyes.

It scared people to see the hopelessness in theirs.

So, they started using the staff's space, sneaking out when no one was there just to take a moment away from it all. When Rosa found Asha sitting out there one day, she almost turned around and left without saying a word, not wanting to accost the young woman with how disheveled she looked, how forlorn. She didn't want the pity that others couldn't help but give when they saw people who looked like that—she didn't feel up to deflecting. But then Asha looked at her and she saw herself in the young woman's eyes. And then it was her turn to feel pity.

That had been two months before.

"A girl your age should be letting the sun touch her face, but instead you sit here all day long, every single day."

The bench where they sat creaked but held firm. It had seen its share of traffic over the years, provided the respite that many a tired nurse or doctor needed to get through their shift. The staff had been welcoming to Rosa and Asha, had shared their retreat with the only two people who were there as much as they were... were probably there even more than they were.

"Where else would I be?"

Asha tried to keep the anger out of her words, but she wasn't sure she had. Rosa had been saying similar things for two weeks already—something about the way Asha's eyes seemed more and more hollow causing her to voice her opinion. And Asha understood, of course she did, but she didn't want to hear it. Not from her mother, not from the doctors, not from this woman who was nothing more than a stranger to her. They didn't understand how much Chris meant to her. They didn't understand how much she owed him.

"Anywhere but here," Rosa answered, her jaw working over the gum she had crammed into her mouth—her third piece in as many minutes. She was trying to beat the smoking habit that she and her husband had formed together as teenagers. Fifty years later it had him laid up with a tube down his throat and her running scared.

"Here is where I belong," Asha said, repeating what she had said the day before that, and the week before that.

"That's what you say but..." Rosa said, letting her voice trail off leaving Asha with assumptions to make.

"But *what*, Rosa? He *is* my family. I said I would always be there for him. How could I turn my back on him now when he needs me? You wouldn't do that," Asha said, confidence bolstering her words. "And I *know* you wouldn't because you're still here day in and day out just like me, and your husband hasn't opened his eyes in nearly six months."

Rosa looked away, her mouth forming a straight line and Asha hated herself for being the reason it was there. They were supposed to help each other, be sounding boards when needed, get each other through. It was a strange kinship they'd formed, but they had formed it and Asha was acting like she didn't care too much about that right then. But she did. It had been one of the only ways she had kept her sanity those past few months.

Asha started to speak, to utter some apology that wouldn't have been enough, but Rosa spoke instead.

"If it was him lying in there, I would agree with you. If there was anything at all to show you that his mind was functioning, that he was hearing you, was present in the room could take a breath of his own—if any of that were happening, I would agree with you," Rosa said, looking at Asha with wet eyes.

"But it *isn't* him, honey. And no amount of wishing it was will bring him back."

Asha knew that Rosa was trying to help her, knew that she didn't intend for her words to cut so deep but they did. They did, and Asha had to think about why.

"What do you—" she started weakly but stopped before finishing.

Rosa nodded, the gesture almost breaking Asha.

"You know what I mean, sweetheart. Your Chris's been gone since the day it happened. You just haven't—"

Don't let her say it.

Don't let her say that she hasn't let herself admit it.

Or that she hasn't let herself believe it.

Dear God, don't let her say she just hasn't gotten around to burying him yet.

"I *have* to come terms with it, Rosa," Asha spat, cutting in. "More than you know. And just because your husband has opened his eyes and grunted a little, maybe shed a few tears a couple of times, that doesn't mean that he's in there any more or less than Chris is. The doctors even told you not to get your hopes up, just like they told me."

"They said Larry's brain was still functioning, even if it's only a little," Rosa said solemnly, and that is all she would say. This was part of the grieving process, the nurse had told her when she expressed concern for the young lady she had befriended in the courtyard, the poor woman whom she had overheard getting the worst news anyone could. They had searched for family, but it seemed that no one had stuck around to help with the odds and ends of closing up the father's house, settling his final debts, deciding what was to be done with the nephew or cousin or whatever Chris was to them. They had left while that poor woman was recovering in her own hospital room, lucky to be alive herself. Her mother had stepped in, asked the staff to ease Asha into it as best they could, this new reality where her intended would likely never wake up, and Rosa supposed they were doing that much. She threatened litigation on Asha's behalf if they kept pushing for organ donation, and Rosa agreed with her on that point. Some of them had been like sharks... better yet, like vultures circling a wounded animal in the woods. Asha's mother had talked about that little girl who had been declared brain dead somewhere up North and how the family won the right to take her body out of there, kept her alive for a long time after. It was all so lawyerly and proper —terms being thrown around that have no place in a conversation about a man's life. But it had worked. And at the time, when Asha's mother had been conflicted about what she had done and it was *her* and Rosa occupying that rickety old picnic bench behind the hospital, Rosa had been proud of her. In awe of her. Asha's mother had done all those things to help her daughter see what was in front of her, give her time to come to grips with what was happening. But instead of easing into it, Asha had latched on to the idea that Chris would wake up one day. Rosa wished she hadn't overheard what the doctors told her mother when she was too sick to visit, wished she hadn't noticed the look of him herself the few times she had gone in the room to visit with her new friend's husband, bring a flower, say a prayer. He was an empty shell hooked up to all those machines: a man with no future at all.

But Rosa didn't say any of those things. She had promised Asha's mother she wouldn't after the woman had approached her, hesitantly dancing around the question of how her daughter seemed one day. Rosa worried that talking to her mother would be like betraying her new friend somehow and even now she felt like a double agent sometimes, but when she thought about it rationally, she really wasn't doing anything like that. She was Asha's friend; their unlikely bond had pulled them both through some difficult nights on the ward. She would always cherish that girl's friendship, even after she was gone. And she would be gone, Rosa knew, just as soon as reality set in about Chris, she would leave—she would have to. There would be no more reason to be there once they turned the machines off.

No, Rosa was no spy stealing secrets and feeding them to the enemy. She, Asha, and Asha's mother were all on the same team.

Rosa looked away, not wanting to see the hurt that she knew stood in Asha's eyes. They had been this far before; once she thought she had gotten through to the girl, gotten her to see reason. But Asha had only been toeing the edge, not looking over it. She wasn't ready to believe that the man she had been about to marry was gone.

Rosa waited for the conversation to pick up, wondering if this time she should give Asha a little nudge in the right direction.

"Mrs. Martinez," the nurse said quietly as she opened the door to the break area. She was a slight young woman with deep set eyes and skin that didn't get enough sun. "I thought I'd find you here. The doctor would like to go over the changes to the nutrition plan with you, if you have a minute."

The nurse smiled at Asha and Asha attempted to return it, felt her lips purse in some kind of way, but was unsure what her face actually looked like. She nodded at her friend as she got up to leave, her face conflicted as if she had something on her mind.

"I'll see you later, ok?" Rosa said on her way toward the door. "We can talk more then."

Asha nodded as Rosa left the table but felt cold as she moved through the door.

CHAPTER 6

Gabby didn't understand.

She had run from the house, her first instinct telling her to look for them, to find her children out there in the darkness, but she couldn't. She had encountered *something* but whatever it was let her pass without showing itself, and for that she was thankful. She could sense it smelling the air—smelling her—and it made the hair stand up on her neck. And she could hear it. The sound, the phlegmy inhalation, the heavy breath... Gabby imaged viscous strands of saliva vibrating with every pull of air, in and out of a gaping maw filled with teeth... It was coming from somewhere in the dark, somewhere close. It was enough to make her jump out of her skin.

If she'd had skin to jump out of.

But still, she didn't run. She didn't hide. Somehow that inclination, which would have been immediate when she was alive, didn't pull at her there.

Hmm.

Gabby was confused about the place she had found herself

in, a place where most of her family had been trying to save her from; a place where she would do the same for her children. It was dark there, cold. It felt evil but she couldn't put a finger on why. At the same time, it felt like where she was supposed to be, where she was destined to be. But she knew she shouldn't want that, shouldn't find comfort in the fact that the place didn't feel foreign to her. There was something wrong with it, The Realm as her father had called it. There was something very wrong there.

Gabby turned around, saw the house in the distance, and clamped her eyes shut. It wasn't real, her father had said, but yet it was. It was a house from her grandfather's memory, nothing more than a sketch really, yet it felt so very warm to her already. It would be different when she went back inside, she knew; her father and grandfather knew she needed to see things she recognized, things she could connect to or else Gabby would never be able to deal with what was happening. They would flesh it out, cull the details from their combined memories, knickknacks here, pictures there, to make it feel authentic. And it would. And Gabby would love it. But she wasn't supposed to.

She couldn't blame her family for trying. They didn't know what to do. They were terrified but didn't want to show it. They were sad that she was there, felt guilty about not being able to save her from the same fate but didn't want to mourn in front of her.

And there was something else they hadn't told her, something they weren't talking about with each other either. Something it seemed they couldn't figure out enough *to* talk about yet.

And then...

Christopher fell.

He fell right before Gabby's eyes.

He *fell.*

And he was there in The Realm... he had to be.

She could feel him.

Gabby didn't understand. It didn't make sense that this man that she saw fall out of the sky, his basket plummeting to the ground though seeming to glide, rocking back and forth so gently one might have mistaken it for a feather floating on a breeze, was her baby. The view had been hazy, distorted, some top-down strangeness that made everything seem surreal... *not* real. Gabby supposed that was for the best; seeing what really happened to her son who was a child the last time she had looked... seeing him fall from the sky without a filter, in real time and in full, unforgiving color, might have been more than her mind could bear. But still, it happened. Christopher had fallen from the sky. And his mother had watched.

She had just gotten there. Hadn't even gotten her bearings yet. Hadn't made her peace with her reality... and now she had to welcome her son to it.

Her husband had been thrown from the basket and she saw that too, had the chance to notice how handsome he looked with gray coming in at his temples and dotting his beard. Gabby had just long enough to see his eyes, wide and frightened as he was sucked out of the basket, away from their son and toward his doom. She fell to her knees as he disappeared from view, felt her stomach twist in a tight knot as realization set in that she would never see him again... ever, because The Realm wasn't for him. Gabby wanted to cry for him, for the pain that he was likely feeling at that very moment but there was no time. Her son careening to the ground filled her view and then there was blood, so much blood, so much destruction. Gabby only had enough time to wish her husband immediate death so that he could be spared what would be in store for him instead if he wasn't so lucky.

Her sobs, deep and guttural, had filled the room as her son bled; her body felt as broken as she imagined Chris's to be. But then, like a ray of light cutting through a storm cloud, a realization came to her. She saw her husband, a good man who hadn't deserved such a painful end; she saw her beautiful boy who died with love in his eyes—love that would paint her nightmares in hues of red and gold... but not her daughter.

Not her precious baby girl.

Where was Autumn?

Gabby scanned the world before her playing like a movie on a screen quickly then slower, with more deliberate strokes.

Nothing.

She called her for, her voice shrill and uncontained, a combination of frantic and delirious that would have been frightening in any other environment.

Nothing.

Her family reached toward her, her father and grandfather placing their hands on her shoulders, letting her know they were there, afraid she wouldn't be able to see them as she concentrated on the whirlwind of emotion. She begged them to show her how to navigate the new world they were in, how to find her child. She clawed at them, slapped at them, screamed when they were slower to respond than she thought they should be because her son had just died right before her eyes and she couldn't find her little girl. When they showed her, taught her how to search the living, she scoured the Earth for Autumn, turning over every stone the way they had advised. Gabby found Autumn's home quickly, noticed the things that gave her comfort in her life. There was no time to process what she was seeing, to take in the environment, because she soon found Autumn, found her daughter, her baby, her sweet girl and she was alive... she was *breathing*... but it wasn't her at all.

Gabby had called to Autumn, spoken to her the way she used to when she was little—the only way Gabby knew how to because she had never met the adult, she was looking at... had never had the chance to meet the young woman her daughter had become. Gabby had called to her gently, then forcefully, then she screamed her name, feigning anger in the hopes of jarring her awake, but nothing happened. Autumn didn't move.

Gabby searched the house they stood in, memories of marathon games of Peek-a-Boo with her baby, tickling the back of her neck, kissing her smiling face.

Nothing.

She had left the house then, looking for Christopher, looking for Autumn, looking for answers. Questions barked at her from the corners of her mind.

Why wasn't Autumn in the hot air balloon?

Why was she living that way?

Was didn't she wake up?

Was she dead?

If she was dead, where was she?

Where was Christopher?

Gabby searched the open space where she had found herself after closing her eyes to the living world.

Christopher and Autumn were nowhere to be found.

Where was she?

Where was Chris?

Where *were* they?

Home. She had to bring them home, bring them to her. They would figure out all the rest of it later. Gabby's arms ached with need; she felt hopeless standing there in the dark—in a place she didn't know, a place she feared as much as she felt welcomed. When she had left them, Autumn and Christopher were children. She hadn't worried about their safety because they were little and they had their father and she had been hopeful she would see them again one day. That was all she could allow herself in the end—that belief. Anything else would have destroyed her. But now their father was dead. She would not see him again, and that broke her heart. He was on the other side, fulfilling his destiny as she was fulfilling hers. Gabby was genuinely happy that he did not have to suffer the same fate as her, existing in a veritable limbo until the end of time.

But her children did, and she would not let them suffer alone. She was their mother. A cruel twist of fate had taken her from them so early that they might not remember the way her voice sounded when she sang to them at bedtime or the way her arms felt when she embraced them, but Gabby was still that person and they were still her babies. She needed to bring them home.

This was home. Gabby knew that with every fiber of her being. This dark, in-between place that left her cold, confused, and frightened—this was where they were always supposed to be.

God help them.

CHAPTER 7

Tara listened to the reunion of father and daughter as the woman saw Doug for the first time since his death. It was touching, but that wasn't the reason she stayed in the shadows; it wasn't the reason she had stayed hidden for so long and listened instead of killing everyone in sight. She did that because she had learned an important lesson in all of the lives she had lived, something that had saved her hide more than once: the one who knows the most knows the best.

There was a story here, something that went deeper than a power play. And Tara was entitled to know what that story was. After all, it had cost her everything she cared about.

The memory of her friends scattered on the ground, their blood black in the moonlight, danced around the edges of her consciousness but she forced it back into the hole it had wormed its way out of. There would be time to mourn them later, time to think about the hair and skin that were the only things left of Sebastian and Kincaid, of Aadi and Qiao. She'd have time to think about Lydjauk, her friend from a world different from her own... her friend whose severed arm, skin iridescent and morbidly beautiful, sat alone in the grass, spotlighted by the moon.

And Mileeha...

There would be time to think about him later too.

She hoped.

But now there were more pressing things to pay attention to, things Tara needed to understand before she made her next move. She listened, taking in more of the story. Doug and Patrick weren't who she thought they were, Tara saw that now. There was something important about them, something she should understand more about before she killed them in Mileeha's name.

And the new girl had something to do with it too.

Hers was the voice Tara had heard when she entered the house and that made her head spin. It was obvious that the woman hadn't been there before, sharing space with them; her voice had seemed to come from everywhere all at once, all around the house and grounds. But then, when she met Doug for the first time, she was in the room with him. It blew Tara's mind how quickly time passed in The Realm. She hadn't taken long to get into the house and find a suitable hiding place, but in those scant few minutes that woman had died in one world and awakened in another. That's why Tara never looked out anymore, never tried to see what happened to the people she knew. She had been there too long: the ravages of time had probably wiped everything connected to her from existence by now.

The woman left the house, but Tara knew she wouldn't be gone long just as well as she knew the Hunters wouldn't bother her. They weren't allowed to—Patrick wouldn't have it. She contemplated leaving the house when the woman did, hoping to slip past the Hunters while they were preoccupied by their new charge but decided against it. Tara thought they might kill her to protect the woman, might be ultra-aware of their surroundings by mandate. No, she'd have to stay where she was a while longer, much longer than she ever thought she would. Tara looked around the space where she'd hidden herself, a pantry of sorts in a kitchen that looked different now that Mileeha's offering to her had been wiped away and replaced with something of Patrick's own making but was still familiar. It would have been a horrible hiding place if they had all been alive—she'd have been a sitting duck among the canned goods and chip bags— but it was just fine for the dead who had no use for such things anymore. As she surveyed the spot, minimally outfitted—just a few cans with worn labels on the shelves; a broom; an apron; a bay leaf taped to one wall to keep the bugs away—an afterthought of whoever had manifested the structure, Tara realized that she hadn't really thought she'd survive to this point. The little detour she was taking; it had never dawned on her that such a thing might occur. Exacting her revenge was the culmination of her plan. When the time came Tara would welcome the true death—nothing about that had changed. But not before she understood everything. Before, Tara had been acting on blind rage, but fate had other things in mind. Like a pawn, she had been led to the house, put in position to infiltrate. But she had also been in position to overhear. And that had changed the game.

She could get answers.

She could get revenge.

She could change everything.

CHAPTER 8

The beeping was always harder to ignore when she came back to Chris's room after having been gone for a while. It seemed louder somehow, more insistent; her mind was more aware of it after the separation she had allowed herself, those few moments away from his bedside. She felt guilty when her senses returned, felt terrible for feeling invigorated by the fresh air or from feeling the sun on her face. All those good feelings were obliterated by the high-pitched beeping, the whirring and hissing of the machines that were keeping Chris alive, the return of reality. It made her sad, made her lonely, made her... Asha didn't want to admit all the things she felt about that room, that place... not even to herself.

She took a deep breath.

Asha found herself looking at the machines, checking levels and numbers to reacclimate herself, get back into the flow, but still the beeping grated on her, irritated her, made itself known.

Normal.

Everything was normal.

Except nothing was normal.

Asha didn't know if it would ever be normal again.

She was starting to sit as the beginnings of the gurgling started. She had about a minute or so before the choking sound would follow and only seconds before they would have company. This ritual had frightened her the first few times, sending her into a panic of calling Chris's name, hovering her hand over the tracheostomy tube wondering if she should touch it, maybe jiggle it a little to wrench whatever was clogging his throat free. She always made herself leave it alone, the fear of making whatever was happening worse stilling her hand, but she got close one time. It was a beautiful day; sunlight streamed into the room and she had been napping by his side. The sound of him choking woke her up and she jumped into action. She had reached out, put her hand on the tube, imagined Chris's eyes flying open in that instant, imagined that she had hurt him, and screamed instead.

It happened every day.

Asha used to leave when they suctioned out the mucus that collected in Chris's lungs and inhibited his breathing, the thin tube going into his tracheostomy hole more than she could bear, but she didn't anymore. She didn't leave when his feeding tube got blocked either, or when they changed his drainage bag. It must have been so uncomfortable for him; Asha could remember him nearly gagging when, in another life when Chris was a walking, talking version of himself, she had playfully depressed his tongue with her finger to look at his tonsils. She hoped Chris would show the nurses how much it bothered him one day, would grimace or tense up when they cleared his lungs or fooled with his feeding tube or did any of the intrusive things they had to do to maintain him. She hoped he would do something but so far he hadn't.

Asha didn't leave the room anymore. Instead, she helped administer the physical therapy he needed to prevent muscle contractures. She talked with the nurses while they worked side by side, making a point to ask questions that would encourage them to expound. She eagerly took everything they said in and looked up what she didn't understand later. That's how she learned more about the dangers Chris was facing by being in a coma for so long. She already knew all about the lack of brain activity that Chris's MRI showed—had learned as much a she could about that early on—but she didn't know about the bleeding that could occur if something went wrong with the tracheostomy tube or the elevated risk that coma patients had of infection.

"That might be what takes him, honey," said a kindly nurse who moved slower than Asha wanted when it came down to clearing Chris's lungs and stopping that gut-wrenching gurgling but kept the perfect pace when cleaning him up and changing his soiled bed pads. She called them diapers but Asha couldn't make herself use that term.

"He's young but in here, pneumonia takes more than its share."

The nurse worked as she talked most of the time, educating Asha in ways she hadn't even thought to ask about. Nurse Bea had told her things it would have taken months to look up and she offered the information willingly, as if she knew it was what Asha needed. It was she who explained that Chris might smile sometimes or cry, that he might do so in earnest sometimes and it would be hard to see those big, fat tears rolling down his face if it happened but she reminded Asha not to think anything of it, told her that just because it looked like emotion, it wasn't. Reflex, she called it, and cursed the way it hurt the people looking on almost as soon as the word had made it out of her mouth and into the world. She calmed Asha down when the students who came in to learn about coma patients threw around slang, words like 'trach' and 'PEG', 'comorbid', even 'M&M'... especially 'M&M'. Asha never got used to the casual sound of those terms; they were nothing more than jargon, terms of the trade, but they still got her dander up. Asha asked Nurse Bea what M&M meant one day and she wouldn't tell her. When she looked it up on her own, Asha could understand why.

Gurgling... a little louder now.

She put her hand on his chest, felt the rattle there. She eyed the leads that reached toward all the machines that monitored his breathing, his heart rate, his everything. All connected. A frown crested on her brow as she wondered what was taking them so long to come to him. She considered reaching for the call button and summoning them herself, lifted her arm to stretch toward the button but got distracted by something that hadn't been there before. Her eyes caught the cover of a magazine that someone had brought in for her and left on the chair—her chair, next to his bed. There was a house on the front, a big, beautiful, three-story thing with a reddish pink façade and a lush green lawn in front of it. The house didn't remind of her any place she had ever been—it wasn't that. What struck a chord was that it was a house.

A *house*.

It was nearing the first of the month. That meant bills would be due soon.

All of the bills.

Even with the programs in place to pay for almost 70% of the hospital fees and Chris's own health insurance kicking in just under 20%, the remainder of the bills were almost as much as their rent every month. Asha hadn't been to work in months

—not since the accident. Within two months, Chris's medical bills had eaten up their savings.

They needed to sell Chris's father's house to pay for his subacute care.

No, not *they*. Legally, there was no they. Not yet.

Not ever, the voice in her head chimed but Asha didn't allow herself to react. Coma patients could hear things and feel things, or so she had read somewhere during one late night research session or another. Maybe not physical things like pain or someone's hand on their skin, but some doctors thought that comatose patients could sense emotion the same way that animals can. The article said emotions flowed from people in waves and that comatose patients could pick up on that, could become agitated because of it, could have some kind of response, like maybe their heartrate speeding up, and Asha didn't want that. She didn't want Chris to know what she was thinking, didn't want Chris to believe she had given up because if he did, he might give up, and then—.

A hacking laugh cut into the room, breaking the silence and cutting off her out of control thoughts. She looked at Chris instinctively, before registering that she hadn't felt his voice coming up through the tube to blare into the room—that it would be nearly impossible for him to do that anyway considering the state of his voice box. It was then that she remembered his roommates; two men he would likely never meet sharing the same air, the same space, the same fate. One of them, the 75-year-old who had been in the subacute unit for eight years already, made loud, involuntary sounds every now and then. They used to drive Asha mad, her emotions ranging from surprise to frustration, but not anymore. Now he was part of the fabric of the place to her, just like she was.

The other man never made a sound.

No one came to visit them, the older man with all the sounds having lost his wife without ever knowing she had died and the younger was a John Doe resigned to that state after bad weather left his car wrapped around a tree two years back. Asha felt bad when she pulled Chris's curtain to have some privacy but she did it anyway. She had gotten used to a lot of things over the past few months, but not to having two bodies in the room all the time, witnessing her grief.

Bodies. It bothered her that she thought of them that way, but she did.

"Ok, Asha, I'll take care of it," the nurse said, pulling her out of her own head. She put a hand on Asha's arm and gently urged her to the side to make room. Asha complied willingly, hardly registering the movement or the absence of Chris's chest beneath her palm, her mind occupied with thoughts of the future and how empty it had become. She had moved back home with her mother already, taking what she could and storing the rest. They had searched for Chris's sister in all the places they could think of. They had reached out to the few family members that would answer their emails and even a few of Chris's college friends to look for clues about Autumn, but no one knew anything. A crowdfunding campaign had brought in enough money to satisfy the bills for another few months but that was just delaying the inevitable. They needed to sell Chris's father's house to keep Chris comfortable for the rest of the time he had left. No, she chastised herself again. Not *they*.

She.

CHAPTER 9

They were impatient.

Patrick and Doug knew why Gabby needed some space, they understood all too well the overwhelming feelings that came with waking up in The Realm, and to see what she saw on top of everything else... Neither of them thought they would ever forget seeing Christopher's body hurtling to the ground. Their hearts ached for him and also for gabby, for every moment she mourned and every tear he shed. But time was of the essence. Soon Christopher and Autumn would be in The Realm with them if they didn't do something to stop it. They had to try; Patrick couldn't live with himself if he didn't.

Patrick thought it might already be too late for one of them. He didn't want to say it, didn't want to give the thought any legs, but he half expected Gabby to walk back into the house holding her son's hand.

So did Doug.

They started looking almost as soon as they heard the door close, searching for Autumn frantically, the unspoken urgency to find the only descendant with a chance at being alive urging them on. They found her when they were on the verge of giving up—right when Patrick had decided to try for Christopher just to be sure. They had looked where they found her already, remembered the squalor she was living in with quiet pity. Doug was looking around her house again, focusing on Autumn one more time to make sure they hadn't missed anything when he suddenly found himself looking at the Sydney Opera House as though from a boat on the harbor. Then he saw a sprawling city, the night sky lit with yellow and blue and white as he looked down on it from above—high up as if from the Empire State Building. He motioned toward his father, thought to call out to him so he could see what he was seeing but Doug couldn't make his voice work. He was too amazed, too awed by the visuals, too confused about what they meant. A few more places flashed in front of his eyes before the idea of calling out to Patrick came around again, limestone cliffs overlooking calm water at sunset; a medieval church, a colorful market bustling with food and fabric vendors... and then he was back in Autumn's house, a drug den in the making. Doug's outstretched hand connected with Patrick's arm unseen and he felt his dad turn around to see it all as new locations flickered, showed themselves in bright colors, before settling back into the dim space where Autumn's body lay. Doug hadn't realized he was still gasping, still staring in disbelief at the wall even after Autumn and her bedroom disappeared. It took his father's tight grip on his arm to snap him out of it. He turned to look at Patrick only to find his mouth hung open in shock as he stared at the wall behind Doug's head. He turned in the direction Patrick was looking and felt his own jaw unhinge and drop open to mirror his father's at the sight.

"Holy God," Patrick whispered, never realizing he had spoken at all.

CHAPTER 10

Asha had never felt more confused, more disoriented, more off kilter. And there was more, another emotion that she was afraid to give credence to, its very existence enough to make her run from the room and never return. But she couldn't avoid it, couldn't leave its presence unacknowledged, because to do so would only be a lie.

Asha was frightened.

Not of Chris—surely he had just been the vehicle for her hallucination, a comfortable place where her mind felt safe enough to go off the rails. Not of the nurse who came in to find her screaming like she had lost a limb, that guttural emission that spoke of extreme hurt or deep emotional pain, discordant from the quiet sounds of life support that were the constant in the room—the sound she felt in the pit of her stomach as it wrenched its way out of her. She wasn't afraid of the men who were subjected to the sudden keening as they lay unmoving, unable to clap their hands over their ears or remove themselves from the room to escape it. Asha was afraid, but not of or for any of those reasons, at least not in any tangible way.

She was afraid for herself.

Because she was certain she had lost her mind.

That was the only explanation for what she saw.

Because she *had* seen it; had heard it too. Whether or not it was a figment of her imagination was a different question entirely. That something happened and she witnessed it was the important thing to consider and that had definitely happened. She was sure of it. She was simultaneously sure that if she didn't calm down, didn't close her mouth and stop saying the things she was saying, they would put her away.

Asha woke up at home, the doctors having strongly urged her to leave, get some rest, and come back the next day. She understood what they weren't saying—that they didn't want the disruption, wouldn't be able to explain it if her screams caused one of the patient's trauma... didn't know if something like that was possible, but definitely, 100% did not want to find out... not that way—and on that point she had to agree. If there was going to be a sound that jolted them out of their comas, she would rather it be the sound of Prince's guitar solo in *Purple Rain* or the climax of Pavarotti's *Nessun Dorma*, not the sound of her sanity fracturing amid the chorus of beeps that had been their backdrop for more years than were fair to count.

Prince of Pavarotti, sure...

Or maybe Bruno Mars.

Anything by Bruno Mars.

Chris would have laughed at the list Asha had put together —that she would have even thought to put Prince, Pavarotti, and Bruno Mars together in the same sentence, but then it would have dawned on him how perfect the connection was. To some the rocker, operatic tenor, and crooner had no business in the same conversation. But to Asha it was melodic symmetry.

Chris.

Asha shuddered, wrapped her arms around herself as she sat up in her bed and it made her sick to realize that her reaction was about him. *Because* of him. Chris. The man she loved. The man she had planned to marry. The man who evoked emotions from her that she never knew existed; more than joy, desire, anger, love—everything hot, everything to the max. Even now, the fear that was brewing inside her stemmed from him, was a response to what he did... what the doctors said he couldn't do. But she knew he had done it, knew that with every fiber of her being, unless she was wrong... unless she could no longer trust herself.

When the nurses ran in, they expected the worst. They sprang into action as soon as they heard Asha, never pausing to wonder why the equipment hadn't alerted them, just reacting to the shrill persistence in her voice, the sharp knife that cut through the normalcy of the ward. He was dying, they assumed. They thought Chris was dying and Asha was seeing it happen before her eyes. It was the scenario they hated most: the loved one in the room witnessing the throes of death. The family always thought they were ready for it; always thought they would remain calm. But death was cruel and undignified. It had a way of weakening even the most stoic. The nurse thought they would have to try to save Chris's life, to prolong the suffering they would both have to endure because their jobs required such measures in lieu of the compassion that would end that poor soul's misery, but when they got to his bedside there was nothing out of the ordinary. They couldn't understand what had made Asha scream like the devil had her by the hair because nothing seemed amiss: not his vitals, not his breathing level, or his color... nothing at all. He was lying in bed as he usually was, flat on his back, nose pointed toward the ceiling. His head hadn't lolled to the side, his jaw had not disengaged to let his tongue protrude. His eyes were still closed and his face was still dry, no tears having wet them. There was no flatline, no seizure, nothing. Chris was the same as he always ways. Yet Asha was inconsolable.

At least she had stopped screaming.

The nurses fluttered around Asha trying to calm her down, give her water, get her to control her breathing, but nothing worked. At least, not until they got her out of the room. She didn't want to go, couldn't tear her eyes away from where Chris lay on the bed. They even had to block her view to stop her from craning her neck to see him as they ushered her out of the room. Her eyes were wild, almost crazed. Nurse Bea told her later, once she had calmed down enough to have tea with her in the nurse's lounge, that they thought they might have to sedate her. She wasn't acting like herself. She was saying crazy things.

"I probably shouldn't put it that way, political correctness and all that, but what're they gonna do this this ole gal?" Nurse Bea said conspiratorially, reclining into her seat as she spoke. "I don't pay them no mind."

Her voice was like a warm biscuit slathered with butter and honey snuck from Asha's grandmother's kitchen. Asha took a deep breath and let it out slowly, letting the feeling wash over her, calm her.

"What scared you so in there, honey? You can tell me," Nurse Bea said after a while.

Asha looked at the older woman, reading her face. She knew what she wanted to say would sound off the wall, knew she had to tell someone about it, but something made her pause, take a second to decide if that someone was Nurse Bea. She couldn't tell her mother—Asha didn't think she could stand the pity in her eyes. She didn't know if she should tell Rosa—she didn't want the only friend she had who understood what she was dealing with firsthand to think she had finally lost herself. The nurse's salt and pepper hair was styled neatly, the curl reminiscent of the ones her grandmother would get when she slept with the pink foam rollers in, bent under itself in a tight spiral. She hadn't combed the curl out; had just let the tight curl stay and somehow that made her seem more real than anything else. Nurse Bea's face was kind and her eyes even more so.

Asha took a chance.

"He moved, Nurse Bea," she started, unable to control the tremor in her voice, "he moved."

Nurse Bea saw her distress and patted her hand gently. There was true compassion in her eyes when she spoke.

"They do that sometimes, sweetheart, but like I told you before, it doesn't mean anything... not as far gone as he is." She paused, trying to decide whether or not she should continue.

"It's just a reflex," she finished.

Asha shook her head rapidly in disbelief.

"No, no this was more than just a reflex. His finger didn't just twitch. His didn't just raise an eyebrow or something like that. He *moved*."

Nurse Bea stayed silent, waiting because there was more, maybe a lot more, and she could see that Asha was ready to tell it.

Asha searched Nurse Bea's eyes for something, anything that would make her bite her tongue, but she found nothing.

She took a deep breath and plunged ahead before she could stop herself.

"He sat up and spoke to me."

CHAPTER II

Nurse Bea was quiet and that was not in her nature. She hoped it didn't worry the girl, didn't stop her from speaking because if anyone needed to talk, it was her. Bea felt sick for the young woman in front her, eyes pleading, sweat forming high on her forehead at the hairline. She really did. The poor girl had sat there day in and day out since she herself had been released from the hospital, sitting next to the man she had planned to give her heart to only to find that he would never be able to take it. By all rights he should have been dead, should have died out there in that field doing the one thing he wanted to; the only thing he could ever do for her again. He had saved Asha's life by landing the way he did and making sure she landed that way too; cleaving her to him in those last moments was a kindness that not many people would ever experience. That man, nothing but a boy really, loved Asha and when it mattered, he tried to give her a fighting chance... even when there was almost no chance she'd live anyway. He didn't expect to make it, but he had. Bea couldn't decide if that was a curse or a miracle.

Nurse Bea was quiet because she didn't know whether or not to snap at the child, try to jar her out of her line of thinking, or cry with her. She couldn't imagine waking up to find out that her love was stuck in the hell of his own mind, dead but laying there still, breathing only because the machines made him do it. Bea didn't know how the girl could stand it; seeing the love of her life lying there motionless, skin shiny and unnatural, like those wax figures at Madame Tussaud's. And then to know that he sacrificed himself so she could live? Bea knew that if her Travis had done something like that and ended up in the state that young man was in, she wouldn't be able to stand it. The guilt would eat her alive. So because Bea couldn't figure out how to react to the poor woman's claim, a claim that couldn't be true, no matter how much she wanted it to be because the man was dead, he was dead but he just didn't know it yet, Bea stayed quiet. She needed to find a way to talk the girl down, get her to stop saying things that made her sound like she was losing her grip on reality. That's what they would say if they heard her talking like that, though Bea didn't know exactly who she meant when she said 'they'. The head nurse? The doctors? Most of them had heard the screaming anyway; it was loud enough to rock the whole floor. The head of the hospital? It didn't really matter who 'they' was, *someone* would say she was unwell if she didn't stop it. They might stop her from seeing her fiancé if they thought she couldn't handle it. Even though no one would blame her for losing it considering everything she had been through, they would still stop her from coming and Bea knew that would be a bad thing. She had the feeling that the girl needed to be there as much as she wanted to be; maybe even more so. She had the feeling that the girl didn't have anything else in her life to keep her grounded, that the dark room and all the machines beeping around her man who was never going to open his eyes was all she had left. Bea had the feeling that keeping Asha away from Chris would be a death sentence.

Nurse Bea lowered her eyes, breaking eye contact with the girl while she thought of something to say. She watched the girl's feet, one flat on the floor but the other with its heel raised, bobbing up and down erratically as she attempted to assuage her own nerves. She was barely holding it together.

Come on, Bea! Help this girl!

Bea couldn't patronize; if she did, the woman would never confide in her again.

She couldn't spout the medical shit again. Lord knows that girl had heard enough of that.

She couldn't mislead her into thinking that she right, that she was on to something that the doctors hadn't noticed yet. Bea knew better. Bea knew if she made the girl believe that lie it could have lasting damage and it wouldn't be right to risk her mental state just so Bea could get herself out of a hard conversation.

So, what the hell should she do?

Bea sat with her arms crossed in front of her, one hand on her stomach and the other gripping her forearm, just like she had before Asha had said that outlandish thing. She hoped she didn't look like a statue, frozen and cold, unable to speak, unable to provide solace even though that's how she felt. And she hated herself for it. In that moment Bea hated all the bureaucratic warnings that were sounding off in her head, hated that she had dedicated her life to helping people but she couldn't help this young woman keep a handle on her sanity. She hated that she looked every bit the part of Nurse Bea, professional helper with years of knowledge to draw upon, but was, in fact, a fraud.

Open your mouth!

Bea obeyed her inner voice, the one that was through with her at the moment, sick of her hesitation to help the girl in front of her; someone who needed her more than anyone had in a long time—and spoke.

"What did you—" Bea started but Asha had decided she was going to tell it and nothing was going to get in her way. Bea admired her; she was strong... stronger than Bea herself thought she would be if the roles were reversed. She let herself get talked over, stopping her words mid-sentence, all the while silently thanking Asha for saving an old lady from making the situation worse. Then she listened, really listened the way no one else would; not the doctors, another nurse, her friend down the hall, or even her mother.

She listened because there was nothing better she could think to do.

CHAPTER 12

Asha felt off-balance as she recounted what happened in Chris's room, but she pushed through anyway. Even as Nurse Bea looked at her with sad eyes and was obviously being careful to keep her face straight as her medical training warred with her humanity, Asha kept going. Because she had to say it out loud, even if she knew how it made her sound. If she didn't, she was afraid that the implications might destroy her.

'He sat up and spoke to me,' was how she started, but that's not where the story began. Asha could feel the hair on the back of her neck standing on end as she remembered it all—Chris's voice, rough from so many months of disuse, tongue thick and heavy: a mouth not expecting to work again. Things had moved in the room when Chris spoke, before she heard his voice, before she was even aware that anything had changed. Papers rustled in a nonexistent wind; the IV rod pulled ever so gently toward Chris, its wheels squeaking. Something whined in the room—a low, faint noise of frustration as whatever it was leaned, reached, was unable to touch. Asha thought it might have been that sound that woke her from the almost sleep she was indulging in, that weird middle place where everything seemed right, like a hazy Sunday afternoon curled up on the sofa, nowhere to go, no one needing anything. It might have been that sound—that yearning keen—but she couldn't be sure, would never be sure, not after what she saw when her eyes focused.

Chris was facing her.

She thought it was the light.

She thought she was still asleep.

She thought it was her hopeful imagination.

But as Asha sat up in her chair, she knew that it was none of those. Chris was facing her. His eyes were open and he was looking at her. He was *looking* at her.

Asha shrieked in what might have been a mix of surprise and fright because even in those early moments of wakefulness she could tell something wasn't right. His face wasn't used to being animated anymore; his muscles weren't used to being active. She had the impression that he was trying to smile at her —the pull of his lips at the corners indicated as much—but he fell short of the mark. Instead of the pleasantness that the look used to impart, the warmth it gave off, the awed kind of love that it used to express, Asha was met with a caricature... no, that wasn't it. Her eyes watered as her mind struggled to define the way he looked but she kept trying. He had looked at her with sunken eyes that shouldn't be that way considering how much fluid was being pumped into him; his muscles had relaxed so much that the flesh on the inside of his lower eyelid showed and it was marbled and raw. His nose, his cheek, his lips split like a gash more so than spread into a smile, hung limply on his skull, like a shirt situated on a hanger on its side; everything seeming to droop... to melt onto the bed. It was horrific yet beautiful at the same time... the man she was in love with was waking up, finally waking up. Chris was finally coming back to her.

Except some part of her wondered if what she was seeing wasn't just a cruel joke: the beginning of the end of her resolve.

"'Chris?' I said at first, but I kept my voice quiet because I was afraid that... that what I was seeing wasn't... wasn't..."

Asha was suddenly scared to continue. She had started the story and there was no turning back, she knew that, but that didn't make it any easier to keep going. She looked down at her hands, at the engagement ring she still wore; the ring she couldn't imagine ever taking off. She could still see him on bended knee with museums at his back and leaves underfoot. She could still hear him singing her favorite song as he asked her to be his.

Nurse Bea put her hand on Asha's shoulder, the rubbing motion a natural instinct.

"Go ahead, baby," she said, professionalism thrown out the door right behind her good sense. "I'm here."

Asha looked the nurse in the eye, saw the wisdom etched in the lines on her face, and knew that if she was going to tell anyone it would be her. She screwed on her courage, took a deep breath, and continued.

"I thought I was hallucinating," Asha continued, buoyed by the woman's kindness. "I thought I just wanted him to wake up so bad that I made myself believe it was actually happening."

"You wouldn't be the first," Nurse Bea offered, letting her arm drop from Asha's shoulder as she settled into the tale. She had seen more than her fair share of people wishing for something to happen so badly that they made more than they should have out of the little things.

Asha nodded. "I thought it was all in my head, you know?

And he just didn't … he didn't look right, so I just stayed quiet… I wanted to give myself the chance to figure it all out."

"Of course," Nurse Bea said, providing the understanding that the girl needed to keep telling her story. She'd have told her how smart a decision that was but felt like the message might be misunderstood as patronizing. She couldn't risk alienating the girl, not now.

"He answered me right away," Asha continued, "told me not to be afraid. I felt so bad when he said that—wondered what he saw in my face that would make him think I was afraid. Because I *was* afraid… I'm still afraid, Nurse Bea. His face was… it was…"

How could she tell the nurse that his face looked like a reflection in a funhouse mirror, elongated and distended… outright wrong? How could Asha tell her that she was afraid for him to open his mouth, afraid to see the teeth that were yellowing beneath his dying lips, or the tongue that she was sure was covered with that stuff she had read about that happens with poor oral hygiene back when she was able to stomach the flood of content on the Internet a little better… that black, hairy tongue stuff… She didn't think she could survive seeing that.

"He didn't look like your man," Nurse Bea supplied, trying to help the girl get the story out. Asha nodded her head reluctantly, almost as if admitting as much was a betrayal.

Her mouth was pasty and sour.

Bea thought she was going to have to say something else to coax the girl into speaking again, say something that would make her feel comfortable enough to continue, but she didn't. When Asha spoke, it was as if she was speaking to Bea from somewhere far away.

"He said… he told me he loved me and that I shouldn't be afraid. It took me a minute to respond but I said I wasn't. He smiled at me that way he used to whenever I said something that didn't sound right; like I might have gotten some term wrong or used the wrong word or whatever. He knew all this random stuff, could just remember all these things from school, words and details that went into most people's ears and out the other. It was almost like he read the dictionary when he was growing up or something, memorized biography details, and his job just added onto it. Chris always hated it when people just looked up stuff on the Internet without even trying to figure it out first or worse, when they asked Siri or Alexa to give them the answer. He thought it was lazy. Or cheating. We used to get into these conversations about moving with the times. I used to remind him that these were his times too, not just mine, and that it was like he was living in the past or something, like an old soul. He would laugh then because it was true. It was ingrained in him; he could be so old-fashioned sometimes.

"Anyway," Asha said, taking a breath, realizing that she had been rambling, had gotten off topic, but it felt so good. For a moment she had been able to talk about Chris like he was real— like he was *him*, not some shell laying in the other room being kept alive by machines. Because that's all that was happening now—he wasn't truly living. Somewhere deep inside she knew that was the truth but she was unwilling to acknowledge it... unwilling to accept it. She wanted to tamp it down, to push it away and live in the fantasy she had given herself over to willingly the moment she had heard that Chris had survived, was still alive. She wanted to stay in that hopeful place that told her he would wake up one day and they would get married, maybe on an island instead of in their backyard as they had planned, and they would have the babies they wanted to have and all of this would be in the past, something they had overcome, something they shook their heads over and hugged each other about when they thought about that thing that had happened all those years before. She wanted to live in *that* world, but reality wormed its way into her mind more and more every day, inching forward ever so slightly as his ECG line rose and fell.

"He smiled at me like that and I smiled back and it was like before, know what I mean? It was like we were out at a restaurant or taking a walk in the city—just me and Chris like we used to be."

Asha stopped talking and pinched her nose to stop the tears from starting up again. Bea picked up the slack.

"I bet that felt good," she said low, almost inaudibly, and she meant it.

Asha nodded and continued,

"But then he started saying things that didn't make any sense."

Nurse Bea had taken to rubbing Asha's shoulder again somewhere along the way and she did so in earnest. Asha was wading into dangerous waters now and while Nurse Bea knew the girl had always been heading in that direction, it was hard to watch it happen anyway. She wanted to tell her that murmuring, mumbling, subvocalization of any kind wasn't possible for Chris. He was more than obtunded... he was so deeply unconscious that no one really knew if he was in there anymore. Most of the nurses on the ward didn't think he was. Nurse Bea would never tell that poor girl that she was one of them.

"Asha... honey, that d—"

"It doesn't make any sense, I know. He's not even alive—I know that's what everyone thinks. But he spoke to me, Nurse Bea. He told me things that I didn't know—things I never even heard about until today. He—"

Asha wanted to take a sip of the tea sitting on the table in front of her, wanted to do something with her hands other than what they wanted to do, which was hold onto her forearms and quell the chill she felt deep inside her, hold on for dear life. But her hands were shaking too much to even try.

"He said that I had to hurry. That even though I was afraid, I had t—"

Asha cut her words off without warning, letting them die on her tongue.

She couldn't tell Nurse Bea about that.

She couldn't tell *anyone* about that.

She tightened her grip on her arms, looked at the mug and realized she might need something a little stronger to deal with what was coming clear to her now, in the forgotten room of tired nurses who stumbled in there in search of something to keep them awake or a place to steal a few winks.

She couldn't say *anything*.

The things Chris had told her made her feel like she was awakening for the first time and finding herself in a different world, a place she didn't understand. That she had been so oblivious to it, this existence that she had never heard of before, frightened her to her core. It was like not knowing what happened around you when you slept or that a spider was nearby, watching you unseen. If Chris was right, nothing that she knew was real—it had all been an illusion. If it had all been a figment of her imagination, if he had never sat up and spoken to her, never told her a story that made her feel insignificant and like she was the last woman left in the world at the same time, then she had definitely lost her mind. Either scenario being true terrified her, yet one of them had to be true.

Asha had never felt more alone in her life.

Her mouth closed with an audible pop as her upper and lower teeth clanked against each other. Asha looked at the older woman, the lingering surprise on her own face slowly being replaced by tacit understanding as she regarded the compassion in the nurse's eyes.

She could say no more.

"Had to what, honey?" Nurse Bea prodded, not liking the resolute set of Asha's jaw. She needed to keep her talking. If she was going to be able to help the woman at all, she had to know more.

"N-nothing," Asha stammered, finding her legs. She stood without warning, fast but sure.

Nurse Bea recoiled, saving the mug of tea she had picked up to drink from Asha's sudden movement. In her surprise, the nurse slammed the mug down, putting it on the table harder than she meant to. She closed her fingers around one of Asha's forearms and squeezed gently. She stayed seated, hoping that might encourage Asha to sit back down too. Bea wanted to turn her away from whatever mission she thought she was on. More than anything Bea just wanted to help Asha process her new reality.

"You said you were afraid—"

"Of his face... you were right, Nurse Bea," Asha said hurriedly. "He just doesn't look like my Chris, as you said."

Asha reached for her mug with the arm Bea held, causing her to let go. Bea hated giving up the connection but she was sure that was what the woman was trying to orchestrate anyway.

As Asha took a sip of the tea that she no longer wanted, Nurse Bea tried other ways to talk her back into her seat, but none of them worked.

"I guess... I guess I've just been spending a lot of time here and I... things just went a little crisscrossed for me is all," Asha yielded, hoping that would be enough to get her out of the room. She needed to leave the hospital, needed to think about what Chris had told her—needed to decide if she really believed that he spoke to her or if it was all an elaborate hallucination. She couldn't afford to lose any of the details and sitting there dancing around Nurse Bea's questions wouldn't help.

"I'm tired," she continued, "and I need a shower. I'll feel better about all of this after I get some rest." Those things were true but Asha knew that sleeping and feeling warm water on her skin wouldn't help—not this time. But her words hit their intended mark and made the impact she hoped they would. Nurse Bea's brow unfurled and she looked visibly relieved by Asha's admission. Good. Now maybe she could leave and get some time alone to think.

"I'm sure you will, Asha. Rest does wonders for the brain. Brings it back to tip top shape."

Nurse Bea looked into Asha's eyes, looking for something.

The space between them was filled with unspoken questions and the makings of lies.

Asha nodded to break the stare.

Nurse Bea, unsure of what she saw reflected in the young woman's eyes, blinked in response. She couldn't keep her there, hold her in place, lock her in the room. She couldn't keep asking the woman questions that she didn't want to answer; if there was any trust there at all, that behavior would surely strain it, if not break it entirely. There was nothing left to do but to let her go.

"You'll feel so much better after a good night's sleep," Nurse Bea finished. She stood, smoothed her uniform, and offered her a smile that she didn't feel, not entirely.

Asha returned it with one that reflected the fatigue that she was feeling but not the reason for it. She left the nurse in the break room to clean up the mugs after thanking her for her kindness and assuring her that she had a way home. As the door closed behind her she looked toward Chris's room. The door was closed as it should be, but her mind's eye saw him lying there, the third bed in a row of insensate men. And he was smiling at her.

CHAPTER 13

At first, she thought it might be cool.

Letting herself do things she never would have done; being aware of what she was doing but uninhibited... she thought it would be fun. She could be anyone she wanted to be, could go anywhere she wanted to go. The world, the universe, the past, the future, it was all open to her. She could create them and peruse them, sample them, revel in them... do whatever she wanted whenever she wanted. She hadn't realized that right away, didn't understand how much she wanted that reality. At first, she was angry, felt betrayed by the guy first and foremost—he was a complete asshole, without a doubt—but also by fate, by her job, by her own self. And she had a right to be. A last-minute decision to go dancing after a shitty day at work and then the barely conceived notion to sleep with the guy in front of her, the one with the Adonis belt she couldn't wait to trace with her tongue, shouldn't have ended with a tab in her mouth and a trip to the fucking moon. But it did. And she kept going back.

Autumn liked the pretty colors the stars made as they cut patterns across the sky; she liked the mischievous glint in Mona Lisa's eye. Her conversation with her great-great-great grand-daughter was unceremoniously cut off when she came down and Autumn was determined to get back to the shores of Mauritius to continue it: the girl with the long black hair and red ochre skin had been about to tell Autumn the name of her second child. She started chasing the feeling, relishing the experience of being somewhere else—anywhere else—more than where she was. She started microdosing LSD to get through the day because work was a bitch and she spent more hours at her desk than she spent at home. But then again, what was waiting for her at home? Nothing. No boyfriend. No roommate... well, at least not before all this. Not even a dog. Chris was the one with the fiancée and the nice job and the future. He was the one doing what was expected of him, making their dad proud. Autumn? She was just taking up space.

She didn't know when she had started thinking of it like that, but she did now.

Autumn wanted to change.

She wanted something new.

Something fun.

Something interesting.

The world behind her eyelids was all of those things and more. She was in control there, could manipulate the world around her to show her what she felt like seeing. So what if she couldn't even find Mauritius on a map in the real world. When she closed her eyes, she was already there if she wanted to be.

There were songs about shit like that. Autumn could finally relate.

Psychedelics.

The good shit.

Autumn lost her job because she tripped at work... more than once. Tongue-kissing a stapler that she imagined was a Nollywood heartthrob was apparently not ok.

She got a roommate, a friend of a friend who like to party sometimes too. Her vice was weed. The roommate had a boyfriend and he did harder stuff but still kept a solid job and always, always had the hook up. They were cool... at least it seemed that way but it didn't matter if they weren't, because the lilacs in her headspace smelled so sweet and the sun was so very warm.

Autumn came to one day to find her house trashed. Her roommate and her boyfriend were in the wind. She didn't know how long they had been gone but they definitely were, and so was most of her shit. The TV was gone, her jewelry too, but the joke was on them if they thought they had gotten away with anything. The TV was old and the jewelry was nothing more than chips of semi-precious stones, some of them lab created. She went on a good trip after that, too sad and pissed off to do anything but go back into the world she created. She met up with a woman who had shown her the Amalfi coast and the inside of Mount Vesuvius. She said she'd show Autumn what the people actually did the day before it blew up if Autumn wanted or she would take her to Rome to watch the games. Autumn knew she would do it, too, because she had made good on promises before. Every single one of them. Autumn hadn't been able to find her great-great-great granddaughter again, but she could find the woman who knew everything almost every time.

When Autumn had woken up and her shit was still gone and it hadn't been a dream, she got angry again. The roommate was supposed to have been there to watch over her when she tripped just in case it was a bad one or if she took too much and her breathing went weird. The roommate was supposed to have been there to hear her stories or just laugh with her when she came out. That was part of the deal they'd made, but fuck Autumn's afterglow, apparently.

Now she was back again—*awake* again—and pissed again too.

Autumn surveyed her place to see just how bad it really was. It didn't take long for her to realize it was worse than she thought. Most of her shit was gone and there was *new* shit in the kitchen. Something the boyfriend had used to cook whatever shit he pumped into his veins and then discarded on her table and floor. Hardcore drug shit. No.

Autumn didn't want any of that stuff laying around—her place wasn't some kind of crack house. She'd need to clean all that up before... before what? Before her guests came for dinner?

The bitter laugh that crawled out of her throat didn't sound familiar to her ears at all.

Thirsty.

Hungry.

How long had it been since she'd eaten?

Autumn couldn't remember but knew it was time to rectify that.

She opened the refrigerator to find that they had eaten most of the food before they made off with her worldly possessions, leaving her with a jar of olives, a half-loaf of stale bread she didn't remember buying, and some ketchup.

Sandwich?

Slice up the olives, toast the bread, smother the whole thing in ketchup?

No. She wasn't that far gone yet.

Autumn tore off a piece of the sliced bread and crammed it into her mouth ignoring the sour bite of stale. She trudged back into her bedroom and shut the door bringing the rest of the loaf with her. She'd closed the door resorting to the thing she did when she was a kid—the only thing that made her feel in control. It had made her feel better to lock her messes away, to shut the door against them and deal with them later when she had figured out what the next step would be. She used to toss the stuff she wasn't ready to handle into her closet, force the door closed, get it out of sight at least until the next morning, but by then she'd be ready. She'd have a game plan; she'd know what to do. Sometimes.

Autumn closed the door to her bedroom, leaving all the shit the roommate and her druggy boyfriend had left on the other side of it, out of sight. There was a lot of crap out there that she'd have to deal with and soon but she didn't want to do it right then. Not when she was wondering what aurora borealis looked like from Venus.

Autumn had just gotten out of bed, hadn't even peed yet, couldn't have been out of her last trip for longer than thirty minutes, but she was going back in anyway. The real world sucked and she wanted out. She wanted to dress like the queen of England and watch red, orange, yellow, and blue powder shoot from her shoes as she hovered over the tidal basin in DC. She wanted to ask the woman who knew everything if there were roses in the air pockets in the Pacific Ocean or if the earth used to have three moons but the other two disintegrated. She wanted to go back to a time where she mattered.

Autumn didn't know how long ago that had been.

All she knew was suspended animation; the blackness of space around her; no forward, no back; a room with books stacked all the way up to the ceiling where touching one spine might make the whole thing come down on her head. All she knew was the ocean outside her window, water splashing high enough to cover it as though she were in a boat caught in a storm.

If she wanted.

She could know a thousand other things too—all she had to do was think of it. In there, she was in control. In there, she was not alone.

CHAPTER 14

Panic.

That's the first word Gabby thought of when she came back into the house. Her father and grandfather were looking at each other with identical expressions of sheer terror on their faces, as though they were mirrors, one reflecting the other. She wanted to ask what happened. Wanted to ask if they found Autumn or Christopher, knew that if they had and they were reacting like this it was bad. The words jumbled onto themselves in her head, tying her tongue. She stood in the entryway to the room unable to move, the memory of the night air cool on her back.

Patrick and Doug noticed her there are the same time and felt the urge to go to her and to shrink away in equal measure. They had an answer to the question in her eyes, the one she was afraid to ask out loud. And it scared the hell out of them.

Patrick looked away, losing a part of his soul as he tore his eyes from his granddaughter. But he had to. He had to think. What they saw didn't make sense. What they did... Patrick couldn't understand how they could still affect the living world after Gabby. But they had and it had been cruel, terrible in a way that neither of them truly understood. What bothered Patrick most was knowing that he would have to do it again.

He heard Doug talking, placating his daughter at first, using the language he might have employed when she was a child; platitudes that might have worked when she was his little princess without an understanding of loss but were empty now, short of the mark. And then Doug was telling her the truth, everything, all the details of what they saw. The machines, the darkened hospital room, the young woman who they had frightened out of her wits. He hoped his son would stop there, leave Gabby with that much and let her make peace with it, but Patrick knew he wouldn't. He would tell her about the café in Paris, the delicate fingers tracing the rim of the espresso cup just above the crema. He would tell her about the shop in Dubai, the colorfully elegant *jalabiyas* windswept on the gentle breeze.

He would tell her about the woman.

Patrick knew that was going to do nothing but confuse Gabby, just like it did them.

But they couldn't keep it a secret; Patrick knew that as well. Even as they had guiltily enjoyed the moment, being with them in a way they had never dreamed of—reveling in the stuff of fairy tales and the fragments of dreams—they still had work to do. They had to save Gabby's children from The Realm. They needed to try to correct their futures and those of their descendants if they could.

But they were Gabby's *children*.

Patrick thought about how he felt when he was trying to save Doug, how his heart ached with worry that he wouldn't be able to do anything: how he felt now knowing that he had failed.

They had to tell Gabby what happened.

She deserved to know.

"He's... I don't know why we could—"

"Could what?" Gabby asked, cutting her father off mid-sentence, the fear in her eyes creeping onto her face. "What did you do to Christopher?"

Patrick rubbed his hand over his face, feeling the skin beneath his palm and wishing he couldn't... wishing that his imagination wasn't so active.

Doug paused.

Patrick thought he might jump out of his skin if Doug didn't say something... anything.

After what seemed like forever, he finally uttered the only sentence that made sense.

"We made him talk."

CHAPTER 15

S o small.

It was as if the bed were too big for him, like he was in a big boy's bed when he was just a child.

Her child.

He lay still, eyes closed. Machines blinked around him. The faint hiss of air whooshed as the ventilator inflated his lungs. He was alone and small and in a room full of machines.

Gabby's hand fluttered to her mouth in an effort to thwart the primordial urge to scream.

"It didn't hurt him," Patrick said, hoping that would help but knowing it wasn't enough. "We saw the nurses come and check him and they said he was stable. They didn't even detect that he had been awake at all."

Gabby rocked slowly, trying to make sense of it all, unable to pull her eyes away from the project of Christopher suspended before her eyes.

"But he's been in a coma," Doug started. "I don't understand how his voice could work at all. His vocal cords..."

Doug stopped himself from talking about how the tracheostomy had likely ruined his vocal cords; either that or the persistent disuse had. He stopped himself from saying more and sounding both callous and clueless at the same time as he marveled over how well Christopher had held up, saying words that his daughter would hate him for—ones that painted his grandson as a specimen instead of his own flesh and blood. Gabby didn't need that right then. What she needed was to know that her son was all right and while Doug couldn't give her that kind of assurance, he knew better than to compound it with ignorance.

"You can't hurt him," Gabby said quietly, her face unreadable. "He's not there."

A new concern dawned on Patrick's face, one that was more fear than anything. Had it been too much? At least he had been able to ease into seeing his son in the living world while grappling with the fact that he was separated from him. He'd also known Doug when he was an adult, had had the chance to watch him grow. Doug hadn't had that time and Gabby had had even less. What must that feel like as a parent, to see their child as an adult who grew up without them? How must it be to search their face to find some vestige of the child they knew? And then to find them in such a state as Christopher was in... dear God, falling from the sky right in front of her eyes, and now fighting for his life? Patrick didn't know how Doug and Gabby could stand it.

And time was such a cruelty in The Realm. It seemed as if the months and years grabbed the baton and sprinted ahead there, ready to take the place that days and weeks occupied when they looked away. People changed from child to teenager and teenager to adult within minutes. Time only seemed to slow when they watched it, when they stared at the screen that was the living world without blinking, trying to capture it in a bottle. But they couldn't do that, be passive in that way, watching, watching, always watching. They had to act if they were going to break the curse. And this terrified Patrick and Doug. If they weren't careful The Realm would be populated with their descendants in what would feel to them like a matter of days.

Patrick watched his granddaughter, a woman who had been born after he had already left the living world, and worried that she might break.

"Gabby?" Doug said, his voice tentative. Patrick turned to regard his son and found the same worry that he felt etched on his face.

"Where is Autumn?" Gabby asked. "Your granddaughter... did you see her too?"

There was an edge to her words... a bitterness.

Doug nodded because he had to. She deserved to know what they saw, but he didn't want to tell her. He tried to think of ways to frame it differently, to make Autumn seem less far away, but there weren't any words to mask the truth.

"She's alive," Patrick started, hoping that would ease her fears, and it did. Her shoulders relaxed visibly and for that Patrick was grateful. She didn't yet understand all of the ins and outs of The Realm—he wasn't altogether sure he did either—so the concept of the true death was still unknown to her and that was good. Patrick didn't think anyone should have to be faced with a concept like that hours after winding up in a place like The Realm. The thought alone chilled him to his core.

"Thank God," Gabby said after what seemed like forever. "I couldn't find her here, so I hoped she was still down there... still alive..."

Gabby bit her lip to stop a wave of emotion from breaking.

"Where is she?" she continued. "Why couldn't we find her before?"

Doug dropped his chin onto his chest and sighed. He looked up at his father without moving his head, raising his eyebrows and scrunching his forehead in a way that was familiar to Gabby. He used to do that when she had disappointed him, had broken something or brought home a bad grade. She felt transported seeing that expression, something she knew, something that was all her dad; it made him seem real to her again ... like more than just a memory. It made her feel like they hadn't really lost all those years together. But at the same time, it caused her to shudder. Because something was unequivocally wrong.

"She's in a kind of limbo," Doug started, searching for the words to explain what they saw. But the problem was he didn't understand what he saw, not even a little, and he saw it with his own eyes. Flashes of different countries, different settings, all as if from Autumn's vantage point. They hadn't been able to see her face in any of the visions, only when she had walked into her bedroom and lain down on her bed. He wanted to marvel in the moment, to look at her and search for traces of his daughter in her face, traces of his wife. But he couldn't. Doug couldn't get over how off-kilter and disconnected Autumn seemed—how she was the very embodiment of hazy. Before he had time to wrap his head around how she seemed, Autumn had lain down, put a piece of paper towel in her mouth, and closed her eyes.

Then she was gone.

Doug was trying to figure it out, to piece it all together so he could say something that wouldn't crush his daughter but he was coming up empty.

"I think it was some kind of drug," Patrick started, trying for sensitive and hoping he hit the mark. There were all sorts of things that looked like they were related to drug use lying around in the front room they had caught a glimpse of before she closed her bedroom door to it all—hardcore stuff that neither of them wanted to ruminate long on.

"Something that would make her hallucinate," Patrick added.

"That's the only thing we can come up with to account for the things we saw. It has to be places Autumn was imagining—Europe, the islands, the Middle East—she's dreaming of everywhere."

Gabby nodded, remembering how Autumn hadn't answered her, remembering the things strewn around her house.

"Psychedelics. Maybe PCP or something." Patrick didn't know what it was. He hadn't so much as smoked cigarettes when he was alive.

"No, not PCP. She didn't seem amped up or angry. She's really mellow, like after 'shrooms start to settle in."

Patrick bristled. It took everything he had not to shoot a questioning glance at Doug, the level of knowledge about drug responses coming out of his son's mouth was unsettling to say the least. He was so busy reminding himself that Doug was a grown man who had surely done countless things that he, as his father, would not have known about was so busy lamenting about how all of it was water under the bridge now anyway, that he missed whatever Doug said to Gabby that made her voice tear through the room as she cut him off.

"Wait, wait! What do you mean she's gone?" Gabby snapped, panic making her words harsher than she meant them to be. "If she's high on something, wouldn't she still be zoned out where you saw her?"

Doug nodded distractedly, reacting to her only cursorily, his thoughts focused elsewhere. Doug's eyes shifting ever so slightly away from Gabby's, peering into his memory as he tried to make sense of what he saw.

"That's what you would think, yeah. Most people just ride the high wherever they are. But some drugs make you wander, investigate, chase whatever's showing itself. That's how people end up on roofs thinking they can fly."

Doug was instantly brought back to the room and out of his own head where concern flashing across his daughter's face was there to greet him. He was deeply disappointed in himself for his insensitive choice of words.

"I'm not saying that's what's happening with Autumn, Gabby, I'm just—"

"I know," Gabby said. She hoped it was enough to keep him talking and stop him from pussyfooting around her. She wasn't a kid anymore and *her* kid was in danger. There was no time to mince words.

"Just tell me what you saw."

Doug ran a hand through his hair before continuing. He listed off what he understood so far.

"She's not dead, that's why she hadn't shown up here. But the way she disappeared makes it seem like she's not totally alive either; or at least not mentally present."

"That doesn't make any sense, Dad," Gabby said, frustrated by the feeling of helplessness that was starting to overtake her.

"I know, I know, but that's what it seems like. I think you were on to something when you said Christopher wasn't there. I think we were able to contact him because he is both there *and* here at the same time, so he isn't anywhere 100%."

Patrick and Gabby's eyes were trained on Doug but he didn't feel the weight of their stares. He was focused on something just beyond his grasp as he tried to piece everything together.

"Christopher is in a coma," Doug said gently, the memory of

all the machines that surrounded his grandson's bedside rolling into his mind like a torrent, "and I think that's why he could be both there and here; I think that's why we could understand him and get him to speak. But Autumn… we can't reach her the same way… at least, I don't *think* we can. There's something different about where she is."

Patrick stepped closer to Gabby. He wanted to put his arm around her shoulders but didn't know if he should. She had never even met him before. The familial connection that he was feeling as he looked into his granddaughter's face and saw glimpses of his son and wife might not be manifesting for her. She might not be feeling anything at all for him. He brought the hand he had raised to touch her down but stayed close.

"She disappeared, but it wasn't right away," Patrick said instead, "it was more like a flicker."

"Yeah," Doug agreed. "I wonder if that means she isn't sick… at least not like Christopher is. He stays solid and visible, but she went away gradually."

"It didn't really seem like she was incapacitated in anyway," Patrick added. "And she was awake. We watched her walk into the room and lay down on the bed just before she disappeared."

"What does that mean?" Gabby asked, trying to keep her voice controlled but it still came out shrill. "If she's not sick and she's not asleep, what is she? Did the *drugs* make her disappear?"

Doug tapped his knuckles against his lips as he thought. "Maybe."

He thought some more, remembering something that was right on the edge of his consciousness… right on the tip of his tongue. He knew what was wrong, why he was struggling to call up the details he was reaching for. It was self-preservation, pure and simple. Doug didn't want to reveal everything he knew, when he had learned about it all, or how. He didn't want them —his father and his daughter, of all people—to judge him for it. The affair, the people he hung out with when he was in that dark place in his life... The period of his life that he would just as soon never think about again. He learned more than he ever wanted to about drugs back then. He did some too. Not a lot of hard stuff, but he saw more than his share of shit. Doug was embarrassed to know what he was talking about, to understand the signs and what they meant. Still, he had to put that aside and tell them what he knew. Hiding it wasn't going to help Autumn, the sweet girl who, even through the dirty hair and sallow skin, he could see looked so much like his Gabby it made his heart hurt. Hiding it wasn't going to help Christopher, his grandson who was named after the beautiful wife whom he had not had the chance to make it up to. Hiding it would be worse than any of the shame he might feel under their accusations.

He took a deep breath that he hoped they didn't notice.

He pushed forward.

"Maybe she *mentally* disappears," Doug said, his voice low enough to be missed.

Gabby turned her head toward him, processing the words.

"Maybe she's imagining that she's actually sitting in Paris or Rome or any of those places we saw flash by but her body is really wherever that bed is. It's... it's almost like she's having a lucid dream."

Doug saw the confusion on their faces. He screwed on his courage and looked his father in the eye before continuing.

"When you trip... when you take LSD, your brain conjures up these images, makes you think you're anywhere in the world, listening to the most beautiful music, seeing the most vibrant colors. You're aware that it's not real. You might think you're asleep and to some extent you are, at least your conscious mind is. And that's the beauty of it. You can go wherever you want, *do* whatever you want because you're imagining it all. But sometimes you can have a bad trip; go somewhere that you don't want to be. Nightmares on LSD are brutal because you think they aren't real so you try to change the script, but sometimes you can't because you're so afraid."

Gabby looked afraid and he was sorry for that, but he had to tell them everything.

"You can have a lucid dream without taking drugs—you just have to be really good at manipulating your REM sleep and most people can't actually do it on cue. But... considering all the stuff we saw on the table in the front room..." Doug looked away from Gabby, unable to shoulder the accusation in her stare. "I just... I think Autumn used something to get herself into that state."

"Is it dangerous? Could she OD? Could she actually die in the dream?" It was Patrick whose voice had taken on the panicky edge of someone who didn't know up from down. Gabby had just gotten there; they had only just started trying to save his great grandchildren. He couldn't handle the thought of her losing her life so quickly... he couldn't let both of his great-grandchildren be damned to eternity in The Realm. He needed time. Patrick just didn't know if there was any left to spare.

Doug shook his head no.

"ODing on LSD is rare; she'd have to take so much... more than she could get her hands on from some run-of-the-mill dealer. It's not even illegal everywhere in the world. The effect is almost entirely psychological. And as long as she stays in her bedroom she doesn't run the risk of walking into traffic or something. She closed the bedroom door and I didn't see any other doors open, so she seems like she's trying to protect herself; like she knows the risks. But we couldn't see her when we looked before and then she disappeared right in front of me and dad's eyes... I really think she does this kind of thing a lot."

"Ok, and doing it a lot... is that a problem?" Patrick asked, hoping the there was a silver lining.

"So what?" Gabby exclaimed on Patrick's heels, out of nowhere, her voice edgy as she looked for ways to protect her daughter from what exactly she didn't know.

"What's the big deal if she likes to fantasize sometimes? That's why people watch movies or read books. If it can't kill you, what's the big deal?"

"The big deal is that sometimes people who dose a lot get... confused. Sometimes they can't tell what's real and what's not; they can't tell when they're dreaming and when they're awake. They might think they woke up from the dream but in reality, they really didn't—they're actually still dreaming; their mind feeds them images that mirror their real lives. This can really freak people out. And if they have sleep paralysis too, the whole thing intensifies. Sometimes you can't open your eyes or you're trying to scream and it's loud in your ears but nothing's coming out of your mouth. Seriously, that can scare the hell out of you."

Doug looked at Gabby quickly as he remembered one of his own experiences, then pulled his eyes away before she could see the fear in them.

"They get stuck in this weird space: it's almost like an alternate reality. And it's a vicious cycle—the more they try to wake up, the more aware of it they become. The dream isn't fun anymore. It's unlike any reality they've ever known."

Gabby's eyes filled with tears.

"Are you saying she could get stuck in there? That she might never wake up?"

"No," Doug said with a sigh, "But she might not realize that. She might think she can't break through and lose her mind trying to wake up. And if she finds a reality that she actually likes better in there, she might not even try to leave. The mind is amazing and terrible at the same time. It might tell her that she's lost forever, might convince her that she's stuck and that anything she tries to do to get out might kill her, and the whole time her sanity would be burning away from the inside."

CHAPTER 16

Tara heard them when they discovered the one they called Christopher, heard the surprise in their voices when he spoke to them. Patrick fell into a seat as if his legs had given out from underneath him. Doug stayed on his feet but Tara could hear his voice shaking and imagined that his body was trembling with... what, exactly? Surprise? Elation? Fear? She didn't know which.

Tara had peeked out beyond the flimsy slatted pantry door but could only see the back of Patrick's back and legs as they were bent in the rickety folding chair.

"Holy God," she heard him whisper and strained to hear more through his rasping breaths.

"C-C-Christopher?" Doug had said, his voice sounding hopeful and confused at the same time. *"Can you hear me?"*

It took a while for an answer to come but when it did it sounded like it filled every space, every crevice in a static rage, like an electric guitar turned up too loud. Before hearing the response Tara thought that was it, that no one would reply, and that the whole thing had been in their heads, but then a voice, tentative and just as confused as Doug's had been, spoke.

"Grandpa Doug?"

That's when Patrick had fallen into his seat and Doug struggled to stay on legs that had grown wobbly. Tara inched closer to the pantry door, trying to hear everything she could.

"Yes, son, yes. It's me." His laugh was full of awe and relief.

"And is that Great-Grandpa Patrick too?"

Tara heard a chair slide against the floor as Patrick stood and said,

"It's me. Yes... it's me. How did you—"

"Who else would it be?" Christopher said and Tara smirked.

There was a pause. Tara cocked her head even closer to the door.

"Where's my dad? Is he...? Did he survive?"

Tara could hear the expectancy in the man's voice and felt sorry for him. She already knew how this part of the story went.

"He's not... he's not here, Christopher," Doug replied, empathy thickening his voice. *"He's not in* The Realm. *He's... somewhere else."*

"Only your maternal line is here," Patrick added. *"My line."*

Again there was a pause, likely because Christopher was taking it all in. Tara couldn't imagine how it must feel to hear that his father wasn't where the rest of his family was... that he would never see him again... for real. She felt pity for the first time in what felt like forever.

Patrick and Doug started to speak at the same time, nervous energy coursing through both of them. But it was Christopher's voice that won out.

"The book... all that talk about The Realm *and people being in limbo... that was real?"*

"Yes," Doug whispered and Tara could tell he was crying.

Tara could hear mumbling coming from Christopher: stifled groans and snippets of words, incoherent in his grief.

"We're trying to save you, Christopher," Doug said, finding his voice. *"You and your sister."*

"Mom," Christopher said as if touched by a metal prod. *"Where's mom?"*

"She's here," Doug breathed. *"We-we couldn't figure it out in time."*

"Autumn... she's ok?"

There was another pause before Patrick spoke.

"She's alive. She's not here. There is still time... for both of you."

Christopher snickered.

"We used to sneak that book... Great-Grandma Joanne's novel. We would read it when Dad wasn't looking. He thought he had hidden it away, thought we wouldn't care about something like that, but... there was nobody left. Mom was dead. Grandparents gone. Great-grandparents... everyone. It was the only way we felt like we had any family at all. And the pictures," Christopher said and Tara could hear the smile in his voice. *"The pictures made you guys real."*

Tara thought of her own family, the pictures that she had cherished until she lost them on one of her and Mileeha's rampages and tasted something bitter at the back of her throat.

"I haven't seen Autumn in a few years. I want... I want to say goodbye to her."

Christopher's voice was suddenly sullen and vacant. Resigned.

"There's time for that. Christopher," Doug said, imploringly. *"There's time."*

"I need to tell Asha I love her. I need to tell her I wish we could have had the life we were supposed to have. We wanted a family. We

wanted a family so badly. We'd... we'd already started trying. I need to tell her I'm sorry."

Tara didn't know who the gasp had come from but she heard it clearly enough. She could hear someone moving, walking. And then Patrick said,

"I wonder if there's a way you can."

There were two people ahead of her.

Asha sat looking round the waiting room hoping the war between excitement and loss didn't show on her face. She didn't think it possible; the idea felt as outlandish as her comatose fiancé sitting up and speaking to her did. But that had happened. With everything she was, Asha knew that to be true. But what he said to her, what he was asking her to do... it just didn't make sense.

Chris asked her to find out whether or not she was pregnant.

Five months.

Five months since they had been together.

Five months for a baby to grow.

Five months that she wouldn't have noticed life inside her.

She hadn't thought it was possible. But Chris had pushed through the haze, fought his way back to her from some nebulous limbo to ask her to do this. Asha didn't have a choice.

And then she found out more.

Asha picked up a home pregnancy test as soon as she left the hospital. She didn't trust the ones she already had at home; they were at least 5 months old, not counting the time they'd spent on the shelf. She took one of the brand new ones that evening and then another in the morning and both were negative. But her research taught her not to rely upon just that, not if she wanted to be certain.

That's why she was in the ER waiting room.

She chose a different hospital than where Chris was staying but wasn't entirely sure why. Getting to Chris with the news would have been easier if she had just taken a test at the same hospital but she didn't want anyone to see her. They might get the wrong idea, might think that she had been fooling around with someone else while her fiancé lay upstairs in a coma. Silly. They couldn't have known why she was there, but on the off chance that someone saw her and decided to talk, Asha didn't want to risk it.

So, she sat in a hospital across town, waiting to be called back.

Waiting, waiting. Alone with her thoughts, thoughts that looped onto themselves, weaving like thread on a loom. Did she remember menstruating? It wasn't really something she had paid a lot of attention to since the accident and anyway, she had always been far from what anyone would call regular in the first place. She was also stressed beyond belief so no one would have batted an eye at her missing a period or two. She hadn't gained any weight; in fact, she'd lost enough for her pants to be loose. Had she been tested when she was in the hospital? She imagined she would have been, just as a matter of course. Had the test issued a false negative? Was it a molar pregnancy? Asha had never heard of that term before, but by that morning she knew it and more things than she had ever cared to about abnormal fertilizations. As she sat there alone amidst the sniffling and moaning, the cacophony of the ER lobby, she didn't know how she felt about any of it.

What *if* she was pregnant? She would have to do it alone. The solemnity of that fact hit her hard and made her inhale sharply, as if catching her breath. It wasn't that she didn't think she could do it; she had watched her mother do it as well as some of her friends. Asha understood firsthand how difficult it could be, the sacrifices that would have to be made. It didn't frighten her; she knew she was capable of raising their baby, if there *was* a baby. What bothered her was that she didn't *want* to do it alone. She and Chris had been so excited to start a family together. They envisioned trips to the zoo, hiking at Great Falls, lunch on the Watergate steps overlooking the Potomac. Now Asha might be doing those activities with their child by herself and that made the sense of loss she was already feeling that much more pronounced. She wanted to get up. She felt like she wasn't ready to know... not yet.

Asha wanted to leave.

The anguish in Chris's voice had made her stay.

His voice hadn't sounded the way it used to. It was raspy now, rough and raw because his vocal cords were dry and rubbing against each other, chafing almost to bleed. The sound came from his head rather than his throat; nasally yet wasted. It was just short of monotone as whatever vocal cords he had left struggled to produce anything other than the most rudimentary of sounds. Chris's voice reminded her of someone speaking through that spontaneous gasping sound that only happened when someone was hiccupping, the one that always surprised people when they realized it was coming from their own mouths.

He hadn't sounded like himself at all... not even close.

When Chris's eyes settled on her, ceasing their wild search of the room, rolling, darting, widening as they found their way again, she thought her heart might break. His expression was everything she felt in a nutshell: loss, anguish, fear, anger. Love.

"We almost had it all," he said as Asha took a deep breath and willed her heart to settle down long enough to enjoy whatever was happening. She was terrified of what was happening. If she had lost her mind, and she wasn't completely certain that she hadn't, that moment might be the only time she was allowed such lucidity in the fantasy. If she was sane, it could be one of those moments where patients get better for an hour or a day only to die right when the people who loved them had started to find hope again. Either way, she may not have him like that—speaking, seeing her, being awake and aware—for long and she wanted to make sure that she was as present for it as she could be.

"We almost proved them wrong," Chris finished.

Asha cried fresh tears as he spoke because a comment like that... it was so like him—the man whose hair she used to run her fingers through; the man who she sat up talking with for hours and hours. There was never anyone to prove wrong. Everyone in their lives knew they were meant to be just as much as they did. They were happy and it showed. Both of their friend groups liked them for each other and so did their families. Chris was just that guy—the one who said something sarcastic when you least expected it, using his dry humor to make people smile even when they didn't want to... Even when he was lying on his deathbed.

She smiled reluctantly, drawn in as always.

"We still could," Asha started, but he closed his eyes as the smile fell from his lips. He shook his head with much effort and she sobbed openly, louder than she meant to. She didn't want to draw attention to them, didn't understand how the machines that beeped around him hadn't already called in the cavalry, but she was glad for it. If the nurses and doctors and whoever else was monitoring the room caught wind that he was awake they will fill the space, take vitals, check his eyes, his nose, his colostomy bag. Their time together would be over. Asha didn't want that. – Not yet.

Watching Chris shake his head, seeing the amount of effort it took to do, made Asha's heart hurt.

"No, baby," he said finally. "We're out of time."

"But we're not," Asha trilled, unable to control the quaver in her voice, unable to control much of anything at all. "You're here. You came back. Christopher, you came back to me."

Asha touched the first spot on his arm that was free of IV leads and tape and protective covering and squeezed, momentum keeping her from recoiling from the feeling of bones and paper-thin skin beneath her fingers.

"No," Christopher said, his eyes reflecting an understanding that she wished he didn't have. "I didn't."

Asha searched his face, let her eyes take it in, let them truly and honestly see it. It was the face of a corpse.

"What do you mean?" she started, her voice rising with emotion, growing louder even as she tried to control her reaction. "Are you saying I'm crazy? That this is all in my head?"

Asha sat back in the chair, gaze averted to the walls as she tried to reconcile everything that was happening.

Incredulous.

Angry.

Afraid.

"Am I fucking crazy now?" she asked of no one in particular, hissing the words because she didn't know what else to do. "Is that it?"

"No, Asha, no," Chris said, straining his voice to try and talk over her, to get her attention before she went on a tangent she might not come back from.

"You're not crazy. It's just... this shouldn't be happening. None of it. I should be dead."

"Don't," Asha said shaking her head. She closed her eyes but hated the picture that waited for her there, the one where Chris lay on his back in a grassy field.

"Please don't."

Chris reached for her hand and she gave it to him, feeling the coldness of his fingertips permeate her skin to settle in her bones.

"It's a miracle, but you know it's true. I did what I wanted to do. You are alive, baby. You can go on. *That's* what I wanted. I never expected to survive."

Chris pulled Asha's hand toward his lips and she anticipated the touch of his mouth on her skin again. It didn't feel anything like she hoped it would.

"All I ask is that you see it with your own eyes—see how beautiful it is, how advanced it was. Just once—that will be enough for me."

Egypt. The place Chris had always wanted to show her; the place she had been excited to explore with him.

Asha's face was hot with tears. "Take me, Chris. Show me all of it yourself."

Chris sniffed painfully.

"I thought I would go back one day as a professional instead of a green kid with a battered travel guide, but it was not to be."

Asha didn't think she would ever breathe properly again after having seen the wistful smile that crept onto Chris's lips as he spoke.

"Chris Adams, BA in Archaeology, MA in Museum Studies, youngest curator in the city to run a facility, dead before he could bring in his first installation."

Chris's eyes were far away.

"I wanted to do something different, Asha. Nobody even talks about Kush or knows how connected Akhenaten was to it.

I wanted to showcase Nubian kings, show people that they were royalty too..."

"Alara, Kashta, Tarharqa." Asha chimed in, grateful for the chance to revel in Chris's enthusiasm for the history he had studied for years one more time. Asha remembered how he talked about falling in love with the glamour of the 18th dynasty, studying everything he could find on Egyptology. He used to talk for hours about how seeing the colossi at Abu Simbel in person changed him; how standing in front the relief of the Battle of Qadesh gave him a feeling of connection to the place that pictures in books never could. His love of Egyptian history prompted him to keep learning, keep uncovering mysteries. It eventually led him to the 25th dynasty and the Nubian pharaohs that he had never learned about in school. Chris talked and talked about it all the time; the culture, the people. Passion and excitement animated his voice every time he told Asha something new. And Asha used to hang on every word.

Chris's nodded and smiled.

"Right. But now..."

"You can still do the work, Chris. You have to believe that."

"No... baby, I can't and you have to start believing *that*. That... I ... I will never..."

Chris paused, let himself settle before speaking again.

"But *you* can walk out of here and live your life. You have to."

Chris leveled his gaze at Asha, his sunken eyeballs disconcerting.

"You're the key to everything."

Asha looked at Chris questioningly, confusion etched on her face.

"The key... what do you mean?"

"I need you to find out for sure and I need you to find out about Autumn too."

She hoped he didn't notice her expression, hoped she had caught herself fast enough to keep her first reaction hidden. When she spoke her voice sounded frightened to her own ears.

"Chris, I can't... I've been trying but I can't find—"

"I need you to find out if you're pregnant, baby. I need to know if Autumn and I are the last or if we'll have to protect our babies too."

"The last? Chris, what are you talking about?"

Asha put her hand to Chris's forehead and it was hot, so hot, frighteningly so considering how cold his fingers were. She felt like it made her own blood boil from the very touch.

"Baby, what do you mean 'protect our babies'?"

"It was all true, Asha. All of it. The place stuck in limbo. It's where I'll go if they don't figure out a way to stop it soon. Autumn too."

Asha wracked her brain trying to figure out what he was talking about but nothing would come. She thought maybe he was hallucinating. His fever felt high enough for that and he had also just woken up from a coma. Asha's own skin prickled. Maybe she had been selfish not calling the doctors in to look at him, reckless even. Maybe she was a terrible person for wanting to keep him all to herself.

"I'm calling the doctor, Chris. You're not making any sense. They need to check you out... make sure you're ok."

Asha reached for the call button on the side of his bed but Chris grabbed her arm in what felt like the clutch of a skeleton.

"No," he wheezed, the sudden movement taking an obvious toll. "Our baby will end up there too. Not Heaven, not Hell... just this in between place where things you couldn't even imagine happen. They told me about the Hunters to scare me into talking to you. Asha... I don't want our baby to end up there."

Asha could tell he meant what he was saying. He believed it

wholeheartedly. His eyes pleaded with her; Asha couldn't even imagine the fear that hid behind them.

"Please baby, find out if you're pregnant. If you're not and Autumn's not, then, well it's just me they have to save. I'd rather it be me than them."

"Save you from what?" Asha asked, afraid to hear the answer but knowing she had to.

"Our destiny."

CHAPTER 17

Gabby took a deep breath, and then another, as she tried to get her thoughts together. Autumn was not dead. She was unreachable... gone... but not dead. And Christopher... he was...

It all sounded so implausible, like a twisted product of someone's imagination, but it was real—she knew that was true as well as she knew her own name. Gabby cried for her son, the way his body had betrayed him, shut down in the prime of his life yet forcing him to remain, to endure life locked in his head until the clock ran out. He was trapped between worlds, mostly dead but still alive, unable to lunge in one direction or the other to find relief. Gabby wanted him with her if only to bring him peace.

But there was some reason for it all, some reason that he was still alive after the hot air balloon crash; some reason he made it instead of the others. Gabby had always believed in fate, even more so now as she found herself suffering from their family's curse. She had always thought that people died when they were supposed to. It wasn't so much that their steps were ordered, but that there was a time that every person would die and that time was definitive and unique. Gabby could hear herself sharing her thoughts when her husband's family spouted off about religion at dinner or on his mother's porch; the inevitability of the conversation was as expected as the sun rising and setting. It was simple back then just talking so matter-of-factly about her logic, when she didn't know how on the mark she was about it all... back when they were just words instead of reality. It made her cringe how flippantly she had spoken about life and death, about free will and preordination. The memory of her own voice prattling on about things she should never have taken lightly made her sick. Still, standing in The Realm, looking at her grandfather, a man who, for her, existed only in stories and recollections, and being in the presence of her father again, in a way that she hadn't for so many years, while they watched her son breathe with the aid of machines like they were watching a movie on a screen, she understood so much more.

There was a reason... Gabby was sure of it.

She wished she had been there to hear his voice. She had missed so many things in his life. She had no idea what he'd looked like as a kid, a teenager, or a man. Her memories are of her little boy, the one who carried his favorite things everywhere he went. And for her, he was that little boy only a few hours ago.

Or was it days?

Gabby didn't know and that was disconcerting. She didn't know if she had been oblivious to time passing because she was searching for her children, meeting her grandfather for the first time, hugging her father after decades of being apart. Or did she not realize how quickly everything was moving because time wasn't the same in The Realm: it could speed up or slow down at random intervals, with no rhyme or reason. She suspected both things were true and that scared her.

Gabby's father had said Christopher sounded fine when he was talking to them; it was as if they were communicating with his inner voice more so than his physical one and that he had a rich tenor that showed no signs of illness or degradation. They would not comment on how he actually sounded when he spoke to his fiancée no matter how much she asked.

Gabby went over what her father and grandfather had told her as she stared at the inanimate shadow her son's body made in the darkness of his room. It was nighttime where he was and the only lights to be seen came from the equipment surrounding the bed. The room she sat in was also dark and she liked that she matched him then. It reminded her of the nights when she would lay with him until he fell asleep, warding off the monsters in the dark he so often imagined were there; those nights when Christopher struggled to relax his mind and fall asleep and Gabby would look around his darkened room noticing how different the landscape was when the lights were off. She would rearrange the room in her head, moving things that might scare him in the night, repositioning toys based on the shadows they cast. She'd let her eyes fall to the pictures he had drawn, their colors indecipherable in the dark but brought to life by her memory. Gabby would breathe deeply of him and the space he occupied, the space they occupied together. But there in the darkened room where she sat staring at the son whose fears she could no longer calm, whose hair she could no longer touch, Gabby didn't let herself notice any details around her. To do that would make The Realm all too real.

Asha was not pregnant. Gabby could feel it. Call it mother's intuition, call it precognition, call it whatever you like, but

Gabby was certain of it. Still there was something else going on, something she couldn't put her finger on, and just as she knew that Christopher's fiancée was not expecting their child, Gabby also knew that whatever else was happening was important. As painful as it was, Gabby went over everything she understood:

- *Her kids were adults.*
- *Her husband was dead.* Dear God, she hadn't even had a moment to properly mourn the man she loved. The pain sat solid and whole in the pit of her stomach.
- *She was dead and had been dead for many years.*
- *Her son was in a coma.*
- *Her daughter was missing.*

Gabby had to stop for a moment to gather herself. She could feel her heart palpitating as she recited the last two bullet points in her head and wondered distractedly why that was. If she was dead, why was she feeling physical pain? Why was she feeling the emotions she was feeling—the despair over her son's condition, the worry over her daughter's whereabouts? Even the joy at seeing her father again shouldn't exist, not if she was dead and gone, her body rendered. It was a cruel trick, being able to feel everything like she had when she was alive. Gabby didn't know if she would ever get used to it.

She frowned. There had to be more to add to the list, more details to decipher. Gabby concentrated, trying to find the needle in the haystack.

- *Autumn wasn't in the accident.* Gabby had a lot of questions about why that would be. She hoped it was a scheduling issue instead of the possibility that she and Christopher were not close as adults. She remembered how attentive Christopher had been with his sister when she was a baby, always trying to help feed her, rocking her when she was fussy, even if she drowned out his cartoons. And from what her father had told her, he was still trying to take care of her. Was it Autumn who didn't want to be around Christopher? Why would that be? Gabby shook the thought away, the idea of it too painful to entertain.

- *Christopher worked at a museum.*

- *Autumn was using drugs.* Something to give her an alternative reality. Why? What was happening in her life that would make her do that? Is that why she wasn't at the engagement party? Is that why she didn't talk to her brother? Gabby hated how easy it was to make that leap.

- *Christopher's fiancée almost died in the accident. Everyone else did.* Was that important? Gabby didn't know.

Her list was all over the place. She needed to organize her thoughts.

- *Christopher knew his grandfather by sight.* That made her smile. That meant that her husband had kept up the practice of showing family pictures and telling stories about the people who had passed away. Gabby wondered what stories he had told the kids about her. Maybe the one about the time she won a limbo contest on a dinner cruise in the Caribbean or when she mispronounced the words she had been studying for weeks before their trip to France, reciting her request so poorly that the taxi driver's sour demeanor cracked and the car filled with hearty, raucous laughter. She hoped he showed them the pictures of her holding them, laughing with them, loving them. She hoped they had been able to call those images up when they needed them most.

- *They had both read the book.* A sigh hissed from Gabby's lips at the thought of them holding the very book she had died reading in their hands. She wished her husband had thrown it out, but she understood why he didn't. It was an heirloom after all—something that meant a great deal to Gabby, especially in those final days. Of course he would have kept it for them, would have cherished it as a piece of their family story. He couldn't have known the truth that lay within those pages, how poisonous it could be. When had they read it? Had they read it together? Those questions and more flooded her mind, pushed her off track, filled her head with so much noise, but one stood out the most, repeating, cycling, crescendoing: had they finished it?

What did it all mean? The list of facts Gabby had compiled didn't seem to lead to anything she could sink her teeth into. She tried again, analyzing what she knew, trying to put the pieces of the puzzle together. Her grandmother had talked about a curse in the book, one based on an ancient wrong... one that would perpetuate in her main character's family line forever, and that turned out to be true. So that meant that someone in her family had to have done something to make them end up in The Realm. God, she couldn't believe it was real, that she had been reading the blueprint for what would be her next phase. Everybody's next phase. How did her grandmother know all those things? She wasn't there in The Realm, not as far as Gabby could tell. And it wouldn't have made sense for her to be because she wasn't part of that familial line. So, how had she been able to pull back the curtain and find out about The Realm? Gabby thought about how engrossed she had become in the story, how hours could go by and she wouldn't even have realized it. She thought it was because of the story itself. It was so vivid and colorful. But maybe it was because the characters were her ancestors and they were speaking to her very soul.

Gabby frowned, concentrating.

Christopher and Autumn had read the manuscript.

Ok.

Gabby searched her memory for other clues that might have been in the story—something... anything she might be able to connect to what was going on now.

- *The story took place on a Caribbean Island.* She couldn't remember which one, but she'd come back to that.
- *They were vampires.*
- *There was unrequited love... or something like that.* Maybe it was that she was more into him than he was into her – Gabby couldn't remember, but there was some relationship problem between the main male character and the evil woman.
- *The evil woman was jealous.*
- *The evil woman was vengeful.* That's why The Realm existed in the first place. That's why Gabby was stuck.
- *The evil woman was ancient.*

Gabby remembered that she was the coven leader and older than the rest of the vampires. She wanted the main male character... Alex? No, that was close but it wasn't right. Eric? Isaac? It seemed like there were only two syllables in the name. Gabby kept hearing the cadence ring in her head. Cameron? No. It was an old name. Biblical.

It rolled off her lips when she spoke it, Gabby remembered. Gabby had mouthed it herself once or twice, mimicking the way that the woman had let it caress her tongue. Strong. Sensual. She was so close to remembering, it was driving her mad.

And what was the woman's name? She too had an old name, one that reminded Gabby of Victorian times, lace sleeves and bustles. Longer than his. She couldn't put her finger on it either.

What was her grandmother trying to warn her family about? Now that Gabby knew that The Realm existed, she was positive that her grandmother had been trying to tell them something. She knew things she shouldn't have and wrote them down for the people who needed to see it. But they had all ignored it, pushed it aside, called it fiction because that's what it looked like. And maybe it had to look like that. Maybe that was the only way that her grandmother could hide the truth.

But Gabby had read it and she understood that it wasn't something her grandmother had made up; some fantasy she had typed out for other people's enjoyment. It was a premonition at the very least, the transcription of a vision at its best.

Gabby just had to figure it out.

CHAPTER 18

The breeze played in Autumn's hair as she looked out over the blue waters of the Aegean Sea. She was at a cafe in Santorini. Her table overlooked the Oia cliffside and was in full view of the blue dome churches of Agios Spiridonas. The churches were backdropped by the most brilliant azure water she had ever seen. It was the perfect seat, as was always the case; every trip was like being front row center at her favorite band's concert and she was happy to share the space with her new friend. Autumn had come to think of her as a travelling buddy, someone to trip with and explore everything there was to find. They had only to imagine a place and they were there. Autumn didn't know if the woman was entering her dream or if it was the other way around, but that little detail didn't matter much.

That day they were in Santorini. The last time they were in Nice. Who knew where they'd end up next?

Autumn sipped her freddo cappuccino and marveled at how well she could actually taste it. Or at least imagine that she was tasting it. When she first started using LSD it was like she was watching a movie playing in front of her eyes... any movie she wanted. But now it was like she was *in* the movie. The sensations were so real; she could actually feel the wind in her hair and the sun on her skin. She could feel her sundress whipping around her ankles. When Autumn started out she would try to make money appear in her hand so she could spend it on whatever she wanted or pick up a guy and have sex without all the pretense but she couldn't quite get it to work. She could see things happening, manipulate the scenery, even interact with some of the people she dreamt up but still they were far away from her, almost like they were looking at her from the stage— breaking the fourth wall. But everything was so different now; the things around her felt real. Tangible. It made her wonder what else she might be able to feel now, since she had gotten better at it.

She'd have to try to remember to envision a sexy guy waiting for her on a secluded balcony overlooking some place beautiful on her next trip.

Again.

Or maybe she should just add that into the trip she was already on. It felt like she'd already been there for a long time, changing locations at least twice since finding out that her roommate had taken off. That seemed like so long ago—she couldn't even remember why she was angry about it, wasn't entirely sure that she had been anymore. Something about rent, about being her babysitter... Autumn couldn't figure out what all that meant, couldn't really pin it down to get a good look at it anymore: the ideas were flying around in her head so fast and were so far away from her grasp that Autumn would just as soon abandon the effort. All that was in the past, whether it was the recent past or distant past really didn't matter.

Except she didn't know how long she had been tripping. And she didn't know if she had any more tabs left to come back in when she woke up.

The tabs.

Where were the tabs?

Autumn instinctively patted her chest, feeling for the pocket on the ratty t-shirt she had been wearing for probably two weeks straight, at least she thought; laundry hadn't been much of a priority recently. She thought she had put the tabs there for safe keeping, that way she wouldn't even have to get up from where she sat to trip again. She knew that was too soon; you weren't supposed to drop back-to-back like that, but she liked the world she had created. She could go anywhere she wanted to, be anyone she wanted to be instead of just being Autumn Adams. Those tabs were her way out and she was cool with that. The real world was overrated.

She patted her chest but she didn't feel the t-shirt beneath her fingertips. Instead, she touched the strap of her tangerine sundress and the tanned skin it sat upon. Autumn smiled. So damned real. If more people knew about it, they wouldn't be able to resist. Autumn wondered what would happen if she told more people about tripping. True, it wasn't legal everywhere, but she could move, go where it *was* legal and maybe be a dealer or an advocate... maybe open a shop and provide a safe space for people to trip—

"What's on your mind?"

Autumn was pulled out of her thoughts and brought back to the present where the breeze was mild and warm.

"Just thinking about how neat this whole thing is," Autumn said, not attempting to hide the amazement in her voice. I can't believe how real everything is. It's like, when I reach out to touch something, I *actually* feel it. I can go to New York and hear the cabbies beeping their horns or go to the movies and smell the popcorn."

Autumn's companion smiled the way she always did. It was becoming one of the things that made Autumn the happiest, seeing her friend smile in agreement. Autumn felt seen in a way that she hadn't by anybody in a long time.

Not since Chris.

She wished she could share the experience with her brother. Chris would love it. He could imagine himself in Aswan, riding a felucca on the Nile or on a dig discovering lost artifacts from Shabaka or Kashta. Autumn couldn't remember which Kush pharaoh he liked most but the names of those ancient people came to her easily after hearing about them so much. He could go back in time too; Autumn hadn't tried it yet but she was almost positive you could do that with LSD. They could explore it all together, just the two of them... like the old days.

"My brother would love this," Autumn said and the way her friend laughed, she knew she had said that many times before.

"He'd love to meet you too. He loves meeting new people and an experiencing something like this... he would love to do it with people who really get it, you know what I mean?"

The companion leveled her gaze at Autumn and had she been looking, it might have been unsettling, but as it was Autumn had looked off in the distance at the projection of the Aegean Sea that she had conjured up. A little greener than the real thing, and far too still, but it was close enough. She had been listening to Autumn talk about her brother for several weeks already, more and more as she sank deeper into her trips, becoming less aware of how deep she was each time. Autumn may have been oblivious to what was happening but the companion was not. If anything, the companion was helping Autumn get into the headspace needed to do what had to be done. Because Autumn was the one; would be the last if she was allowed to live outside of the bubble that the companion and the drug had created for her. If Autumn stayed on the outside in the real world she would die, either by mistake or on purpose as self-destructive as she had become, and it would be soon. And that simply would not do.

The companion sipped her own drink, a mimic of Autumn's... an effort at flattery that she was sure had worked on the impressionable girl. So needy, this one. So starved for affection. Autumn had separated herself from her family for reasons that amounted to jealousy from the outside looking in; reasons that had long narratives and detailed asides that the companion did not have any interest in. She hadn't told them she'd lost her job, hadn't told them what was going on in her life—had chosen, instead, to stay away from them. Autumn hadn't talked to her father and brother for a long time. Months? Years? It really didn't matter. What was important was how easy Autumn had made it for someone to step in and fill the empty space. She was vulnerable and wanting. It had been simple to provide her the connection she wanted so badly. The companion thought Autumn should consider herself lucky. At least she wasn't being abused or anything like that.

She was just being kept.

It wasn't against her will, not really. Autumn had just said it herself; she really liked it there. The colors, the landscape, the people, the freedom that a trip allowed—this disconnect from reality. Autumn considered herself lucky to be able to experience it. She didn't realize that she had been gone for days this time, had retreated into her head, into her imagination so completely to the point that she had burned the images in, wallpapering the walls of her mind with it. Every time she dined in the trip, whether on *petha* in Agra or on escargot in Paris, she also ate in real life, bringing old bread that she had lain on her souring bedsheets to her mouth and tepid water to her lips. She urinated on herself, defecated off the side of the bed, unwilling to leave the space she was in because in the trip she might have been dancing on the moon. And her companion, this new friend whom she was able to find every time she put a tab under her tongue and dialed up a destination... this friend who always seemed to be going the same way she was, who was always game for whatever, witnessed it all.

"I'll call him before I come back in next time, tell him about this. He'll probably balk, though. Chris is so damned strait-laced. But I'll tell him how safe it is. He'll see how I'm doing, see how it isn't messing me up like what happens to crackheads, and then maybe he'll want to try it for himself."

The companion nodded as she had the last time Autumn had hatched the same plan.

"And he'll definitely be interested once I tell him about you and all the places we've been together. You're... whoah," Autumn laughed self-deprecatingly, snorting into her hand. It took everything the companion had not to suck her teeth in disgust.

"I can't believe this, after all the time we've spent together, I-I don't know your name," Autumn admitted with innocent eyes.

It was almost cruel.

The companion watched Autumn's face quiver as she waited for a response, seeming less and less sure as the seconds ticked by. The companion dragged it out, wanting to see Autumn's composure first tested then fail. She enjoyed watching as Autumn's eyes began to search her own, to peer at her face, looking for answers all the while trying to keep her own countenance casual, curious, calm. But by the time the companion started speaking Autumn was anything but calm. There was something about the companion's face that Autumn suddenly didn't like, something that seemed unnatural, fluid underneath, as though something else lived beneath the skin... something covered in a paper-thin sheen.

The fear starting to creep onto Autumn's face was divine.

"My name?" the companion asked, lingering, enjoying the new weight to the air.

"Y-yes," Autumn replied, trying not to stammer.

"I — I just realized I don't actually know what it is."

The companion nodded, sipped her drink.

Autumn shifted in her seat. The wind caught the hem of her sundress and pushed it off her knee.

"I mean, you know mine, right? It's Autumn. Autumn Adams."

Autumn's eyes darted from side to side; she looked every bit the drug addict she was.

"So it's only fair that I know yours too... right?"

The companion traced the rim of her mug with her finger, allowing a smile to form.

"Indeed," she said low, her voice dropping to an almost inaudible husk.

Silence.

Unbearable.

Confusing.

Autumn wondered why she suddenly felt like someone was tickling her from underneath her skin.

"I have used many names, but this one I will keep," she started, looking off in the distance at the sea from Autumn's imagination.

"For a time I needed something that would keep their eyes away from me, keep them blind. Later, I needed something that was common, something that labeled me as one of many, no different from them. But when I awoke 2,000 years after the end of my mortal life to hear of a celebration for a beheaded Italian girl who had incurred the wrath of a prefect, I knew that what I had been looking for was a name that spoke to my soul. So, I took hers. I take a different body when I need to and did so the first day I called myself by her name. There are so many beautiful vessels to choose from that I have never had trouble finding one that suits me, but the name was much more difficult to decide upon. But that was in the past. This name is mine now and always will be. Cecelia. It's lyrical; pretty. It suits me almost as well as my first name does, the name given to me by a King."

Cecelia.

That name was familiar. So familiar it caused Autumn's breath to hitch and her heart to feel like it might stop in her chest.

Why?

Where had she heard that name before?

Why did hearing it frighten her so much?

Autumn almost didn't realize that her breath had quickened.

"Where... where do I know that name f—"

"I want to pick our destination this time," Cecelia said, cutting in.

"I have the perfect place in mind." Cecelia smiled.

Autumn wasn't altogether sure she liked the look of it.

"I want to show you something amazing."

The freddo cappuccino in front of Autumn disintegrated, slowly dissolving like the table, the blue dome churches, and the Aegean Sea did. Autumn had seen that happen before when she hopped to another location during the same trip, so that wasn't what made her nervous. It was the bodies that came into view in place of the Greek paradise that had occupied the space before, wrapped in discolored linen, some with splintered masks decorated with faded color, some with broken digits and limbs, the sight of which nearly drove her to her knees. Stacked upon each other in haphazard rows, their tombs ransacked and their mummies stolen and hidden away, those who ruled Egypt lay in a heap of decay. Autumn gasped in surprise as her companion—Cecelia—led her deeper into the cache, forcing her to step over mummies and fallen amulets that had been loosed from wrappings when the graves were disturbed. She guided her into a hidden room within the chamber where two mummies waited for them. The mummy on the floor lay prone, wrappings frayed, and vulnerable. Autumn had time to notice Cecelia regarding it lovingly before she saw the cracked sarcophagus behind it where another mummy lay concealed, the façade etched with symbols she could not understand.

Cecelia cast an appreciative glance at the mummy inside the sarcophagus before reaching out to stroke the partially exposed face of the mummy that lay on the floor.

CHAPTER 19

For a moment, she didn't know if she'd be able to get through it. The way the nurses looked at her when she came back into the hospital, some with eyes that showed concern, others with sadness: Asha almost couldn't make it to Chris's room, the hallway seeming longer than it ever had before. She lost her composure for a second and asked one of the nurses if something had happened to Chris while she had been gone. She thought she would know if something had, that she would feel it somehow. At the very least, she was certain that someone would have told her that he had taken a turn for the worst, would have said something to her when she got off the elevator instead of letting her walk into his room unaware if he… if… Asha got in front of one of the nurses, the quiet one who kept to the perimeter when she walked, almost as if she wished she could blend in with the wallpaper. Asha got in front her and made the nurse look up before she asked if Chris was ok. He was, of course he was, but she almost kissed the woman for confirming as much. She was on edge; hadn't realized how much until then, when she could feel the air on her skin prickling her like needles, could sense each and every hair on her forearms. Asha had to get hold of herself. She had to pull it together before she bumped into Nurse Bea.

She took a deep breath, smoothed her hands on her legs.

Chris was ok.

He was *ok*.

She breathed in deeply again for good measure.

Asha walked into his room without encountering Nurse Bea or anyone else; they gave her a wide berth and she guessed she understood why. She had screamed bloody murder and then been gone for a full day. She had never done anything like that before. She was usually quiet and cooperative. Her screaming like that and then leaving the premises was a huge departure from the norm. Most of them had never seen Asha cry let alone show such volatility. Maybe that would earn her some privacy, a longer stretch of undisturbed time with her fiancé instead of their usual hourly intrusions. Maybe they thought she was ready to say goodbye and would let her do so in peace.

She wasn't. There wasn't anything further from the truth. If Asha had seen Rosa before going into Chris's room... had she locked eyes with her friend, the cat would have been out of the bag. Rosa would have been able to look past the melancholy expression she had worked to perfect and noticed the excitement in Asha's eyes. Asha would have had to shoot her a pleading glance, one that asked her to act like she hadn't seen... to play along for her sake. But she hadn't seen Rosa. She was ashamed to be happy about that.

Quiet. Nothing but the sound of machines harmonizing with each other to break the silence. As usual.

Asha went in and made her way to Chris's bed without so much as a sideways glance at the other two men. Some part of her felt badly about that; she almost always said hello to them as she moved toward the space that Chris occupied. Hers was the only voice they ever heard outside of the doctors and nurses charged with giving them care. No one had visited either man since Asha had risen from her own hospital bed to take up residence next to Chris's. She felt badly, but she was single-minded right then. She moved into Chris's space and closed the privacy curtain. She pulled her chair next to the bed and sat down, all before uttering a word. Staring into her would-be husband's immobile face, she said, her voice barely louder than a whisper,

"I'm here, baby. I'm back."

CHAPTER 20

Asha looked at Chris, trying to detect movement... an eyebrow twitch, a nose flare... something.

Anything.

But there was nothing.

She looked around the room, wondering if she had noticed anything different there the first time he spoke. Had the light changed? Had a shadow crossed the wall? She couldn't remember. The only thing that filled her mind was the memory of waking up and seeing Chris looking at her. As disconcerting as that had been, she would pay anything for it to happen again.

Right now.

"Chris?"

Asha felt silly whispering but she did it anyway. She scooted closer.

"Babe, I'm back. I found out I'm—"

"They told me you were here," a voice said fondly, though it sounded loud and obnoxious to Asha's ears at that moment. The way the curtain was ripped back, removing any semblance of privacy that Asha had hoped to create… first it scared her out of her wits, made her jump in her seat, but then it pissed her off.

Nurse Bea appraised Asha, trying her best not to let on that she was doing exactly that. She looked fine, like her usual self, even if her eyes were a bit wild. But what else was to be expected? Nurse Bea had scared the heck out of her when she burst into the space—she could see that. And that was ok. The older woman had been going for the element of surprise.

Nurse Bea wanted to see how Asha really was, not be greeted with feigned pleasantness. She like to think that she would have seen right through it, but there was no sense chancing it surprising her when she least expected it, right when she was whispering whatever it was to Chris and feeling like no one was around was the best way to see what was real and what was fake.

So far so good.

She had slept—that much was clear. Asha didn't look jittery or nervous. Just irritated and Nurse Bea figured that was ok. The routine was important. She wouldn't take long.

"We missed you yesterday," Nurse Bea hedged, waiting to see where Asha would go with it.

Asha felt like she wanted to roll her eyes but knew that was the wrong response. Nurse Bea was being nice and didn't deserve the frustration that Asha was leveling at her. She took a deep breath and spoke, hoping she was speaking the way she would have before.

"Ooh! You scared me!"

Asha giggled because she felt like she would have on any other day.

"I didn't even hear you coming!"

"People always said I was light on my feet. And hospital sneakers don't help any." Nurse Bea turned the instep of her nursing shoes toward Asha revealing a heavily cushioned sole. She motioned toward her foot and explained,

"So we don't wake the patients in the middle of the night."

Nurse Bea smiled.

Asha smiled back.

Normal.

Regular.

Usual.

Hmm.

Nurse Bea went on, "Where'd you go off to yesterday?"

"Nowhere. Hung out around the house mostly. Took a walk, went to the grocery store, actually cooked dinner for a change."

Asha had been ready for that question. She hoped her answer didn't sound rehearsed.

Nurse Bea nodded, busied herself with something at the foot of Chris's bed. Both women knew there was nothing there to fiddle with; the sheets were tucked in just as tightly then as they were when the bed was made earlier, but neither commented.

"I bet that felt real nice," Nurse Bea said and she meant it. That was all the girl really needed – some time away from the hospital to feel the sun on her face and the wind in her hair... to feel like *herself* again. There was no way to tell her that and Nurse Bea knew that if the roles were reversed she would be doing the exact same thing but it was a fact. She could only hope that the taste of life she had gotten outside the day before would be enough to remind her that she was still among the living.

"Yeah, it did." Asha said, cutting her comment short in an

effort to send a cue. She was done talking, at least to Nurse Bea. She wanted to speak to Chris. That's why she was there, not to chitchat with the nurse on duty.

Nurse Bea looked at Asha, registered her growing irritation, and decided she had seen enough.

"Ok," Nurse Bea said, standing straight and giving the woman a smile that meant a lot of things at the same time. "I'll leave you to it."

Asha replied with an appreciative smile that she hoped didn't look too eager.

Nurse Bea nodded.

"He was good yesterday. Numbers stayed level. Nothing out of the ordinary."

Asha thanked her quietly while berating herself inside. She hadn't even thought to ask about how Chris had been.

Nurse Bea waited, for what she didn't know.

Asha shifted in her seat, felt her smile falter.

Nurse Bea shook herself out of it, whatever 'it' was and moved back toward the opening she had created in the curtain.

"Ok, I won't take up anymore of your time. I know you missed him... I know that's true."

Asha smiled self-consciously and suddenly couldn't meet the woman's eyes anymore. She looked into her lap as she nodded, fighting to keep the tears at bay.

Nurse Bea's smile was one of compassion as she left Chris's space so that Asha could once again be alone with her fiancé. She pulled the curtain together and left the room soundlessly.

When the door to the room clicked shut seconds later Asha let go of the breath she had been holding. She stared at the space the nurse had occupied moments before, her body still as she listened... waited. There was no sound in the room other than the usual din. Nurse Bea was really gone.

Asha turned back to Chris and leaned close, closer than she had before.

"I'm not pregnant," she whispered, searching his face for understanding.

"What now?"

CHAPTER 21

"Oh my god... Autumn," Chris said to no one in particular—more of a reaction than anything else—and Gabby felt her jaw slacken.

Her son.

That was her son's voice.

Rich and well-rounded; a velvety tenor that was so expressive, Gabby could imagine it singing Big Band classics like he was from another era. The last time she heard her son speak he was a toddler navigating inflection, choosing opposing emotions most of the time.

She was in awe.

"I haven't spoken to Autumn in... She wouldn't..."

Chris couldn't finish—it hurt too much to say it out loud.

"We have to find—"

"Christopher."

Chris stopped speaking mid-sentence, his mind setting aside its current panic to allow the scent of lavender to fill his nostrils, the gentle touch of a hand on his cheek. He had always shied away from that scent, never allowing himself to breathe of it completely for reasons he could never connect to anything tangible. He would clear his throat or cough or otherwise make a fuss when he encountered it by mistake, like if it was lingering on the air after someone had sprayed it; he would walk out of the room if the scent was particularly strong. Chris never bought candles or room deodorizers that had lavender fields on the bottle. But now, as the scent engulfed his senses, filling his head with feelings of warmth and love if not clear images of the source, Chris felt innocent, felt a joy that he hadn't experienced since he was a child.

She was there. After so many years of wishing he could feel her arms around him, of wishing he could talk to her, see her face, she was there.

"M-mommy?"

Gabby's elation colored her voice as she laughed with pure excitement. She stumbled toward the space where his visage was most clear all the while speaking to her son, seeing a grown man but remembering the young boy she had adored so much she felt her heart might burst.

"Yes, baby, it's me. It's me! Oh my God, Christopher... you're all grown up."

Chris was smiling so hard his cheeks hurt. Because now he could see it all playing in his head like a movie, all the memories he had locked away, thought he had lost forever. He remembered racing his mother in the tall grass and her giving up and falling over, seemingly engulfed by the wildflowers. He remembered sharing ice cream with her and playing Tic-Tac-Toe. He remembered watching movies with her and stories at bedtime. Chris remembered how she smiled at him from a bench when he played at the park, how she smelled when she kissed him goodnight. Lavender.

He started to cry.

"You look just the way you did when... when..."

Gabby didn't need to feel the tears on her cheeks to know she was crying too. She could feel her chest heaving, could hear herself fighting not to sob. Dead shouldn't be like this. Dead should be different. Death should mean the end of pain.

Her son was dying yet he sat crying over his mother who had died years ago.

But it was only a few hours ago.

Only a few...

"I love you, baby. I love you so much."

It was the only thing Gabby could say.

CHAPTER 22

They needed to find Autumn.

Patrick's heart was warmed by what was happening between Gabby and Christopher, but he couldn't shake the feeling that they needed to hurry. That they were even able to hear Christopher in The Realm—that he was able to interact with them at all—scared him. It could only mean that his great-grandson was nearer to death than any of them cared to admit out loud. It meant that they were running out of time.

Doug seemed to think that Autumn was in some dream state and couldn't get out. Patrick thought there was more to it than that. There was something he heard Gabby talk about when she was reading Joanne's manuscript; something Joanne alluded to before she died for the second time... something... some*one*...

Autumn wasn't just some drug addict who had gotten too high and locked herself in a confused haze. Patrick was sure of it. Someone was keeping her there, hidden away, invisible. What could they gain from holding her?

A chill ran down Patrick's spine as he drew connections and saw a picture start to come clear. Whoever was holding Autumn captive in her own mind had plenty of reason to do so. Autumn was the last in his line; the only descendant with a chance at a future because Christopher was dying and his fiancée was not pregnant. But Autumn—she could either become pregnant or already was. Patrick felt himself shiver involuntarily as the dots connected.

They were already too late.

Whoever was keeping Autumn under knew about The Realm and had a vested interest in keeping it going. The only way to do that was to make sure that there would always be someone from his bloodline to rule.

There was something in the story that Gabby had read that mentioned this, something about the backstory that connected to what was going on, but his mind had snagged on something else, something that was taking all of his attention... something that required all of his will to process.

If someone from his lineage had to be born and die to make sure that The Realm always remained in the family, did that mean that Mileeha was his ancestor? And what did that mean about Mal?

Mal, the one who had so brutally dispensed with Mileeha when he tired of him.

Mal, the one who made he and Doug an offer they could not refuse.

Patrick felt his knees buckle. How foolish they were to think they could play this game with such a seasoned opponent. Patrick feared that by agreeing to take the reins and rule The

Realm with his son he had walked right into Mal's trap and ensnared his family forever.

He grimaced as emotion welled up in his chest.

He knew what had to be done.

They had to find Autumn.

They had to break the cycle even if it meant destroying her.

CHAPTER 23

"My sister did everything she could," Cecelia said, her back turned to Autumn as she strolled among the columns etched with reliefs that told of trade agreements with bordering lands. She ran her fingers along the stone, tracing the images, feeling the gritty cuts made to settle her story into history. Cecelia cast her eyes up to view the cornice. It was adorned with gold and lapis and ornately carved; she had approved of the design herself.

"She moved me twice before she died, even carrying my body on her back once to a boat surreptitiously placed where the Nile met Karnak. Nefrubity took me to Sais where she buried me among traders who died far from their homes."

Cecelia chuckled ruefully.

"After all those years of building, all the blessings and curses laid upon it to warn people about disturbing my resting place and I never even used Djeser-Djeseru. For all of the work I did to bring riches to my people, in the end I couldn't surround myself with it."

"You... you're...?" Autumn stuttered, unable to believe the conclusion she was drawing.

"For hundreds of years after my sister died they continued to move me," Cecelia continued, cutting Autumn's stutter-starts off. "The priests who respected the ancients were vigilant about preserving those who ruled. Did you know that people used to unwrap us at parties, decorate their houses with us, grind our bones with a mortar and pestle and *eat* us? How disgusting your lot have been.

"And then there was Thutmose to worry about. Just as Nefrubity left instructions for the continuous movement of my remains, so did Thutmose task his ancestors with finding and destroying my body and my legacy. But they were not successful and now they never will be. No one has looked upon my face in centuries even though they are staring right at me."

Autumn shook her head, trying to make sense of what she was hearing. She knew the people and places Cecelia was talking about. Her brother had talked about them so much after his first visit to Egypt that she felt like she had been there too, right alongside him. Thutmose, Djeser-Djeseru, the relief Cecelia had been touching—Autumn had seen that very one in Chris's pictures.

Cecelia.

The name was coming back to her as she stretched her memory to call up the details of hers and Chris's conversations and flesh out the story being told to her.

Her and Chris.

They had been so close growing up. They would be close now if she would let it happen. He tried. She saw his attempted calls, his texts, his emails. She just didn't respond. Yet he still tried. It hadn't always been that way. They used to be like two peas in a pod, always together, always chattering about something. Even when they got older and made friends outside of each other, they still found comfort in the inherent under-standing they shared. They got into things together; prying open closets filled with old clothes, dusting off books on the bookshelf that hadn't been opened in years; poking around stuff hidden away in boxes... boxes that were pushed into the corner of the attic and covered up with moth-eaten blankets and old draperies meant to obstruct it from view. It was always just the two of them. Autumn was ashamed of herself for letting her own insecurities get in the way of their relationship but she was damned happy that they meant so much to each other... still.

Because now she knew what was going on.

Now she knew she was never getting out of her head.

Cecelia.

Autumn knew that name was familiar.

She was the woman from their great-grandmother's story. The one who started it all.

She had been so angry at Aaron because he was unsure about what he wanted, she created The Realm and damned Aaron and his whole family to it.

And now she was keeping Autumn in a world that was beautiful and exciting but altogether made up, outside of the real world: another place of her own creation.

So... the story was *real*?

Autumn bit her lip to keep the gasp rising from her chest from escaping her lips.

Autumn didn't understand how that could be possible. When she and Chris snuck it out of its hiding place and read it they were amazed by the detail. There was this whole action/thriller vibe that kept them interested. And vampires—Autumn's favorite. They wondered why it had never been finished, why their great-grandmother wasn't some famous author. But that was all, they just thought it was neat story they could tell their own kids one day: that there was an amazing author in their family, blah, blah, blah. They never thought the story was *real*. Vampires and immortals—why the hell *would* they think it was? But now Autumn was stuck in her imagination with a woman who kept showing her shiny things to make her stay, places and people that were much more exciting than anything Autumn's real life had to offer... except the mummies. Those weren't so pretty to look at. Some of their wrappings had been torn, enough so that she could see their withered faces and gaping maws. She could smell the dirt floor and something cloyingly sweet on the heavy air, could feel the air as it entered her own body and sat like a rock in her lungs.

Autumn wanted to leave but she was stuck there. She was being *kept* there in that imaginary place tucked deep in the recesses of her mind... she was sure of that now. And it was because of a woman claiming to be Cecelia. This Cecelia was older than Autumn and Chris would ever have been able to conceive of as kids reading the manuscript typed out on loose, yellowed paper. An ancient who lived in a land so far away it felt intangible, like a fairy tale in a book. And if she was who Autumn thought she was, she was one of the most formidable women in the world.

The relief on the wall. Autumn recognized the pattern of the hieroglyphics.

The cobalt blue stone and gold.

The mummies.

Thutmose.

Cecelia wasn't just any ancient woman.

She was a pharaoh.

She was Hatshepsut.

Autumn looked closely at the woman standing before her

and noticed that she appeared younger than what Hatshepsut was supposed to have been when she died, at least, based on what she had learned from her brother, but that made sense. To even be standing in front of her thousands of years after her death there must be magic involved. Chris had come across a lot of spells during those early days of researching all things Egypt. It made sense that a pharaoh would have access to the best of the best, from gems to magic. In the manuscript Cecelia was written as a vampire, a coven leader though Autumn thought that might have been contrived now that she knew who she was dealing with. She could not imagine a woman like Hatshepsut deigning to drink from someone's neck. But vampires were also shapeshifters, and that would account for the different look. This was not her body. Autumn was considering the significance of this when Cecelia spoke again.

"Smart," Cecelia said appreciatively as she watched recognition dawn on Autumn's face. Autumn snapped out of her reverie to find Cecelia staring at her with a curious smile on her lips... a smile that Autumn didn't like one bit.

"We're going to get along fine, you and me."

Autumn wasn't sure what facial expression reflected on her own face. All she could do was bat aside the questions that were bouncing around in her mind in rapid succession:

Who was Vernese supposed to be, then? The love interest and the cause of all Cecelia's problems in the manuscript, who was she in real life... in *Autumn's* life?

Who was Aaron?

How was her family connected to Hatshepsut?

And if The Realm was real, what do *they* have to do with it?

CHAPTER 24

Doug hated having to break up the reunion his daughter was having with her son, but he was afraid that if he didn't, she would be seeing both of her children in front of her in that very room before long. If they lost Autumn and Chris to *The Realm* everything would have been for naught.

"I'm so sorry to do this, but we have to focus on Autumn," Doug said, his mind coaxing his mouth to utter the thought that he wasn't sure was fully formed yet.

"It's Autumn," he continued. "She's pregnant or she could be, physically, I mean. I mean she's capable of having a child."

Doug clamped his mouth shut to stop himself from rambling on, making it worse. He had never been good at expressing his thoughts, always felt so nervous under pressure that his words just jumbled up when they came out of his mouth. But he wanted to talk now. He needed to express what he was feeling so they would understand Time was of the essence.

"What I'm trying to say is that she is the person most capable of continuing our line." He looked at Chris with sadness in his eyes.

"I'm so sorry, son."

"I know what's happening to me," Chris said, his voice thick with emotion. "I don't know how I've lasted this long. At first I thought it was to save Asha—to make sure she would be ok. Even then, it doesn't make sense that we survived... either of us. Not after what happened."

The fear that crossed his face made Gabby's stomach twist.

Her poor baby.

"But now I'm not so sure that was the reason."

Chris struggled to find the words, to put them together in a way that would make sense.

"Asha is fine. Perfectly fine. She can walk, talk, do everything the way she used to. And while I can't talk to her, not without help, I *can* talk to you. And you can see everything. There has to be a reason that I can see you, talk with you, think the way I used to even though my brain is... is..."

He couldn't bring himself to say it.

"Too many things that shouldn't have happened have come together to get us to this point. I wouldn't have been any use to you dead or fully alive. I think it had to be this way."

Gabby knew what Chris was saying was true but she couldn't figure out why it had to be her son. What would have happened if they were in different positions when they fell to the ground? She hated herself for thinking that way, but it was there, nonetheless. But so was the answer; if Asha had hit the ground first she might have died and ended up somewhere other than *The Realm*. Chris might have died also and he would be there with them, without a connection to a person in the living world. And Autumn might still be held captive to ensure that *The Realm* always had a leader from their bloodline. They wouldn't have been able to do anything to change it.

Chris was right. It had to be this way.

There was nothing fair about The Realm.

Chris turned his attention to the woman he would have married if given the chance and Patrick followed his gaze. She was beautiful and she obviously loved Chris dearly. They might have had a happy life together were it not for the curse that plagued them, the curse that he hadn't been able to break before his great-grandson fell out of the sky. He bit back the sob rising in his throat.

Chris was stunned to find that so much time had passed. It was a different day. Asha was dressed in different clothes and midday light shone into the room leaving different shadows on the floor and walls than before. It was disconcerting the way that things seemed to move faster when he was conversing with his family in The Realm. It was like watching one of those old TV shows where the minute hand made its way around the clock in triple time and the characters on screen aged, white hair growing where dark hair used to be, wrinkles appearing on skin that was smooth only seconds before. Only the people he was looking at didn't age with the passage of time. Because they were all dead.

Asha was sitting in the same chair she always sat in, flipping through a book. She held her hand beneath the front cover, keeping it raised off the table ever so slightly as she brought it closer to get a better look at whatever she was reading. Chris cocked his head and squinted at the cover. The blues and golds looked familiar to him, but the rest of the detail was left in shadows. He leaned closer but Asha lowered the book before he could make anything else out.

"We should try to connect to Autumn again," Doug said,

hoping what he was thinking was true. She couldn't stay under forever. Even if she was being kept away from them, once the drug wore off it might be easier to reach her. Her hallucination would be the only thing keeping her away then and maybe they could take advantage of that and break through. —Unless whatever was binding her in the lucid dream was stronger than Chris's newfound ability, an ability that none of them understood or knew how to control. It was a long shot but they had no other choice.

Chris nodded his agreement and searched his mother's eyes for the same. She didn't want to give it, didn't want to endanger him, the need to protect her son rising inside her unbidden, unexpectedly strong. She feared what the strain would do to him, didn't think she could watch him transition from one of the living to one of the dead while she looked into his eyes. But at the same time she knew that if he didn't, her daughter would remain in peril... in a mortal danger all her own. What if Autumn refused to procreate... what if she *couldn't*? Gabby didn't know anything about the drug she was using; what if it impaired her ability to conceive? What if she was already pregnant and she lost the baby? What would the one who held her do to her then?

Gabby shuddered and Chris wished he could reach out and touch her. But he couldn't. He realized that if he could it would mean that he had died and he would be of no use to his sister then.

He couldn't wait any longer.

Chris averted his eyes from them, looking toward the back of the room, into the kitchen, just past the pantry where Tara still hid. He was seeing but not seeing, searching without knowing what he was looking for. His grandfather had told him where he might find his sister, pointing Chris's gaze in the direction where he was looking then. He focused his attention there with nothing other than thoughts of his sister, memories that only they shared, on his mind. Chris would use them like a beacon, something for her to see in the darkness. He would use them as a bullhorn if he had to, would pelt her with memories of their childhood, of their escapades, of their connection. He couldn't let her run away from him this time, not now—not ever again. There were no more tomorrows. He and Autumn only had the moment they were in.

He had to make the most of it.

Chris stared but saw nothing but the darkened house beyond where his family stood, the layout vaguely familiar. He was sure he had seen it before, wanted to call up the memory of it from the recesses of his mind, but he didn't have time for that. He closed his eyes, took a deep breath, wondered what he must look like to Asha as she sat by his bedside. Unmoving? Statue-like, his skin appearing hard like stone? The same as he had every day since the accident? Yes, he was sure of it. The realization brought tears to his eyes.

Chris breathed in deeply through his nose and then out of his mouth slowly. He did it a second time, hoping it would settle his mind and bring him back to task.

He looked at the room over his mother's shoulder again, let his eyes relax. The room was relatively empty, just a chair jutting out into the walkway facing one of those desks built into the countertop. He couldn't see what was on the desk but tried to anyway, focusing on the shadow of what looked like a picture frame. Plain, unfinished wood floors that seemed to dim, become less distinct, almost fall away once they ventured past the space where the refrigerator would be. Closed pantry door, pulled to but not fully shut, one hedging out the slightest bit beyond the other, the result of an old house perpetually settling. Peeling wallpaper on the walls. Hazy, everything hazy... too far away to be sure of any detail. Like static, a gray cover infiltrated the black, lightening the room, but confusing the images before his eyes even further. It was as if he needed to blink; his eyes became scratchy and irritated, as they tried to make out something, anything that would lead him to his sister. The gray moved like smoke, cascading over the countertop and chair, engulfing them, obliterating them from sight before seeming to regurgitate them back out, changed. The summers of his youth filled the pockets the gray touched and he was a child, tired from playing in the sun, sitting on the sidewalk. Traffic was minimal on his street nestled so deep in their neighborhood that no one other than the people who lived on it and the occasional delivery person ever used passed by. It was hot; the sun was hot even though it was late in the day and Chris felt like he was melting. Someone was grilling already; he could smell the meat from where he sat, rich and full. Steak. His dad was grilling steak and it was summertime at his childhood home.

If he turned his head he would see the smoke coming off the deck, billowing off the back of the house as he opened the lid to flip the steak and turn the onions in the grill pan.

If he listened closely he might be able to catch his father's voice bouncing off the exterior walls, bounding through the corridor created by houses set closely on quarter acre lots. He'd be talking to their neighbor who always seemed to be grilling at the same time. They'd each have a beer in one hand and tongs in the other, talking about sports or politics over the sizzling and licking flames.

Chris knew there would be a black Honda Accord in the driveway, a late model sedan with smoke-tinted windows that his father had applied himself on a day not unlike that one.

He knew these things because they were part of the fabric of his life. But he couldn't look at the memory, couldn't enjoy the comfort it would bring. The logical part of his brain, the part that felt the onslaught of things that were decidedly illogical happening around him, so much so that he envisioned himself being driven to his knees under the weight of it all—that part of him knew that everything he was seeing was orchestrated for his benefit. It felt too normal, too natural... too good. He could feel the warmth of the sun on his skin, the rough concrete on the underside of his legs where the shorts hiked up to reveal untanned skin. He touched a blade of grass to test the theory and he could feel it under his finger. The sensations were real, pulled from his memory and presented to him as new with such detail that he could assume, could honestly believe that he was experiencing them right then and there.

He was nine years old without a care in the world.

Chris couldn't allow himself to revisit that place he loved, couldn't afford to let himself hear the sound of his father's voice even if he knew he'd never get the chance to again.

He was nine years old and he had decades to go before he fell out of the sky.

Chris couldn't get sidetracked or else he'd never save his sister.

He was nine years old.

Where was she? His eyes tripped over the scene before him, marveling at the trees, the weathered shutters that bordered the neighbor's windows, the anthill near his heel. On a day like the one he found himself in, where he could see the wave of heat coming off the asphalt as it hovered, shimmered, sweltered, his sister would have been right beside him, colorful chalk in hand working on a butterfly or a rainbow. Her legs would be crossed as she sat on the sidewalk where loose rocks had been wriggled free, rocks that undoubtedly cut into the soft flesh of her legs, indenting her flesh every time she moved. Autumn might have been humming, a tune caught in her little girl head, one that was only kind of close to a nursery rhyme she had learned, but mostly not. One that wouldn't be the same if someone interrupted her and she had to start again. She might have had her bottom lip clamped between her teeth as she worked, her eyes focused on her creation, fingers stained with chalk residue. But she wasn't there, not then.

Mistake.

It was a mistake going there, letting the dream manifest itself the way it wanted.

It was a mistake to let himself be pulled in.

"Who knows if they can do it," his father bellowed from the backyard. *"He hasn't pitched a no-hitter all season..."*

His father's voice was as he remembered it with his kid ears, solid and strong. The strongest man in the world but now he was dead, dead, dead.

"But wonders never cease, am I right?"

Laughter erupted from the backyard from the neighbor who had shared those afternoon talks with Chris's dad for the better part of 15 years... the neighbor who had been dead since Chris's junior year in high school.

Laughter, full-bodied and hearty.

Laughter that couldn't exist.

Not anymore, unless...

unless...

"I'm dead," Chris forced himself to say out loud, his voice coming up from his throat with the force of a shout but sounding weak to his ears. "Oh god... I died."

"No!"

The sound was loud and sharp, like the clank of a sword against its metal scabbard as it was unsheathed to cut through the air. Chris turned his head toward the sound; it was behind him, where the house he grew up in was... where his father who couldn't be there, couldn't be back there laughing with his long dead friend was. Chris turned toward it immediately because it sounded like his sister. It was anguished and afraid and sorrowful and frightened. So very frightened. He'd never heard her sound like that before; indeed, he hadn't heard her voice in over a year, but he knew that's who it was. He would know her voice anywhere. He always would.

"Autumn?" he called as he spun his head toward the house, but it was gone. Soon everything was, evaporated like effervescence from a freshly poured glass of soda, gone like the figment of his imagination that it was. In its place was like something out of his dreams, somewhere he had dreamed of returning to.

The room was vast, overlooking a courtyard filled with fuchsia Lynchpin, red and yellow Celosia, and brilliant cornflower. Creeping Myrtle and poppies ringed an ornate fountain where lotus flower dotted the water. Reliefs inlaid with gold lined the walls painted with pigments of brilliant cobalt, light blues, muted oranges, and maroons. Columns with palm capitals adorned the room, each reflecting a pharaoh giving offerings to different gods. Through the door to the antechamber Chris could see the colossus situated at the far end of the room and thought, not for the first time, that the wonder the ancients left behind gave more than passing credence to the possibility that humans were once giants. He had seen them before, giant statues of kings and of the gods, had stood before the Colossi of Memnon, and the statues had never ceased to give him pause. But this one was different. His eyes fought to latch onto the image, so far away, almost out of his line of sight but close enough to tantalize him with the possibilities. He felt his mouth drop open as he squinted.

The sound of her laughter was silky.

Chris turned toward it, wishing it was the sound of his sister's voice but knowing it wasn't. Distracted. He had been distracted by the grandeur; the room created for him to see so reminiscent of his beloved Egypt that he might have laughed at his own simplicity had he not detected something in the woman's voice. Something that struck a chord... something that frightened him.

The owner of the voice was a beautiful woman. Her hair was pulled into an elaborate bun, the delicate twists combining to create a texture that drew him in. Her skin was golden and vibrant, seeming to glow from within. Chris saw her shapely lips form the smile beneath lipstick the color of crushed red roses. She was gorgeous, sensuous in way that spoke of a confidence that many never possess. But it was her eyes that impacted him most, that froze him in place, scared to move but terrified to stay.

Chris caught a glimpse of the relief on the wall behind the woman because he saw movement beyond it and averted his eyes from hers in search of his sister. Black and shadowed; someone seemed to be clawing, reaching for something just beyond their reach, writhing in place as they lay on the floor.

"Au-" Chris started before the hiss of a word wrenched his eyes away from what distracted them and back to the woman before him. But he saw it all. Something on the floor. Something curious on the relief. Something... Chris saw just enough of the relief to know there was something written there, that he was seeing a cartouche instead of a different kind of hieroglyph.

The sound of her voice almost made him forget it all.

"Back," the woman said, her voice like a serpent's, her eyes ever more.

She raised a hand to him and Chris could not resist the urge to flinch, to squint his eyes, to bow his head in a supplication that he didn't understand. When he raised his head again, it was to meet his mother's worried eyes.

CHAPTER 25

Chris's eyes were unfocused, confused when they looked into Gabby's and she wanted to reach out, to touch his cheek and reassure him like she would have before. She frowned involuntarily, her eyebrows knitting as she searched his face for something, anything.

"Christopher?" she said hesitantly, trying not to startle him but needing him to come back to himself. "Honey?"

"Christopher, what happened?" Patrick asked, stepping forward, closer to Gabby, closer to the space that Chris was able to occupy. "What did you see?"

Chris had been looking at his mother, trying to bring his brain back to that room, that place, even though he didn't understand where he truly was or how he could be there. He had been staring at her not for answers, but for grounding, so when his great-grandfather spoke it surprised him, jarred him as if he had forgotten there were other people in the room. He turned his head toward Patrick, his eyes wide. Then he looked back at his mother. He could read the question in her eyes. He didn't know how he was going to answer it.

"She was there... at least, I think it was her," he started because that was the truth. "I heard her—I'm sure of that—but when I looked for her, I couldn't tell..."

Chris's voice trailed off as he tried to explain.

"What do you mean?" Gabby urged, nerves twisting in her stomach. Something was wrong. He... he looked so nervous...

"Someone was there, but they were too far away, in the shadows. But I heard Autumn's voice before that, at the house. Well not there, but right as I was leaving... before I got to the palace."

"The palace?" Doug asked, confused. When he saw Autumn she was in her house. It was dark and shadowed there too because she had been sitting in the room without the lights on so when Cristopher mentioned it being hard to see her, it made sense. But he would never have called that room, with clothes littering the floor and chip bags and dirty cups stacked up on the nightstand a palace... not by any stretch of the word.

"Where were you, baby?" Gabby asked, sensing that this was where they needed to focus. The way his head moved as he tried to sort through the recollection... how troubled he looked; Gabby knew something was bothering him about this part of the story. They needed to find out what that was before he would be able to talk about Autumn. Maybe talking about it would lead him to his sister.

"I-I don't know," Chris said as he met his mother's eyes again. "It felt familiar but not like I had been there before. More like I'd *seen* it somewhere before, but... but... there's no way I could have."

Patrick stayed silent, hoping that was what Chris needed to

continue. It took everything he had not to ask him what the hell he was talking about but he tamped the urge down.

"I don't know if I made it up or something, combined things I've read with what's been excavated, but what I saw was... was magnificent. The columns, the courtyard, the inlaid gold and rich hues etched into the walls... it was what we hoped it might have really been like. It seemed like it came right out of our dreams."

He looked at his mother, his grandfather, and his great-grandfather. They weren't following.

"I'm an Egyptologist. I've consumed everything I could about Egypt since I was young."

The wistfulness in his mother's eyes was almost too much to bear as she heard details about her son that she had not lived to find out firsthand.

"I'm a museum curator, was ready to bring in my first installation when all of this..."

Chris took a deep breath. He couldn't let his emotions derail him—not now.

"I was bringing in a 25th dynasty installation—the first of its kind—when I had my accident, but I got my feet wet in 18th dynasty history. The pomp and grandeur, the glitz of it all... I couldn't resist it."

Blank stares.

"This is the era of King Tutankhamun," Chris explained.

"King Tut is what most people call him."

Chris smiled at a memory before sharing it with the people in whose eyes he could see his past.

"Asha never let me call him that after I told her his whole name. She said it was horrible to shorten it—disrespectful in a way because people shortened it because they didn't know how to pronounce it. She said it was pure laziness... and then she proceeded call me Chris instead of Christopher."

Everyone in the room smiled with Chris as he remembered his intended, feeling they would have loved her instantly if given the chance.

He looked for Asha then, needing to see her, terrified suddenly that he might never get the chance to again. He wanted to tell her he loved her one last time, wanted to see her smile at him the way she used to, full of love and trust and honesty, not the veiled thing she gave him now when she looked at his withered body, the one that was there to hide grief and loss and fear but couldn't quite manage it. He had decided he wouldn't speak to her again, not while she was awake and looking at him. It was too much to ask of her sanity to do such a thing. He shuddered to think what he must have looked like, eyes yellowed and sunken, skin like that of a doll's, lips pulled into service, stretched thin over stained, neglected teeth. He probably scared her to death. It must have been the worst of feelings to see the man she loved, the man she had been keeping vigil over day in and day out, the man who had been inanimate when she went to sleep, suddenly awake and speaking to her in such an urgent way. Surely Asha thought she had lost her mind. It was a horrible cruelty that he did not intend to repeat.

Her eyes... they had been so relieved, so surprised... so frightened... so sad.

Chris figured it was better that she thought it was a dream than believe it was real and find renewed hope only to watch him die in a day, a week, a month.

Chris could feel his body rotting—it would not be long.

But still he wanted to see her, needed to.

It was dark in the room that would bear witness to his last breath, but he searched for her anyway. Part of him knew he wouldn't find her there; the staff had allowed Asha to stay in his room overnight a few times in the beginning, but they had returned to protocol in the last month. They let Asha stay as long as she liked during the day, beyond visiting hours if that's what she wanted, taking meals with him and napping in the chair as often as she liked but no more overnights. They were trying to help Asha remain in the real world. They did what they could to force her to go outside, hear the sounds of the city, breathe in fresh air, and for that he was grateful.

It was nighttime. Asha wasn't there.

He was disappointed but he understood. She shouldn't be there, not all the time, even if they let her be. Soon she wouldn't have to be there at all anymore.

Chris was about to turn back to his family and try to describe the figure that lay on the floor in the shadows, see if they could make sense of it together but before he pulled his eyes away from the room, before he gave into the compulsion to find a reflective surface that might give him a glimpse of his own form lying the hospital bed, might let him see the horror that Asha was treated to every time she stepped foot into the room, Chris noticed the books she had left behind. They were stacked on the table—nothing more than a tv tray really but they left it there all the time so that Asha could have a place to set up her laptop, leave magazines, whatever she might not feel like lugging back home every day. Sure, the table was in the corner and out of the way, but it was probably against the rules too. It warmed Chris's heart to know that the hospital staff showed his fiancée such kindness when she needed it most.

He scanned the book titles. Books about Mummies. Books about Luxor. Books that covered the 18th and 19th dynasty pharaohs, those with reliefs and inscriptions from many of the pharaohs from the period on the covers. A book displaying a collection of the artifacts found in Tutankhamun's tomb; one book showing an oversized full-color spread of what was found in Ramesses II's on the cover. Even though he had developed an interest in the 25th dynasty, Asha was as enamored with the 18th and 19th as much as he had been when he first found it. Ramesses II had been her favorite, though Chris had never been entirely sure if that was because of the pharaoh himself or because of Yul Brynner's interpretation of him in *The Ten Commandments*. He scanned the table once more. There was nothing there from Kush. Made sense. She'd have been hard-pressed to find many titles about the 25th dynasty pharaoh's anyway; there were only two or three in the house. Chris had planned to fill the museum bookstore with as many 25th dynasty titles as he could find—would write one himself one day to round out the research. But that day would never come.

The image on the book on top featured a close shot of a queen wearing a bejeweled blue crown, the diadem touching the skin painted gold. The queen had full lips, copper skin, and a perfectly symmetrical face: the most beautiful woman in the world. Nefertiti. He remembered seeing her bust at the Neues Museum on a trip to Berlin, the trip he took for that expressed purpose, remembered thinking and it was even more beautiful in person than it was in pictures.

Nefertiti.

Chris remembered going through all the printed material they had available at Neues about the authenticity of the bust, wanting to understand why Egyptologists had debunked certain theories and had settled upon identification. He had the opportunity to view the House Altar relief there as well, actually took a magnifying glass to it and apply his burgeoning translating skills on the hieroglyphics, corroborating what had been proven long before he was born: Nefertiti, who sat across from her husband, the pharaoh Akhenaten in the House Alter relief was the same woman in the bust. She wore the same crown, had the same features, and she was so named in the relief as the Great Royal Wife.

She was named.

Chris's brow furrowed as he looked at the book cover, seeing but not seeing, his mind combing through details from the past as it tried to make connections that seemed just out of his reach.

He squinted, tried to bring the memory closer, clearer.

"What is it?" Gabby asked, alarmed. His face was contorting in ways that she didn't know if she should be concerned about. "Christopher, what is it?"

"The cartouche… I saw it. Just the edge of it, but I saw…"

Patrick looked at Doug, a question etched on his face. Doug shrugged and looked back at his grandson, hoping he would explain.

But he was silent, his eyes searching the room, scanning images that existed only in his memory.

Gabby looked like she was going to jump out of her skin. Christopher wasn't saying anything, nothing that made sense to any of them. The whole thing seemed to be agitating him in ways that she wasn't sure his body could sustain. She was worried for her son, worried that he wouldn't get the opportunity to help his sister, wouldn't get the chance to share space with his fiancée again…would end up there with them in short order because they didn't know how to help him through what he was experiencing.

She opened her mouth to speak but felt her grandfather's hand on her shoulder, quieting her. She didn't look at him—didn't have to—to know that he was concerned too. She took the guidance that the touch implied and held her tongue.

Chris's eyes seemed to be reading things in the air as though consulting a whiteboard they couldn't see, comparing. After what felt like hours, he spoke again, talking through what he was grasping at, his comments more for himself than for them.

"Something about the cartouche was so familiar. The god Ra was on the first line but many pharaohs identified with Ra in some way, even before Ahkenaten's monotheistic rule. But the second line... the seated figure... I've seen it somewhere before."

Mumbling. It all sounded like mumbling. Gabby understood the words individually but they meant nothing to her in the combination Chris used. If they weren't up against the wall, so pressed for time, she would have a moment to be thoroughly impressed with her boy.

Chris seemed to lean in as if staring closer at something they couldn't see. He turned his head, frowned, squinted his eyes, twisted his lips as he flipped through the repository of images in his head. Gabby, Doug, and Patrick waited in silence.

And then Chris jumped as if he had been stung.

"Oh my God! Oh-oh my God!"

He looked at them with eyes that were both excited and confused at the same time.

"I don't understand this, but if it's true, this is... this is... holy shit."

It was Doug who asked this time. "What is it, Christopher? Tell us."

Chris took a stabilizing breath before he continued, his mind racing.

"When I was in Berlin I saw Nefertiti's bust and I tried to figure out how they knew it was her, right? It was because she was wearing the same headpiece in other depictions of her and those had a cartouche on them that named her as Queen Nefertiti. A cartouche is like a name plate that says who the person is.

Cartouches like the one that named Nefertiti were only reserved for royalty.

"When I was looking for Autumn, at first I was out in front of our house. It was like I was there, really there, in the front of our house on a hot summer day. I could even smell what dad was grilling in the back, could catch snippets of his conversation with the neighbor."

Chris tipped his head toward his mother instinctively and she felt a smile cross her lips.

"Frank," she supplied and Chris nodded.

"Yeah, Mr. Frank. I could hear everything and it all felt so real. But Autumn wasn't there and I knew she should be. I wanted to stay so badly, but I knew I couldn't because something about it was wrong."

The words were coming in a torrent.

"I started to think I was dead. I even had time to think that it might be ok that Autumn *wasn't* there because I had to be dead and that meant she was still alive. But then I heard Autumn scream."

Patrick's hand reached across Gabby's back to grip her other shoulder. He instinctively pulled her closer to him and she leaned into her grandfather's chest.

"It's like she was trying to wake me up, to snap me out of it or something. Autumn yelled 'No!' and then, all of a sudden, I was in another place. My house was gone and I was in the courtyard of a palace. A royal palace... in Egypt."

Gabby was sure her face mirrored everyone else's looks of confusion.

"What? How?" Doug asked, confusion knitting his brow.

"I don't know, but I'm sure I was in a royal palace because I saw another cartouche. That's what I was trying to make out; I didn't see the whole thing because I noticed it on one of the reliefs on the wall at the same moment that I saw the person on the floor in the shadows. But I've seen a lot of cartouches in my research and I... now that I've seen her and the place where she felt most comfortable, I can't believe what I'm saying but I think I know who she is."

"What do you mean you've seen *her*?" Doug asked "I thought you said you were in a palace. If you saw Autumn where I saw her, you wouldn't be calling *that* a palace." Doug was afraid the words were too sharp, accusatory almost, but they were out of his mouth before he could phrase them differently.

"I don't mean Autumn. I think she was there. That shadowy figure on the floor might have been her or maybe she was somewhere else in the room... I don't know. I never got a good enough look to know for sure. But that's not who I'm talking about now. There was someone else there. Someone regal and poised. A woman who was beautiful with knowledge in her eyes that spoke of confidence. I think she's the one keeping Autumn from us—the one who trapped her in her own mind."

"Why? What happened to make you think that?" Gabby asked.

"She only spoke one word to me but it was filled with such control and finality. almost like a decree. And if I'm right, that makes all the sense in the world."

Chris looked at his confused family and, for the first time since meeting them there in that place to which they were banished, he wondered exactly what any of them could have done to incur such wrath.

They stared back at him, each of their eyes imploring him to explain... to continue.

"Even though the god Ra is commonly linked to the pharaohs of many dynasties, only a few take the name as part of their royal titulary. In the 18th dynasty there are only three that come to mind that have Ra occupying the first line of the cartouche. In fact, all three of them share the god Ra in the first position *and* the seated figure in the second. But where Nefertiti's cartouche holds something that resembles a cross-stemmed spoon and Amenhotep III's has what looks like a bowl on its third line, only one has what I caught a glimpse of. It's the symbol of *ka* or the soul."

Chris paused, seeing the cartouche again in his head.

"It looks like arms raised in praise. That's what was on the bottom of the cartouche in the palace. That cartouche belongs to the most formidable female pharaoh to ever have lived. Lady of the Two Lands. It's Queen Hatshepsut."

CHAPTER 26

His hand moved.

Or at least she thought it had... hoped it had.

Chris always looked the same when Asha came into the room in the morning; head facing the ceiling, hands on the bed by his sides, legs stitched together, as straight as they could be. Only his feet showed dissonance, added a bit of personality to the visual that was so very unnatural. They cocked out to the side, one in a deeper arc than the other as though being pulled toward the mattress by a string.

A string wrapped around his toe.

Asha hated herself for the image that reference called to mind.

The lighting in the room was usually one of two ways also: fluorescent and too bright or muted, almost blue. It was enough to make her think she was looking at a photo still or a video on pause. Maybe she was even dreaming it all on a perpetual loop. That would be better, infinitely better than the reality. But her mind wouldn't let her indulge in that fantasy for long.

This was Chris now. This was their life, not a bad dream or a cruel joke.

This was reality.

But not that day.

When Asha walked over to kiss Chris on the cheek the way she did every time she came in, even before putting down her purse and laptop and whatever else she might have brought in with her, she almost didn't notice that something was different. She leaned in to kiss him, shutting her eyes the way she used to when he was animate and would raise his chin so that his lips could reach hers and they had never stepped foot in a hospital together before, but her eyes caught on something before the lids fully closed. She opened her eyes lazily to look directly at what had caught her subconscious's attention, still hovering over Chris's flesh, flesh that was always wrong; too cool, rubbery... not right.

And then she saw it.

Chris's hand was against the bedrail.

Asha pulled up slowly, keeping her eyes on it, trying to make sense of what she was seeing. Maybe it was nothing, she told herself. Maybe he got jostled around after his sponge bath that morning: she could smell the fresh yet still slightly medicinal scent of the body wash the hospital used so Asha knew they had been in there already. Maybe one of the nurses took his pulse and let his hand flop down instead of placing it back where it had been. She hated that some of the newer, younger nurses did things like that—scrubbed at the patient's skin when washing them, squeezing their trapezius extra hard during pain response checks, moving them roughly, almost without regard when changing their gowns. Treating them like they were just another chore to be handled. She always said something when it happened to Chris and got the nurses changed out. She felt terrible for the patients who didn't have someone to stand up for them.

She'd have to do it again, get some new nurse swapped out. It wasn't a big deal—his hand was only a little out of place—but that was how it started. Nurses like that, they don't speak to the patient, they treat them with disdain, start to resent them, disrespect them. Asha shuddered to think about what went on after visiting hours.

"I'll be back, babe," Asha said, standing up to her full height. She put her things down at her makeshift desk, mumbling, "I'm gonna nip this in the bud."

As Asha headed out of the room, the rustling of bedsheets was muted and far away, like it was happening in another unit.

By the time Asha had taken the few steps it took to get from Chris's bedside to the nurse's station, her dander was up. She approached the nurse's station ready to do battle with someone, anyone—the nurse in question, if Asha was lucky. She was ready to tell them how Chris was a human being and that they had better work on their bedside manner because it was trash in its current state. She was ready to show the nurse how she was not having it, that Chris had someone there who loved him and she was not putting up with any bullshit from someone who was supposed to take care of him. Her speech was prepared and sitting on the end her tongue but something else called her attention away from the nurse's station just as she was about to launch into her diatribe.

Rosa looked like she was in a daze. She was standing in the doorway of her husband's room, eyes unfocused, clothes disheveled, looking as if they had been slept in. Her mouth hung open as if she had been about to speak but lost the words. She turned to eye the doorjamb, ran her hand over it, feeling the cool metal beneath her fingers. Then she snatched her hand away, clutched it to her chest as though she had been burned. Rosa whipped her head back to look into the room; Asha could see her head moving, imagined her eyes scanning, searching.

Oh no.

Asha moved briskly to her friend's side, called her name gently so as not to frighten her. When Rosa turned to look at Asha it was with eyes that were utterly lost.

"Larry?" Rosa asked Asha, and they both turned to look into the room. Larry's bed had been stripped of the bedding he had laid upon. The machines had been repositioned against the wall and turned off. Everything was still, terribly still. The very air seemed to have been sucked out of the space leaving it cold and barren.

Larry was gone.

"Larry?"

Asha embraced Rosa and felt the older woman's legs give way as she fell into her arms. She cried then, letting her own fear, her tension, her grief, her empathy flow as her tears wet her friend's cheek and hair, as the other's dampened her shirt in kind. The nurses ushered them into a space where they could have privacy and Asha listened as her friend spoke of hers and Larry's love affair, their biggest arguments, the life they shared together. Asha rubbed her hair when the tears came again as she recounted the moment Larry drifted away. She cried her own tears for her friend who was never able to hear her love's voice saying her name again. She tried not to see herself sitting on the opposite side of the table one day soon.

"I went to see my sister yesterday. She had been here for two weeks already and it was her last day before going back home. I hadn't spent any real time with her yet, not more than 30 minutes the whole two weeks she had been here, so I spent the day with her. It was like we were kids again. We did everything.

Went shopping, got our nails done, got massages, ate more than we should have. I even had a drink. I haven't had a drink in years."

Rosa's wistful smile broke Asha's heart.

"I haven't felt like that—like I was 20 years younger... 30, maybe—in a long time. I felt guilty about being out in the beginning, but my sister... she can be persuasive when she wants to be."

Rosa paused, took a deep breath.

"I had *fun*, Asha. Real, honest to goodness fun. And now my Larry is dead."

Asha reached for her hand, noticing the brick red nail polish on her friend's newly manicured hands when she did. She couldn't block the unwanted images of Rosa scratching at that red nail polish when night fell and she found herself alone, ripping at her nails, tearing them off the nail beds.

"No, Rosa. Don't do that. Larry would have wanted you to go out and have a good time. He knew how dedicated you were to him. If he could have, I'm sure he would have told you to go out and enjoy yourself sometimes. He loved you and he knew how much you loved him. Nothing can change that."

Rosa nodded distractedly. Looking at the table, she continued,

"They called me last night and told me I should come. It was late and I was still feeling my drink, but once I heard what they said I was completely sober again. My sister drove me here. She's getting the car now. She'll stay longer to help me plan the..."

Rosa didn't finish. Asha didn't finish the sentence for her: there was no need to.

"I just wish he had opened his eyes one more time, had told me he loved me. I haven't heard his voice in so long, and now..."

Fresh tears came and she let them trail down her face.

"I hope he knew I was there, holding his hand just like I promised I would be," Rosa said, resigned. "I kept my promise."

Asha held her friend for what would be the last time. She would not be attending Larry's funeral or visiting Rosa at her home. Asha's presence, though a comfort while they were together in that controlled space, would not be welcomed in her world, in her next . The reminder would be too great. When her sister came upstairs to collect her, Rosa said goodbye as she left the corridor and moved toward the elevator, hoping that her eyes imparted the gratefulness she felt toward Asha for the companionship as well as the hope that she too was prepared for what was to come.

Asha watched until the elevator door closed with a mix of emotions swirling around in her head. She wanted to block them all out...- needed to or else she would collapse right there in the hallway. Larry had died. Just died. He hadn't gotten sick; nothing about his health had changed at all. He just died. Asha didn't know the details of how or why. She didn't need to. What she did know was that the other day, when she had passed by Larry's door to see if Rosa wanted anything from the cafeteria, he had been laying there looking the same way he always did. And now he was gone.

Would the same thing happen to Chris?

Would she be at home one night and they'd call her back, telling her his vitals were falling and she needed to hurry?

Would he die without fanfare one day while she napped in the chair next to his bed?

For a second, the absolute quickest of moments, Asha was frozen in place, afraid to go back inside Chris's room.

Asha shook her head; she couldn't let herself think about that. If she did she would never move from that spot. Wiping her tears, Asha went into Chris's room, deciding to forget about the rant she was prepared to have at the nurse's station, wanting only to be near her fiancé, to hold him, to touch him while she still could.

She pulled the curtain closed behind her and approached Chris's bed slowly, wishing they weren't in that hospital at all, wishing she had never met Rosa and her husband, wishing all the pain and sadness in that place didn't exist.

And Chris's hand was through the bedrail bars.

CHAPTER 27

Confused.

Tara was confused and she hated feeling that way.

When she was alive, being confused would make her stop listening, make her bow out of the conversation, deem it unimportant and stupid. When she felt that way she would decide that the people who were talking about the things she couldn't wrap her mind around were just trying to sound smart but in reality, they were talking about shit they didn't understand. Either that or they were making it all up as they went along. It didn't matter when everything was said and done. Tara got exactly what she wanted out of those interactions: the asshole talking about the shit she didn't care about would eventually shut up about it all and she would go on about her merry way, usually richer than when the whole deal started, lifting a little something for her trouble. But this time she wanted to understand what the hell was going on.

This time was different because she actually believed them.

No one could fake the pain in the new woman's—Gabby's—voice. She was suffering seeing her son the way he was and the prospect of him dying and joining her didn't bring any consolation to her worried soul. Gabby might have been happy to see her father when she got to The Realm, might have been excited to meet her grandfather. Those moments might have even made her accept the fact that she was dead a little easier, but seeing her son on his deathbed negated all of that. And to have one child close to death and the other one missing, unreachable, as lost to her as if she had died and ended up somewhere else... Tara didn't know how the woman was still standing. Tara imagined that now, what seemed like a strange new reality to Gabby had turned into a full-on nightmare. And Gabby would be right to think that. If she knew what monsters lurked just outside the door, she would be terribly afraid for her children and for herself. Tara couldn't help but think about the old women in her family who used to carry themselves to church every Sunday for service and Wednesday for bible study, making sure they 'got right with God' before that 'great gettin' up morning' when they would be called up. If they only knew what might be waiting for them, how impenetrable the dark could be, they may not be so ready to call the Lord to take them home.

No one could fake that kind of anguish.

And there was more.

Something was going on with Doug. At first he had struck Tara as one of those guys who acted like he knew everything and that nothing was a big deal. He had an attitude, a bravado that rubbed Tara the wrong way. But he was different now. Thoughtful in a way that didn't seem to come naturally to him. Cautious. At first Tara thought it was because his daughter was there now, and while that could still be part of it, that wasn't the whole thing. Doug's father had been there before Gabby and that hadn't changed his tone, so Tara didn't think it was the fear of being seen acting that way that did it. She couldn't put her finger on it, but something was different now with him. And Tara definitely noticed.

She had been in the pantry for a long time.

A hell of a lot had happened since she snuck inside the house and found herself stuck in that cramped space.

Tara couldn't help but laugh at herself hiding there in a corner like a little kid afraid to get caught with her hand in the cookie jar. She supposed that was more the truth than anything else. Tara snickered quietly. She was having the time of her life after death.

CHAPTER 28

Dad... and Hatshepsut?

Pharaoh Hatshepsut?

Doug had never been a history buff and didn't remember much about the whole Egyptian craze that happened in the 70s when King Tut's riches were paraded around museums in the United States and Europe drawing crowds the same way that concerts did, but he knew what a pharaoh was. He had even heard of Queen Hatshepsut, though he would have been hard-pressed to come up with her name on his own. But now that it had been said, uttered in that strange in-between place they were forced to call home, he remembered her clear as a bell. Hatshepsut had been born into royalty and ascended to the throne when she married. Her stepson was supposed to be pharaoh, but her husband died when the boy was a child so Hatshepsut first ruled with him, and then in his place. Doug didn't remember the details of how or why she had taken over reign but he remembered the aftermath. When Hatshepsut died, her stepson took over the throne and broke all of the statues that she had erected in her likeness, wiped her name from the book of pharaohs, if there was such a thing: acted like she never existed, let alone ever ruled Egypt. Doug remembered the detail that stuck in his mind—probably the reason he remembered Hatshepsut in the first place. The visual was too brutal to easily forget. The stepson threw her mummy into the Nile and let the crocodiles have at her.

How could his father be involved in all of that? Doug knew it wasn't his father directly, that it was Mal that had to have had a relationship with Hatshepsut, but the logistics of it all kept tripping over themselves in his head. He bounced between thinking of his father, of Mal, of the Aaron character in the manuscript his mother had written all those years ago, the one that Gabby was reading as she took her last breath. All of them were the same person, intertwined, inextricably linked. And that was confusing as hell. But with what Chris had figured out two things had become crystal clear: the curse was incredibly old and they weren't dealing with a garden variety grudge.

This was a pharaoh who reigned over a vast kingdom, was the most powerful person in all of Egypt, and had, through some kind of magic spell or incantation, figured out how to become immortal. This was the person who had been spurned by some version of Doug's father, who had cursed his whole family to live in limbo after they died... who was holding his granddaughter captive to make sure that happened.

Holy shit.

She had set all of those things in motion; orchestrating their demises, creating The Realm itself if the story was to be believed. She was holding all the cards.

And Patrick didn't have any idea about any of it.

Doug realized then that he would have to tell him. Maybe Patrick knowing could change things somehow, force Mal out of the shadows. But who would Mal confront? Hatshepsut or Cecelia or whatever she wanted to call herself? While that would be ideal, Doug feared the outcome his mother wrote about. But what if Hatshepsut decided to deal with Mal a different way? What if she turned her sights onto Patrick and decided to break Mal down starting there? Doug was afraid of what that might mean.

But still, Patrick had to know. Keeping him in the dark was cruel. He was already tormenting himself for whatever he thought he had done to doom his family to The Realm. He needed to know that it wasn't his doing – that it was some version of him who was responsible. But then would that mean that Patrick wasn't truly himself? That he was never anything other than a version of Mal, the seemingly omniscient entity that he and his father had witnessed killing their predecessor? Would that mean that he was Mal, the one who Doug had never believed, never trusted. It made him sad to think of his father that way, but he had to if he was going to be able to help Patrick get through it. He had to if he was ever going to be able to explain the glint he saw in his father's eyes from time to time—the one that spoke of excitement where there should have been disgust.

Doug had to tell his father the truth.

As Patrick stood listening to his great-grandson talk about the woman who was having her way with them, Doug realized how much he loved his father in spite of it all. Maybe even more so because of it.

CHAPTER 29

Dark room.

Big room.

Orchestra onstage, two cellos situated in front, chamber music filling the concert hall. Between classical sets a tenor speaks to the audience, one of the duo, quipping, engaging, laughing with the people who have paid to see him play. The language was familiar to Autumn, though she couldn't pick out any words. Settled in and comfortable, the man addressed his audience with the ease of a person using his native tongue with people who have known him all his life. She felt the swell of her cheeks and noted the smile that crept onto her face as Bach's Double Violin Concerto in D minor, first movement started up.

God, she loved late Baroque.

Should have been a music major. Should have never given up the violin. Shoulda, woulda, coulda. Water under the bridge —a bridge she no longer had to cross anymore if she didn't want to. Except...

Chris hadn't looked right. He was drawn, pale, the kind of skinny that came from illness, not diet and exercise.

Something was wrong with her brother.

She needed to see him, find out what was wrong with him... help him. Autumn wouldn't be able to do that if she stayed there in that nothingness that had turned into everything she had ever desired in her whole life. He had come looking for her. She didn't know how, but Chris had come looking for her and she was there, right there, but something held her back, silenced her voice, blocked her from view.

No.

Not something.

Someone.

Cecelia. Hatshepsut. Whatever name she wanted to go by. She was keeping Autumn there, keeping her away from Chris, keeping her entrenched in the fantasy.

The tempo increased and she felt her back arch. It was remote; it almost went unnoticed as her soul swayed to the music. Her fugue was literal and all-encompassing.

Autumn touched her stomach before she realized what she was doing and it made her jump. It wasn't so much the act itself nor the sensation that called her hand into action, but it was the fact that she was *aware* that she had done it in the first place that surprised her. She hadn't been aware of much of anything for a long time, longer than she could even try to calculate. Autumn had been blissfully living in her own little world, not paying attention to anything but the scenery, the way the air felt on her skin... the fact that the air of her imagination felt like anything at all. She had been caught up in the fantasy and was loving every second of it until she realized she wasn't in control of anything anymore.

Until she realized she couldn't get out.

Until... now.

Intricate bow work: the cellists lured her with techniques her heart leapt for.

No!

She had given in enough; the lure of the mountains, the beach, of sex, of excitement... she had taken the bait every time. She just took another tab, placed it under her tongue, and let herself fly away. And her companion had always been there to greet her, to see the sights with her. She was Autumn's road dog, her partner in crime. Cecelia. Hatshepsut. The woman who... who... what? Autumn didn't know exactly. But Chris knew, and she needed to find out.

Autumn looked around herself, saw that she was seated in the balcony of a concert hall among a dozen similarly clad people all decked out in tuxedos and evening gowns. Their faces showed the same appreciation for the music that she felt; some even had their eyes closed to take in each note.

But something was wrong.

Very wrong.

It was almost perfect, but off enough for Autumn to catch on, especially in the heightened state of awareness that she was experiencing. If she was right the cellists before her would not be speaking the language that she thought she was hearing— Croatian or Slovenian... she couldn't be sure which, but she was leaning toward Croatian—if they were in a concert hall of such grandeur where she could sit in the balcony and watch. They might speak Italian or Russian, even, but not Croatian or Slovenian—not in *that* concert hall, because the concert hall they would be playing in where they could speak Croatian to an audience that understood them without translation did not have balcony seats. Those ornate armrests carved into flower stems and seats the color of crimson simply didn't exist in that concert hall; the web searches she did during music theory class proved that much.

Or did they?

Were the seats a more vivid red or perhaps a deep blue? Were the armrests really flowers or were they the claws of a bird of prey?

Even then Autumn was unsure.

That was the thing about LSD: the trip could only go as far as your imagination could and what you didn't know showed itself whether as a faulty creation or as a blank space.

Autumn stood up, her black, sequin-embellished gown clinging beautifully to her form. She saw the mermaid hem and almost gave in, almost allowed herself to stay a little longer. She had never owned a more gorgeous dress in her life and part of her wanted to relish it just a little while longer. But then she touched her stomach again, impulsively... instinctively... and found that her hand rested upon it where she hadn't expected it to.

"Four months, by the looks of things, but time is so different in here. One moment we are at the symphony," Cecelia said from the seat next to Autumn. She was wearing an antique gold, form-fitting, off one shoulder gown that was utterly jaw-dropping on her shapely form, "and the next we are looking at a painting in the night sky."

The woman snapped her fingers and transported them from the concert hall to the cold Alaska countryside shrouded in darkness save for the aurora borealis lightshow overhead.

"And then we're on a catamaran off the coast of Bimini."

Autumn felt the warmth of the sun on her exposed shoulders before she saw the breathtaking turquoise water. She hated herself for reveling in it.

"I remember when it happened, though I doubt you do,"

Cecelia intoned as Autumn's mind forgot to find the moment in her memories. Where had it happened?

Milan?

Kyoto?

Dubai?

With who?

She'd met men in a lot of places in her headspace and thought she could enjoy them without worrying about any aftermath because, well, they were make-believe. Some part of her always knew the whole thing was a dream and that everyone in it was part of the fantasy. She thought that realizing that, keeping that in the forefront of her mind, was what had kept her sane.

When she met Cecelia she wasn't sure where the woman had come from at first. She tried to dredge up whatever memory had fleshed her out, made her part of Autumn's story. They met randomly, in front of the train station at the Colosseum. They talked about how cool Italy was, what places were worth seeing, normal tourist stuff and Autumn thought she had just created this woman to build in some normalcy to it all; that she was there to add a little color. Later, when she would see Cecelia in the crowd at a baseball game or in the previews of movies as her mind began experimenting while she tripped, seeing what kind of details is could create, Autumn thought maybe she hadn't made her up—that maybe there was a woman sitting in her house in some other part of the world tripping with her. And she thought that was cool—nothing more, nothing less. She never thought it mattered if she was alone or with someone else because in real life she was alone in her house and the people she encountered, if she truly had figured out how to tap into a shared trip, were sitting in their respective places too. So, they could do whatever they wanted, their brains couldn't get too drunk and throw up, catch a disease, get pregnant. It was just all fun and games; VR x 1,000.

Now she wasn't so sure.

"I rather like this place," Cecelia said as she stretched her body across the trampoline, the sun kissing her golden skin. Her bathing suit was a one piece with a plunging neckline that went almost down to her navel, like the green of a peacock's feathers and just as iridescent. Autumn wondered if she looked that good.

"I could live here forever," Cecelia breathed as her eyes closed contentedly.

How often had Autumn uttered similar words?

Autumn looked around. Everything was perfect. The water, the sun, the cloudless sky. Picturesque. Exactly the way she liked it.

How many times had that happened?

The concert had been perfect too: classical music played expertly in a place where she could be anyone she wanted to be. All of her trips had been good, even the very first one where she lumbered through an alley that was painted in a repeating rainbow like the one she had seen one day riding the bus home from school. She hadn't experienced any bad trips like the ones some people had described to her, oversharing as they tried to come down, to process, to navigate their hangover the best way they could. She'd heard terrible stories about scary things in the dark, people's faces melting, horror movie type shit and she had always been afraid that something like that would happen to her but it hadn't yet. Nothing weird had happened except this; being stuck in the fantasy, locked in her head, the way out blocked by someone with an old grudge, if the story was correct. The *story*... a made-up thing left in a box to rot. She snickered at the absurdity of the idea but then stopped laughing almost as quickly as she thought about all of the stories that read like works of fiction but in actuality, ruled the world.

Had it all been planned? Had she been a pawn on a chessboard the whole time? And if she had... why?

Autumn looked at Cecelia questioningly and Cecelia laughed.

"Come, come, child. Don't look at me that way. You're far too smart to give up now when you are so very close."

Autumn recoiled as if slapped.

"Why are you doing this to me?"

"Doing what? You chose to be here, to let yourself get caught up in all the pretty, shiny things. I was just here to enjoy them with you, encourage you to see what else you could dream up."

Autumn looked out over the water hating the woman for her matter-of-fact honesty with every fiber of her being.

"That's not the question you really wanted to ask anyway... is it?" Cecelia cocked her head to look at Autumn inquisitively. She let her stare linger for a moment before sighing and resuming her relaxed posture, every bit the sunbather soaking up the rays on a hot summer day.

Autumn looked at her, not knowing where to begin. She wanted to know everything all at once, wanted to know how she could get her family out of whatever hell they were in—how she could get herself out of her own head. Autumn called up the details of that forgotten manuscript, wishing Chris was there to help her. He had a head for things like that; her brother remembered everything.

But he wasn't there, by her side, standing next to her the way he used to be.

Autumn had to do it alone.

"Am I really pregnant?" Autumn started, trying to figure out where to start. Between that, asking why Cecelia was involving her family in a lover's spat, and how the hell can she be a pharaoh who died over 3,000 years ago, Autumn thought that was the safest bet.

"You are. Can you not feel it?"

And suddenly Autumn could. She felt like herself but more... full in a way that she hadn't been before. She felt the bulge in her lower abdomen but didn't feel the urge to suck in like she usually did when she noticed more weight than she would have liked. Autumn felt different and wasn't entirely sure what she thought about that. If she was pregnant, why hadn't she snapped out of the headspace she was in? Wasn't she doing it to herself, allowing herself to believe she was still in a dream? That had been what she wanted before, though that seemed long ago now. Couldn't she just wake up now that she had more important things to worry about?

Where was she in the real world, still in her bedroom? She could see herself there, didn't know if she was looking at a memory or seeing the space as it was in real time. Dingy. Dim. Stagnant. All that would have to change if she was going to have a baby.

A baby...

Whose baby...?

"I-I h-haven't eaten in so long. H-how long have I been here?" Autumn stuttered, suddenly afraid. If her mind had been tucked in on itself, what had her body been doing?

"You eat the food you've stacked around yourself. You're quite the grazer, I must say," Cecelia chuckled and Autumn realized that she didn't feel hungry at all.

"My house. My job. What...?"

"You lost that job a long time ago. No need to worry about that anymore. And your roommate came back and gave you money for the bills she skipped out on. She had a crisis of conscience, I assume."

Yes. She kind of remembered something like that. Checking the balance in her account, going online and paying the bills, packing her bed with food. All of it seemed like it had happened to someone else.

Autumn had gone back, jumped back into herself for a short time to fortify for the next trip. And when she did, she saw Chris. Is that how he found her? In that moment of lucidity, is that how he had been able to find her only to end up in that same strange limbo she was in? Was he still there?

Shh. No.

She couldn't allow herself to say the rest out loud... couldn't let herself buckle under the possibilities. She had more thinking to do about Chris and where he might be.

"I have to go back. The baby... it can't exist here. There *is* no 'here'... it's... it's all in my head."

Cecelia shrugged noncommittally.

"That's not entirely true though, is it, Autumn? You know that. You've always known that."

What? Autumn didn't feel like she was following, didn't know what Cecelia was talking about. Chris would have. Chris would have known and he would have been able to save himself. But Autumn felt less and less confident that she would ever get out of there.

"I need a doctor," Autumn said emphatically.

"Yes, and you will have one when the time comes. Consider this bedrest, dear. Kick your feet up. You deserve it."

The laugh that spilled out of Cecelia's mouth was as an entirely unpleasant cackle.

"Why are you doing this? What does my family have to do with all of this? I read the story. You had some problem with some guy and banished him, right? My great-grandmother didn't say it was you, but it was, wasn't it? Your name is Cecelia, just like in the book."

Cecelia stayed silent, letting Autumn talk it through.

"What I don't understand is how my great-grandmother could have known all of those things. Or how you could be Queen Hatshepsut."

Cecelia leveled her gaze at Autumn. It took everything Autumn had not to look away.

"That's who you are, right? I remembered all that stuff you talked about from when Chris was studying about Egypt. The places, some of the names you said—I could recite them in my sleep, I heard them so much. You're a *pharaoh*. What... what could you possibly want with us?"

Cecelia smiled and Autumn wondered what wickedness she was thinking about when she did.

"Your great grandmother," Cecelia sighed, "a thorn in my side in perpetuity, or so it seemed. I guess I have your great-grandfather to thank for getting rid of that problem for me, don't I? His devotion incited Mal's rancor in a way that I hadn't foreseen. But not before she set all this in motion."

Cecelia shook her head before finishing.

"Such a troublesome shedding."

Autumn's blank expression made Cecelia smile.

"You don't know what any of this means, do you?"

Autumn hated that she could only shake her head in response.

"A shedding is most closely related to the concept of reincarnation and your great-grandmother is one of them. She is a shedding of the woman that Mal..." Autumn could see the anger flooding Cecelia's face before she was able to push it away and suddenly understood the magnitude of the situation her family was in. This was so much bigger than any of them knew. Sitting there, lost in her head with a woman who should no longer exist, Autumn wasn't sure there really *was* a way out.

"She is the woman," Cecelia continued, freshly composed, "that Mal decided to play with. And I let him, at first. I entertained the idea of free will, especially considering how he came to be immortal, that brutal attack at the hands of a new vampire leaving him to die on the road. I understood why he needed to be in control of something for himself. But when he chose that woman instead of coming to me—"

"Vernese?" Autumn blurted out, recalling the name from the story and being unable to stop herself from saying it out loud.

Cecelia scowled at her.

"*Vernese.* That is a character in a book, Autumn," Cecelia chastised, "though I am amazed at the clarity your great-grandmother had to get so close. She was clairvoyant, that shedding. Saddled with a gift that would curse her descendants with knowledge."

Cecelia looked at Autumn, her eyes suddenly softer than they had ever been before.

"It would have been better if you had never known."

Autumn was afraid. She was very afraid. But she had to continue.

"Known what?"

"What your ancestor did to you."

She didn't know who Cecelia was talking about. In the story it had been Aaron who had fallen in love with Vernese. He had done it even though he was a vampire and couldn't be with her without killing her, not in the long term. But Aaron was just a character in a book.

Except...

Cecelia said that her great-grandmother was clairvoyant

and she too had heard similar stories about that while he was growing up, but they were coming from her father, a man who had married into the family and was relaying stories that his wife had heard from her father when she was a child. There weren't any real details, no specific story to point to that would prove it. It just sounded like the supernatural stuff you could hear in any family. But there was the manuscript that she had written and Cecelia had just said that her great-grandmother had gotten close with the name. She frowned. Autumn felt like there was something there, something just beyond her grasp.

"My ancestor," Autumn hedged, just to keep the conversation going while she tried to figure it all out.

"Mal."

Mal.

Autumn shook her head.

"And he is *not* a shedding?"

Cecelia snickered and raised up onto her elbows.

"No, he is the original. My love. The one who was not ready to rule."

"Rule... Egypt?"

The tone of Cecelia's voice felt like a slap.

"No, no, girl. He is not from my time; there is no one else who can lay claim to be. It was too late to use Heka's magic on Senenmut. He had not been as carefully prepared as I was even though he was part of my royal court."

Emotion thickened Cecelia's voice.

"He had already traversed Duat and stood before Osiris. His... his body was too damaged to perform the rite; his *ka* could never have inhabited it again and the rite demanded that it do so before transferring to another."

Cecelia took a deep breath and closed her eyes before speaking again.

"Mal is from my awakening. He is the love I chose to rule this world with me, the night creatures and immortals, side by side. He is the original. He is the one upon whom I laid the curse."

Autumn remembered the curse from the book, remembered how it damned Aaron and the rest of his lineage to an in-between world that they could never escape.

The Realm.

She had to know if that was what Cecelia was talking about. She had to store it in her mind so she could warn Chris if she could figure out how.

"The curse?" Autumn asked, hoping that she hadn't overdone it with the innocent tone she had affected.

"Yes. The reason you are here. The reason your family is stuck in *The Realm*. The reason you will all find yourselves there until the end of time. I gave him what he wanted. He would have Severna, the one your great-grandmother called Vernese, in every version of his life; each of their sheddings would find each other in some way and each would suffer the other's loss, feel the despair, the longing, and the pain over and over, forever."

Cecelia looked past Autumn and at the turquoise water, feeling the weight of her words, the weight of what had come to pass.

"I created the illusion of control in The Realm to give Mal a taste of what leadership could be. At first. I thought, at least in the beginning, that I would come for him after a while. I would make him suffer there with people who embodied everything he detested—so moral, so virtuous my love was—and then remove him from it so he could take his proper place by my side. But then I saw his answer."

She worked her mouth as if tasting something sour.

"Mal rules The Realm," she continued resolutely. "It is utterly and irrevocably his. And now he has a shedding who is a worthy co-regent. He could close the circle with this one, remove all opposition and claim dominance forever. When the original and the shedding become one there is nothing that can stop them. He won't need to wait and find another: it is evident that his perfect match is standing before him now and Mal knows it. He wants this and before too long, his shedding will come to know how much he does too."

Cecelia stopped speaking then, leaving Autumn to decode what she had left unsaid.

Autumn felt sick, that unsettled feeling that one gets in their stomach when they are extremely nervous. She was starting to piece things together, starting to understand what was at stake. When she spoke, her voice was little more than a whisper.

"My great-grandmother was speaking the truth when she wrote that manuscript, because she is a shedding of Severna. So that means that my great-grandfather Patrick was a shedding... of Mal."

Cecelia's smile was wide, so very wide... too wide for her face.

"Grandpa Patrick is the one you're talking about," Autumn continued, letting the awe of such orchestration render her voice airy.

"He is the one who will rule The Realm with Mal," Autumn surmised, dimly aware of a bitter taste as the tab that she didn't remember placing beneath her tongue dissolved.

"Child," Cecelia said with her poisonous tongue, "Patrick *is* Mal."

CHAPTER 30

Chris felt drained and exhilarated at the same time. There were varying degrees of understanding on his family's face about everything he had said, his great-grandfather didn't know what he was talking about at all but was trying to figure out the connections; his grandfather's face showed recognition but of which part of the story, Chris didn't know; whatever his mother understood was tinged and tempered by the concern she was feeling for him.

He had to make them understand how big this thing was.

"The book," Chris started, backing up, hoping to give them a handhold on what he was talking about. "The manuscript in the attic. Do you rememb—"

It felt like a track bolt was being pressed through his temple to lodge itself behind his eye. Everything was searing and white; blinding and all-encompassing. He could hear himself panting from the pressure, whining low in the back of his throat from the pain. And then she was there, in the room, her form flickering, sputtering, fighting to come clear.

Autumn.

Oh my God.

"Autumn?" Chris asked, forcing his eyes open to look at her as she struggled to break through. Her struggle gave him time to wonder what it meant that she was there.

"Where... where are you?"

Gabby was looking at the place that Autumn fought to occupy, looking as if she wanted to reach out to her. Patrick and Doug were surprised, awed by what was manifesting in front of them, their eyes wide as they watched Autumn fight through the field that separated her from The Realm. That they could see her too scared Chris to his core.

"Autumn?" Gabby started and she leaned toward what looked like the re-materialization of Autumn's energy pattern and Doug cautioned her against reaching toward her child.

"She shouldn't be here," Doug said quietly. "If we can see her, that means something's..." He couldn't bring himself to say it. He couldn't watch the hope die in his daughter's eyes.

"I'm afraid if we touch her, she might—"

"Chris? Chris, are you here?"

"Autumn?" Chris said, through gritted teeth, the pain shooting through his head in sharp flashes. "I'm here. Can you see me?"

"No. I-I can't see anything."

Chris could see her looking around for him. She was frail, her eyes sunken and her skin pallid, but that wasn't the thing that upset him the most. His sister was afraid.

"I'm here, M. It's ok," Chis said, hopping the nickname he had used since they were kids would be enough to calm her down.

"I... I don't have long. Chris, I'm so sorry for not talking to you, for disappearing like that. I...I just... when you still came to find me even after all of that... I realized how... I was so stupid."

"It's ok," Chris said again, meaning every word. "I'll always find you, M."

It looked as if Autumn tried to smile but the visual kept jumping, contorting.

"You're si—"

"Don't worry about me," Chris said, cutting her off.

Autumn nodded and continued,

"The woman you saw. It's that pharaoh you used to talk about. Hatshepsut. It's really her!"

Chris leaned closer through the blinding pain and said,

"I knew it! How can this be? Where are you now? Are you in her palace?"

"I don't know. She took me all over. I saw a bunch of mummies and then somebody's sar... sar... whatever you call it —you know what it is. There were so many mummies, Chris. Some of them were unwrapped. It was..."

Autumn's voice trailed off and Chris could imagine what she was remembering. It must have been a gruesome sight.

"Where were the mummies?"

"I don't know, but listen to me," Autumn replied urgently, looking over her shoulder. "I took another one. She made me take another one, I can feel it."

Autumn's breathing increased. She was almost panting in fear.

"Chris..."

"I'm here!" Chris yelled, his voice desperate, his head feeling as if it had been split wide open. "I'm here! M, tell me!"

"The body," Autumn said with considerable effort as the drug started to take effect. "She said the *ka* had to go back into the body for the rite to work. Something about Heka. She couldn't do the rite because the body was damaged."

The body...? Chris tried to figure out what Autumn could be talking about, who's body she was referring to.

"Find... -dy, Chris. Maybe if you d-... come out."

Autumn's form was growing dimmer by the second. Soon she would be gone and Chris was terrified about what that would mean for her.

"Who's body, M? Who?"

"Also said gran-... -al. The... -ok. It's all t-... -s. It's all true."

She was nearly gone but they heard her shriek anyway. The sound reverberated inside each of their heads.

"Autumn!" Gabby screamed and lunged at the place where her daughter's image was fading out.

Autumn turned toward the voice, her face fading, dissolving, disappearing from view with every passing moment. Gabby saw her eyebrows furrow, watched her as recognition dawned on her features, felt tears stinging her eyes as her daughter uttered "Mom" before she disappeared completely.

CHAPTER 31

"Who is she talking about, Christopher? What body?" Patrick started, trying to give them all something else to focus on other than watching Autumn fade away.

Chris shook his head, the pain subsiding rapidly but the memory of it still clear as a bell.

"It has to be Hatshepsut's. She talked about mummies and I saw the cartouche with my own eyes."

"But her body was destroyed," Doug said, as shaken as everyone else by what they had seen. Autumn's body was so frail and her skin looked sallow and thin, malnourished. And her stomach. She was definitely pregnant but she looked more like she was carrying a football under her shirt than making a home for a baby. She was unhealthy, malnourished; Doug didn't know how she was even standing.

He cleared his head of the image... he had to.

"I remember reading that her stepson threw her body in the Nile for the crocodiles to eat," Doug supplied.

Chris shook his head, piecing it all together. "That's what we originally thought since Thutmose III went to such lengths to eradicate her image from every statue and relief in the kingdom. I'm sure it was something that people whispered about back then too, especially since no one knew where she was buried. It probably worked just as well as any spell, warning about what could happen if you go against pharaoh. But Hatshepsut's body was actually found..."

Chris's eyes grew wide. He was on to something.

"She was found at the turn of the 20th century by the same guy who found Tutankhamun's tomb. He just didn't realize it."

Chris was thinking, animatedly connecting the dots and his mother, grandfather, and great-grandfather let him do it undisturbed.

"Carter discovered her tomb and found it empty in 1902 but then he stumbled upon a huge find in 1903 that included Hatshepsut's mummy but he had no idea who he was looking at! It was a huge mummy cache—maybe 30 mummies. They were all stuffed in one room and that's not counting the mummified geese and cats that were in there too."

Chris tried to sit upright, feeling more mobile in his excitement but his body, still stuck in a comatose state back in the living world, would not comply.

"He walked right into the chamber where all the mummies were shoved in and staked unceremoniously. They were probably hidden there to evade robbers or something like that. He went into a room off the back where the bulk of the mummies were and looked right in her face but he didn't know who she was. There was a sarcophagus in there with a mummy in it. The person inside of the sarcophagus was Hatshepsut's wet nurse. She was not royal so they left the mummy alone. There was also a mummy on the floor with nothing on it to indicate who it was, so they ignored that one too.

"Years later, and I mean like 80 years later, –Egyptologists went back in and took the wet nurse's mummy and her sarcophagus but left the other mummy behind again. Later they found a tooth in a box tucked inside that same sarcophagus. When it didn't fit her mummy, they went back in and tested it on the one lying on the floor."

"And it was a match," Gabby supplied.

Chris nodded.

"They took the mummy to the Cairo Museum and tested the DNA against the mummies they found in the front room and the one that was supposed to be Hatshepsut's wet nurse, but it didn't match anyone. That's when they looked in the royal lines of that family, testing her DNA against the kings and queens of Egypt."

"So that's how they found out they had a pharaoh on their hands," Patrick said amazed by the level of confusion surrounding the whole identification process.

"Not just any pharaoh. Only the second female pharaoh to ever rule Egypt. The only one to have such heralded success. Hatshepsut was an amazing ruler and her legacy was stolen from her. And someone left her to rot in the open air."

"Seems unlikely that they would have kept ignoring a mummy," Doug said skeptically. "Especially after that whole mummy unwrapping thing that went on in Europe."

Chris nodded, "Yeah, or when they would grind up the bones and take the powder like it was medicine to cure headaches and things like that; I know what you mean. It's almost like there was some kind of hex on her mummy—some kind of masking spell that hid it from view—at least for a while."

"Magic," Gabby said in awe. "But if that were true, why did it wear off?"

Doug shrugged.

"It's over 3,000 years old."

Chris shook his head.

"Maybe it didn't wear off. Archaeologists kept going in there and not seeing her, not noticing that she was a pharaoh... not even thinking about bringing her mummy to the museum to figure out who she might be. Anonymity. Maybe *that* is the spell that was cast on the body. We wouldn't know who she was if a tooth hadn't been found and science hadn't compelled us to check the only other body we hadn't identified. And, I mean, sometimes science *feels* like magic. Maybe this is like oil and water not mixing or magnets repelling, particles and molecules... Maybe the two can't exist in the same space."

Gabby's smile took over her whole face. She wished she could thank her husband for raising their son to be such a thinker.

"All I know is that after identifying the tooth, they noticed all sorts of things that should have made them investigate further when they found her the first time. Her arm looked like it had been moved from a position on her chest; a position only reserved for royalty. It had nearly been broken off in the process. There was also a tiny swathe of linen covered with execration text naming, among the Hittites rulers and Punt vendors who disproved of the dynasty tax, her stepson Thutmose III, the would-be king, as one of her enemies. There was something that looked like a game on the floor near the body, discarded like it had been kicked aside. It was later identified to be from the time when Hatshepsut would have lived. All of that had been sitting right there the whole time but they missed it."

"Magic," Patrick whispered.

Patrick wondered what it all meant. What was their connection to Hatshepsut? He couldn't figure out why a pharaoh would be interested in them. He was about to ask the question, set the conversation on that path, when Chris spoke again.

"We have to find Hatshepsut's body."

His eyes had grown cold, focused.

"Christopher? Honey, what is it?"

Gabby could see the change in her son and she didn't like it. Something was wrong. Something was very wrong.

Chris would not meet any of their eyes.

As he was talking, his mind was still working on the puzzle that they were dealing with. That was something he loved about studying the antiquities. So many things were unknown. Sure, there were artifacts left behind, clues that could help researchers draw certain conclusions, but the number of things that could actually be proven were few. Anyone who tried their hand at genealogy knew that to be true. So many times assumptions were made based on memories and stories handed down over time—stories that were unreliable at best. How many people had the presence of mind to write down chronologies of their life, keep detailed journals complete with names, dates, and enough information to paint a clear picture of what was going on in the world when it was penned? And of those people, how many of them thought to store it in a way that would ensure that the paper it was written on would not decompose over time, become so much compost to be trampled underfoot? Chris wagered that very few people had that kind of forethought, whether then or now. So, he approached every puzzle from the past with an optimistic skepticism, allowing for the ambiguity that was bound to surround everything that seemed to be concrete evidence.

Except this time he saw the evidence with his own eyes.

As crazy as it seemed, he knew he wasn't hallucinating; his brain was alert and his body hurt... the process of shutting down a slow and arduous one. He didn't know how he was there in The Realm talking to his family, but he knew that he was. He didn't know how he had been in a room that looked like an Egyptian palace talking to a pharaoh, but he knew that to be true as well. Beautiful coincidence or not, it was all happening and he had to let himself be present for it, be open to whatever was going on. And he was. Oh, he was, and that's how he knew.

He knew he'd have to face Asha again and run the risk of ruining her memory of him, replacing his smile with a death mask.

He knew what was in store for Autumn if they failed—what was in store for himself regardless of what happened.

He knew it all.

God help them.

"Something Autumn said at the end when she was breaking up. She was talking about the book. She said it was true."

Gabby looked at Doug and Patrick, cold dread creeping up her spine as she thought about what happened in the book— thought about what that could mean for them all.

"We have to find her soon," Chris said, raising his eyes slowly to look at each of them. "It might be too late already."

CHAPTER 32

It had been days since Chris moved his hand, days since the nurse dismissed it as the way he had been left after being changed into a fresh gown, dismissed it as nothing: a mistake. But Asha knew the truth. So, she waited to see if it would happen again.

They wouldn't let her sleep over. She had really freaked them out that day when she started screaming so they were less open to bending the rules so soon. But she made sure that she was in his room pretty much every minute of her visit, bringing in whatever food she could pull together out of her meager pantry instead of going to the cafeteria and waiting until she couldn't take it anymore to go to the bathroom. Asha didn't want Chris to start moving again and she was somewhere else, maybe standing in line at the cafeteria talking to one of the other visitors who was out trying to stretch their legs. Normally she welcomed the interaction; it gave her a chance to talk with someone other than the nurses she saw day in and day out. It had been especially refreshing to chat with her friend, take a break with her, and let the sun kiss their faces, but that was over now. While she wished Rosa hadn't had to go through her husband's death, Asha was happy that she was gone, happy that she didn't have to make excuses for why she couldn't spend time with her. Asha didn't know what it was but something was happening with Chris and she needed to be there for it.

Asha stared at him, willing him to move again.

Chris was still.

Asha spoke to him about what was going on in the world, read to him from his Egyptian books, played his favorite songs. Then she tried playing contemporary jazz for him, read the gothic horror stories he used to devour, watched movies that he used to like and talked through the social context like he used to. She brought him tidbits about anything she heard about Egypt, watched documentaries, and thumbed through his books to talk through discoveries. Asha did the things Chris used to enjoy, tried things he had never done before, but nothing worked. He stayed still, so very still, looking smaller and smaller in his hospital bed by the day.

Hours passed and Chris stayed still in his bed the way they said he would... the way he always did. She touched him, hoping that the feeling of her hand on his skin would bring about some kind of response, but that didn't work either. Anyone else would have given up; she was sure she was inching toward obsession territory, but there was nothing Asha could do about that. She knew what she saw. Nothing could make her think differently about it.

Asha noticed that Chris was looking back at her but it didn't register, not right away.

She was looking at him while she thought about that day, what he had said. No one believed her. They continued to remind her how impossible him waking up and talking was, and as time passed Asha began to challenge her own memory of it. That, in and of itself, felt like betrayal, but she couldn't discount the improbability of it all. Very much like an apparition, she had woken up to find the love of her life staring at her through sick eyes telling her things that wouldn't have made sense to anyone but her. Wasn't that enough reason to think she had made it all up, was manifesting her needs in this grotesque way?

Possibly.

But still, through it all, Asha believed.

Her vision shifted as she went over those moments again, trying to validate herself... trying to be sure. Her eyes blurred out much of the room save for his hand, the thing that she had been focusing on so determinedly, willing it to move again, move for the first time maybe if the nurses were right about how it had been knocked out of place before... move at all, damn it. She studied his once strong fingers, traced with her eyes the veins that used to show just under the skin, affecting the treasure map that she used to love to explore but that now stood out like massive cords beneath his paper-thin flesh. Her senses were occupied in this pointless loop of discovery and despair when he awoke and looked back at her. She didn't see the moment when his eyes opened and he focused on her— that moment that would have allowed her to react with grace instead of the surprise that startled her, made her jump out of her seat. Because he didn't look right—still didn't—and some part of Asha's mind knew that he couldn't look right and never would because she was looking at something that shouldn't be animated anymore, a husk that was long past the point of viable. Chris was gone and she only had those few moments where his soul jumped back into his body to talk to her left. She focused then, willing her pulse to relax and let her be there with him as he was: atrophied, deteriorated... wasted away.

But it was so hard to see how difficult it was for him to use his withered voice, how his yellowed eyes struggled to focus.

"Chris? Honey?"

Asha forced herself to move toward him.

Chris blinked in response.

"I started to think I had lost my mind. I thought I was right about your hand moving but after you didn't move again for so long, I just... I thought my mind had finally snapped."

Chris wondered how long it had been since he had tried to wake up, to move, to reach out to her. A day? Two? A week? He couldn't tell. All he knew was that he was very tired and that he hurt. He couldn't have raised his hand to touch her face if he tried.

"Maybe that's still true," she was saying and Chris tried to pay attention, though a haze was creeping in, usurping his vision, making it harder and harder to concentrate.

"Maybe I've lost my mind and I don't realize it. You wouldn't really know you were crazy, would you? All the things you'd be making up, it would just be normal life to you, right? But I have to be crazy because you can't be looking at me right now. You couldn't have told me to go and get a pregnancy test, of all things... after so much time. You can't because..."

Asha was crying and he couldn't do anything to help her. His voice felt like it was fighting to surface from the bottom of a deep, dark well.

"You're dead, aren't you baby? You're dead and I'm hallucinating and soon they're going to rush in here to try and revive you but it's already too late, isn't it? You're – you're saying goodbye."

He was wheezing.

It was difficult to breathe.

It had been easier to exist in The Realm. His breathing wasn't labored there and his mind was clearer. He could feel the pain that caged his body, but it wasn't sharp and stinging there the way it was in the waking world. Each time Chris stepped into the existence he once knew the world fought against him with everything it had. And it was winning. He felt worse, as though he was falling apart, decaying with every breath. Speaking to Asha the first time had taken a lot out of him. Finding Autumn had too. Chris wasn't sure if he would have anything left after this.

Asha thought he was already dead. It frightened him how close to the mark she really was.

"Nnnnnohhhh," Chris said, muscling through the resistance his body put up against him.

"M'not dead... not yet." He tried for a smile, realized too late that it probably made him look like a grinning skeleton. He closed his eyes so that he didn't see her recoil... so that she *could* recoil if that's what she needed to do.

"Chris," she whispered emphatically, eyes wide and teary. "Baby."

Chris opened his eyes to find her sitting close, so very close, her face close enough to kiss. And then she did kiss him. First his lips and then his cheek, leaving her tears behind in her wake. She laid her head on his chest, pressed her forehead into his neck, nuzzled into him the way her used to.

She hadn't back away.

Chris felt his own tears spill from the corners of his eyes as love and appreciation welled inside him for the woman who held him as if it were the last time she ever would. And it was. Something inside him knew that this was the last time they would ever be like this; the last time he would be able to feel her touch, smell her hair the way he did right then. There would be no happy ever after, would be no meeting her again in the after-life, no seeing her in the next lifetime because he was going to *The Realm* and she was going somewhere else. Even if Asha could manage to save Autumn, there was no saving him. Chris would die soon and wake up next to his mother and grandfather and great-grandfather far removed from sight, if the manuscript was right. And he didn't even have time to mourn for himself or to be afraid. If he didn't move quickly, there'd be no chance of saving Autumn from that fate either.

His throat tightened with emotion sending a fresh wave of pain through his neck and shoulders.

No, it wouldn't be long now.

Chris mind screamed with the realization that he wouldn't have the time to tell Asha how much he loved her, how she had changed his life for the better, how he had envisioned having children with her, raising their little family, travelling the world, growing old together. His body couldn't hold out, couldn't give him the time he needed. He looked at her, his eyes desperate. She knew how he felt, right? She knew that from the moment he laid eyes on her he knew she was the one, the only one he'd ever want, right? Chris was suddenly afraid that she didn't know; that he hadn't done enough to show her how much she meant to him... that he hadn't been enough.

He started to shake.

"Ahhhsh-"

"You don't have to speak, baby. It's enough for me to just lay here with you."

Asha's arms grew tighter around his chest and Chris wanted to sink into the warmth. But he couldn't. He shook his head; fought with himself to do what he went there to do.

"No... have to talk. Have to tell you... I know... not pregnant."

Asha lifted her head from Chris's chest to look into his eyes. They searched for hers, had trouble settling. She wished she could take all his pain away.

"You heard me?"

Chris nodded.

"I always hear you. Just can't always speak."

"How is this happening? How are you talking now? Your voice – you shouldn't be able to..."

"I know," he said, cutting her off, knowing he didn't have enough in him to veer away from the main conversation.

"Don't understand either. But it is. This is real."

He tried to squeeze Asha's hand but wasn't sure if he did.

"I need your help, baby. I need-need your help to save... us all."

Asha's eyes grew wide as she looked at Chris, trying to understand what he meant but not able to put it all together.

"What's real? You said that before, that everything was real. What are you talking about?"

"Chris's breathing was labored but that didn't matter anymore. He had to say it. He had to say it all.

Chris told her about his grandmother's manuscript and how he and Autumn had snuck it out to read it cover to cover. As he spoke his body rallied, operating on pure adrenaline to level his breathing enough to let him tell his story without many pauses and for that Chris was grateful. He had to say what he went there to say and he needed his body to cooperate in order to do that. He told her that the place he had spoken about before was where he would be going and he thanked God that she wasn't pregnant, told her how thankful he was that he didn't have a child destined for that place.

"But Autumn *is* pregnant, Asha. And she's in trouble."

"She's... alive?"

Asha hadn't thought so. She was sure that Autumn had died somewhere and that's why they couldn't find her. She had tried to reach her once more from the hospital room, calling all the numbers that Chris had for Autumn in his phone, finding a friend on Instagram, sifting through all the pictures she could find of people who knew her, but Autumn was nowhere to be found.

"She's alive but she's not really in the world, otherwise I wouldn't have been able to see her."

"You saw her in... The Realm?"

"No. She's still here, but she called me to some other place, someplace that seemed like a memory at first – our house... the place where we grew up, but then we were somewhere else and she was on the floor in the shadows and I couldn't see her and she didn't answer me when I called her—"

Asha put a hand on Chris's chest to still him. He was nearly panting from the effort and a light sheen of sweat had formed on his forehead, his nose, his lip.

"Slow down, babe... please," Asha begged, hoping he didn't overexert himself so much that he couldn't continue.

Chris nodded and took a deep breath before starting again,

"They think it might be a drug. Maybe LSD."

"*Who* thinks that?"

Asha felt like she was missing something.

Chris smiled wide, knowing how amazing his answer would sound.

"My grandfather."

Asha's eyes widened in a mixture of awe and joy as she looked at the same reflected in his.

"Your grandfather? Oh my God, Chris. That is amazing."

"My mother... she's there too. She looks just like I remember her. She's so beautiful, Asha. I just want to hug her."

"You haven't?

"No," Chris said, shaking his head, the mood shifting back as the weight of the situation settled on his shoulders again. "They're afraid to touch me because it might affect me here. I'm in my own limbo; I have one foot in both places."

Asha rubbed his arm, hoping that feeling her touch would bring some kind of comfort.

Chris cleared his throat and immediately wished he hadn't. The taste of his blood was slicking his ruined throat.

"Grandpa thinks she's taking LSD to get into a dream state but that she's being kept there by this woman who is the whole reason we're in The Realm in the first place."

"What?"

"She got angry at one of my ancestors for choosing to be with someone else and created this purgatory space between Heaven and Hell where all of my family's line is destined to spend eternity."

Asha's face registered her confusion.

"It's a lot, I know. And I don't have time to explain all of it, but just... one day, after all of this is over, find my grandmother's manuscript in the attic and thumb through it. You won't believe your eyes."

Asha nodded, trying not to qualify it as a deathbed promise but knowing it was.

"Ok, so this woman is somehow keeping your sister in her head, making it seem like she's still hallucinating on the drug?"

Chris nodded.

"I don't know how she's doing it, but she is. She wants the baby to be born, wants to make sure that our line keeps going so there's always someone there to populate The Realm... always someone there to torture."

Asha shook her head, looking at the machines connected to

Chris, trying to put all the information she was hearing together in a way that made sense but failing. She was only distantly aware that the numbers tallied his status were slowly changing for the worst.

"And she's not just *any* woman. Babe, she's Queen Hatshepsut."

Chris could have said she was ancient or that she was a vampire, which he wasn't 100% certain wasn't true, but he thought her identity might make him look the least delusional, if only slightly. He didn't think there was anything he could say that would, make his story sound plausible, like anything less than the fever dream of a dying man.

Asha sat back in her chair heavily, a cloud of confusion encircling her. None of what Chris was saying made sense, but the fact that he was saying those things scared her more than anything. She had heard of people seeing things before they died, speaking to long-dead relatives as if they were standing in the room with them. At one time she had thought those visions were helpful to the person seeing them, thought maybe family and friends had come to take them home and maybe that made their transition to the afterlife easier. But now, listening to Chris's story about the things he was seeing, feeling the emotion the whole thing was bringing out of him, so much her soul ached, she wasn't so sure. Asha had a choice to make: whether she was going to believe Chris and let his mind rest easy as he left her or if she was going to struggle to get him to see that he was imagining it all and waste their last moments together fighting.

She chose to believe him. And silently kiss her love goodbye.

"Hatshepsut? The pharaoh?"

Chris nodded.

"The one in the book over there on the desk."

Asha didn't need to turn around to see what book he was talking about to know which one he meant. She wouldn't have taken her eyes away from him then for anything in the world.

As Chris went on questions started to form in her mind—questions Asha wouldn't dare interrupt what could be his last words to ask.

How did he know what books she had with her?

Had he been watching her from the place he had talked about—The Realm?

Asha suppressed a smile as she imagined Chris showing her off to his family, talking about how they met, about the plans they'd had. She hoped they were pleased with his choice.

"I don't understand," Asha said, deciding she'd engage with the one person she'd hoped to banter with forever for one last time.

"What does a pharaoh have to do with your family? Are you saying *she's* the one who was in love with one of your relatives?"

Chris nodded, knowing how wild it all sounded, hoping she believed him enough to do what needed to be done.

CHAPTER 33

The Hunters were waiting, still and unmoving in the woods surrounding the house as they had been when he left it hours before.

Curious.

A family reunion was in progress, and he knew there would be much discussion and many tears, but to not have surveyed the kingdom yet? Mal didn't understand it but for Patrick and his ilk, it made sense. Unlike others of his line that littered The Realm, lost in their aimlessness and base in their stupor, this shedding had been perfect in almost every way; intelligent, physically strong, resilient. Mal had challenged Patrick in many ways since he stepped into The Realm and he was pleased with what he saw. Merging with him would be a wonderous occasion, one that would close the loop of control, ensure the perpetual dominance of the place to which he had been banished but where he had flourished as ruler, and Mal was eager to finish the process. While Cecelia had anticipated much when she sent him to that in-between place lifetimes ago, she had not considered the covetousness that could be experienced by the ones who were controlled, the insidious nature of the coup d'état always there, always threatening, just under the surface. And there had been many challengers, tenacious condemned who thought they should run The Realm instead of him.

Distractions.

He'd put Mileeha in place to deal with those nuisances, separating himself from the minutia as a leader should, but while he didn't deal with those who might challenge him directly, he still understood that there would always be another. Merging with Patrick would change all of that. The past and the present would come together to flank the gates of The Realm, emblazoning their seal on it for eternity, ruling together as host and shedding; the two becoming one; the one manifesting as two.

And he was close, so close to making this a reality.

Patrick loved the power, would soon be drunk on it, if Mal had his way. He was surrounded by family and was driven by his love for them. These emotions were ones Mal could work with. It was the desire for something else, something that was part and parcel of the upbringing for many of his time, that made his conversion easier. The concept of religion was not part of Mal's own youth; it was not part of his psyche to make measure of his afterlife. Mal had no preconceived notions about what would happen to him after death. He could hardly remember when he walked the earth as a living man; his clearest memories extended only as far back as waking to find blood wetting the collar of his shirt from a vampire's bite. But in that knowledge, he knew more than Patrick did. He understood that the inherent unfairness of living well and being charitable, trying to help as Patrick had in the moments before he was struck down by an unseen hand—all of his good deeds netting nothing in the end. Patrick still found himself in The Realm as his family did, right alongside people who had committed crimes and been unable to change their ways. He was still stuck in the in-between with Mal.

The reluctant immortal.

The damned lover.

Would that Cecelia could see him now.

Mal thought of Cecelia, his beautiful queen, and wondered what she would think of him. He thought about how things had changed and wondered what their dynamic would be like if they were face to face again. When they met, she was in control of all who roamed the night; Mal had been lucky that she took him in. And when she wanted more, he was happy to oblige; her beauty was an elixir that was only punctuated by her power. But as he found his legs in the underworld that was his new existence, it was Mal who wanted more. Not power, necessarily—that had been an acquired taste for him—but choice. Mal wanted to do what he wanted to do, go where he chose to and with whom. He wanted to experience immortality and the spoils that came with it without tether. He wanted a freedom that being the queen's manservant could not offer. Would she want him to simply kneel now, press his mouth to her foot and supplicate like all the others or would she see that he was worthy of standing next to her, making decisions alongside her as well as choosing the company he kept?

Would Mal choose her now, after everything?

There were times when he didn't think he would, but others when his heart cried out for Cecelia.

But she hadn't come to him. She hadn't answered, though he knew she heard. And The Realm kept filling with his descendants, innocents seated alongside depraved souls from universes untold.

Mal could hear Patrick's heart crying. He could feel his own doing the same.

Mal could see himself in Doug's face, could feel the same pull toward Gabby as she walked by him that he had felt with each of his descendants as they moved through The Realm. He had gotten good at pushing that feeling aside, ignoring it, not allowing it to take up residence in his mind because if he did, he would be inundated with a sense of loss that was so heavy he didn't know if he could get out from underneath. Because these were his family members, his bloodline. Because he was the reason they were there. Mal tried to rationalize that they were all together but that was only partially true. Husbands were separated from wives; children were separated from one of their parents. In each scenario Mal's family members had to deal with the fact that the promise of that great reunion of souls they had been taught about would not exists for any of them. And he was the cause of it.

That could stop now. Mal rationalized that it could be over with the merging of himself and Patrick. There would be no more need to search for a proper shedding to combine with because Mal and Patrick closed the loop and solidified their rule. He felt optimism now where he hadn't before, anticipation about the positives that merging with his shedding would bring... the things that could happen. But slowly, as it always did when his mind traversed this track of hopefulness, the reality that the need for unification had been *his* line of thinking, *his* way of rationalizing the continued influx of his descendants coming into The Realm—not Cecelia's. She didn't care if rule was consolidated. She didn't care if Mal got used to being in charge or not. None of the people who had suffered mattered to her. Cecelia had sent him there intending to punish. And it seemed that she still felt penance was due.

Mal had watched as Gabby went back into the house, could feel the tension in the space she occupied prickling his very skin.

This new batch of people, from his blood but so very far removed, were curious indeed. He wanted to know more.

The Hunters watched Mal's approach, bowing their heads as their lord passed, beasts with rows of teeth as large as a proboscidean's tusks, retractable and sharp, behaving like house pets. As Mal mounted the steps, registering the stress inside anew, he considered what it meant to control everything he touched, to wield the power of life or death with a simple word. He wondered if there wasn't some wisdom in Patrick's hesitation after all.

CHAPTER 34

She had to move.

Tara's spot in the pantry wouldn't be good enough to see what was going to happen if their plan went the way they hoped and she hadn't spent hours hiding away, eavesdropping on the most sensational story she had ever heard, just to miss the grand finale. She thought about everything they had talked about, everything they had planned before Christopher had left again to talk with his fiancée and if they could really pull it off, well, it would be something Tara definitely didn't want to miss. She wondered if Christopher would see it all from the room where his mother, grandfather, and great-grandfather stood, joining them in The Realm for the fireworks, and figured he would. The way he looked, Tara was surprised he had enough gas in the tank to make another trip to explain everything to Asha.– She didn't really think he'd get all the way through it before keeling over and joining everyone else in the room. He might be rendered mute right at the point in the story where things got interesting. And then what would happen?

It was all like a movie, one of those mystery/thriller flicks where the cast mattered less than the story. Tara was on the edge of her seat, invested now in a way that she wasn't sure would mean anything after all was said and done but she was willing to stick around and find out. Only listening wouldn't be enough. Tara wanted to see. The ending they had planned was going to be epic and she didn't want to miss a second of it.

Tara looked through the slatted door and stared at their backs a moment longer, listening to the voices as they spoke, trying to gauge how likely they were to start moving out of the room, to turn toward where she had hidden herself and catch her coming out of it. That wouldn't do, not now. She had gone into the house ready to kill them all but now she wanted to know more about what they were talking about—wanted more details to be sure she would be slicing the right throat. Getting caught now would force her hand and she didn't want that... not yet.

Tara listened.

They talked quietly as they waited for Christopher, whether to find out if his fiancée would do it or to welcome him home.

Tara waited, peeked out, saw their backs again.

She had to move.

She cracked open the door expecting the creaking hinges to scream from the movement, but it didn't happen. She waited a moment before pushing the door even more, wide enough for her to get through.

She stopped, forcing herself to be still.

None of them turned around.

Tara scanned the place she had been thinking about since the idea of getting a better seat dawned in her head. The under the sink crawlspace was snug but she thought she could wriggle her way in there. From what she could tell the double cabinet doors that blocked from view the cleaning supplies and extra garbage bags that usually resided there was broken in her favor; it had a perpetual gap that she could watch the fun through without having to manipulate the door herself. Perfect. She wondered if all the wire pads and supermarket bags and sponges and drain plugs—the litter that made up people's lives—would really be down there or whether Patrick had neglected those finer details. Tara was thinking about that as she took a step out into the darkened kitchen, counting on the shadows to mask her escape as she scampered across the floor, just another shadow among many.

But then she felt it.

A cold realization like ice on the back of her neck. Menacing. Tara felt the ominous presence as keenly as if it had crept into her nose and mouth to slither down her throat.

She remembered.

She had felt it before.

Tara almost gasped out loud and knew that if she had, that would have been the end for her. That frightened her more than she thought it would.

Tara's heart was pounding in her chest, a sensation she still couldn't reconcile even as long as she had been in The Realm, but it was real and it meant everything in death that it had in life. She was terrified. She pulled back, halting the forward momentum clumsily as she tried to remain silent and unseen, hunkering down even closer to the floor than she had been before as she backtracked. He wasn't in the kitchen yet, at least not all the way, and would not be able to see her as she crouched behind the cover that the center island provided—the one she had been cursing moments before for blocking her view of the under the sink space. Tara thanked whatever deity might be listening for the obstruction now though; had Mileeha's rendition of her uncle's kitchen still stood in tribute, only a table with rickety legs would be there to provide cover: she might as well have stood out in the open and screamed his name had that still been in place.

Tara slid the pantry door open slowly and slipped back inside.

She looked through the slats to see if she had drawn anyone's attention.

She had not.

Tara took a deep breath as she closed the pantry, hoping against hope that she would find the same luck closing it soundlessly as she had opening it.

She did.

When the door was finally shut, Tara slumped into the wall, her muscles unable to hold her taut anymore. She was hidden again and that was a good thing; she would have no excuse that would make sense to Mal if he found her there. She doubted she'd even have the chance to explain herself. Their day would come—somewhere in the back of Tara's mind she always knew that—and while she understood that she might die trying to kill Mal, she also knew she needed to prepare for the battle, couldn't just be thrown into a fight with someone as formidable as that. Not if she hoped to have any chance at winning at all.

So, she hid.

Tara calmed her breathing and made herself small, so small... indetectable.

Then she thought. What was Mal doing there? Why would he waste his time in that house with people so mired in what Mal most surely would think was a trivial problem?

Tara wondered.

And she listened.

CHAPTER 35

It was still incredibly warm long after the sun went down. The flights had been hard; Asha hadn't been able to sleep much on the leg that counted most, sitting awake for the entire red-eye to France and almost falling asleep during the layover. It was nighttime when she landed and the streets were lit up in greens and reds. People lounged in front of street cafes, and the night was abuzz with a language she didn't know. Her taxi moved through downtown Cairo on its way to Haram where she had booked a room for the night, passing by the seedy hotel in the city where the roster also held her name. She doubted she would even see the front of the hotel in Maadi where she had also rented a room. Asha wouldn't lay her head in any of them. Once the taxi had dropped her off in Haram, once the taillights were out of sight, she would get into another one and head to the bus station in Cairo proper where she would pretend to sleep in her chair as she sat on her money pouch and pressed her backpack flat between herself and the wall like a backpacker who hadn't had enough cash left to find shelter for the night. She wouldn't even have time to enjoy the view of the pyramids backlit against the night sky.

Another time, maybe. This time she was there for business.

By 5:00 a.m., Asha would be on her way to the Valley of the Kings, the barren land of the Western Desert the backdrop, as her bus travelled to its destination several hours away, armed guards flanking either side of their caravan. There, on that rickety bus creaking with age and overuse, she would sleep because she needed to, even though she was afraid of what waited for her in her dreams.

In what she knew was their last conversation, Chris had begged her to save his sister and her baby, begged her to do what no one else could. He told her that he wouldn't be able to thank her, wouldn't be able to show her how much just listening to him meant because he wouldn't be there when she got back and Asha believed that was true. The smell of death was in the room with them: it was coming off his skin in waves.

She had been skeptical at first; anyone would have been. But as Chris explained, as he shared the horror of what was happening to his family, she transitioned from just placating her dying fiancé to believing his truth. Asha believed Chris when he said he had spoken to his sister even though he was in a coma. His body was lying in a hospital bed in front of her but his mind traversed a whole other existence. She believed him when he talked about *The Realm*: the fear in his eyes was real. So she told him she would do what he asked. Asha said she would do what he couldn't and try to save her would-be sister-in-law, and she would because she loved him and wanted to fulfill his last wish, but also because she believed. Asha laid her head on his chest and cried before leaving because she was sure she would never speak with her love again. He would be dead when she returned. Either that or he would never wake up and speak again, even if the audience was limited just to her. She wished the latter was what was in store for Chris but she knew better.

But what he had asked her to do…

"People think she's where she's always been. They never brought her upstairs to be displayed with the others, so people just assume Hatshepsut's mummy is still in the basement. There will be guards everywhere, of course, but even more now because they're getting ready for the move."

"The move?" Asha had asked, mostly to give him time to catch his breath.

Chris nodded before speaking.

"The National Museum of Egyptian Civilization. Remember? I was going to take you there one day, once the museum at the Giza complex was finished. It would have taken us days to get through everything. I wanted to show you the jewels and the gold, the statues… there's this statue of King Hor from the 13th dynasty that always bothered me. His eyes… they were made of quartz and, I don't know, they just always gave me the creeps."

The way Chris's own eyes shone, glassy from emotion, broke Asha's heart.

"I wanted to show you all the things I love, but…"

Chris stopped himself then, took a shuddering breath. Asha waited. She would wait forever if that's how long he needed.

"It's been rumored that there's gonna be a parade to move the mummies from the Cairo Museum over to the new place," Chris said when he continued, forcing himself to leave the emotion he was feeling behind and get back to the details he had to share with Asha. Maybe, if there was enough time, he could let himself talk about what might have been… maybe…

Chris talked about archaeological happenings like other people talked about spilling the tea and Asha couldn't help but chuckle. Everything was cloaked in shadows and only those "in the know" had heard about it. It was like he was in some kind of secret society or something where rumors were passed in whispers and, even then, only on a need-to-know basis. Considering some of the things he'd told her, maybe he was.

"They're calling it a golden parade," Chris continued and Asha realized she had missed some of what he was saying. She wouldn't ask him to repeat it; she didn't want him to think she wasn't listening.

"There will be horse-drawn chariots and pressure-sealed funerary cars carrying the mummies to their new digs."

"Wow," Asha said, in awe. She envisioned cobalt blues and gold, celebratory music and women dressed in period garments, all chiffon and linen—all the regalia a pharaoh might require beneath ultramarine lights. The only word she could think of to describe it was majestic.

"There are supposed to be 22 pharaohs making the trip through Tahrir Square including Ramesses II, Sequenenre Tao II, Queen Tiye, even Seti I. The convoy is also supposed to have Thutmose I, Thutmose II, Thutmose III, and-"

"Hatshepsut," Asha breathed.

"Father, husband, son—the whole family... only they won't all be there."

"What do you mean?"

Chris lowered his voice conspiratorially when he spoke next.

"Some of the mummies won't be in the convoy. Word circulated a few years ago that some of the mummies had been taken out of the Cairo Museum to help with cataloging. They were kept out to reduce the risk of damage that could come from moving them so much. But construction took longer than expected. They've building the place for years, kept facing delay after delay. Some of the mummies have been out of the Cairo Museum for over a decade."

Asha nodded her head, remembering a conversation she and Chris had had before about there being hundreds of mummies in the basement of the Cairo Museum that hadn't been identified yet, some offsite, some onsite.

"I don't know how the decision about who was going to go into the museum first was made but some of the mummies are coming from Saqqara, some from Minya... some as far as Luxor."

Asha looked at Chris, wide-eyed.

"The Valley of the Kings?"

Chris nodded with some difficulty and Asha noticed. He swallowed as if it hurt to do so.

"They ran out of room and were forced to take some of the mummies to other locations. Keeping them all together like that was risky anyway; the temporary space wasn't fortified for long term use. They put her in her tomb. Hatshepsut and Tutankhamun and a few others, they put them back in their tombs to wait for the new museum to be ready. They'll bring the mummies to the new museum later under the radar so they don't disturb all the pomp and circumstance of the event and no one will ever know. No one will be looking for them: people will assume they're part of the procession, lying in their sarcophagi like the rest of the royalty. All eyes will be on the parade and not on the necropolis... not on Djeser-Djeseru."

That's what Chris had said and he had been right.

The plan was good, even down to her ending up in the guide tent, the bubbling sound of the shisha reverberating in the space as she pulled apple tobacco smoke through the pipe. Asha knew all the steps she'd take; she'd pass by Ramesses III's tombs and marvel at the vivid colors that still remain on the ceiling and walls; she'd see Ramesses V & and VI's massive burial chamber and Tutankhamun's mustard-colored wall and Seti's sketches, shuffling along to 'ooh and ahh' with the rest of the tourists. She would go over to the Valley of the Queens too, make a show of deliberating over buying a ticket to see Nefertari's tomb, and file in behind the others who shelled out more for the chance to see her colorful walls. She wouldn't run, even though that's all she would want to do... run out of the West Bank, run away from Egypt, from Africa, from the other side of the world. She would, instead, consult her guidebook out in the open, pretend to listen to the facts being rattled off by the tour guide, stare at reliefs of people she knew nothing about. And then, after a suitable amount of time, she'd leave. If anyone asked her where she was headed next, she'd say she was going to the light show at the Temple of Karnak, would smile with them if they said they were going there too and even part ways saying she'd see them later that night. Or she might even say she was heading to Alexandria to check out the Bibliotheca Alexandrina or to comb through Royal Jewelry Museum, add to the "girl power" story she might use to spin things should she ever have to. She would say just enough to sound like an excited tourist working her way through Egypt and people would believe her.

If she did it right, no one would ever suspect her.

If she did it right, Chris would be able to rest in peace.

Asha had left a smeared dot of it on the bench at the bus station, had let her finger work it into the chipped paint.

She had left a small brush with a bit of it dried on the wooden handle on the floor of the taxi to Haram, watched it roll under the driver's seat to mingle with the bottle caps and wrappers there.

She had left little bits and pieces around, selections from her personal cabinet of curiosities scattered about like breadcrumbs for someone to follow if they stumbled on her trail, even down to the story she told Nurse Bea about how she wanted to experience the things Chris loved and come back to tell him about it. Asha had told the nurse about how she wanted to do the very thing Chris had always hoped to do with her – said that she wanted to see Egypt so that she could know the place he loved, feel closer to him there in that environment. This statement, though true, was purposeful, deliberate, calculated. It was yet another clue that someone could pick up if they chose to, if they thought they saw something more in the picture than what appeared on the surface. But they wouldn't. To get to the point where someone would suspect her would take a whole lot of reaching and require a ton of conclusions to be drawn. It would all seem too implausible to be true, too fantastic. And besides, she was everywhere and nowhere, seen but unseen among the masses. No one would think of a quiet female backpacker when the shit hit the fan. She would be miles away by the time anyone noticed, likely old and gray, on the other side of her life before the next round of specialists decided they needed to perform the latest test, confirm something they had uncovered. And by then any trace of anything she had done or anywhere she had ever been would be gone, like dust in the wind.

If she was lucky.

"*Caput Mortuum*," Chris had said, his voice growing heavy, gravelly. "Egyptian brown... *mummy* brown."

Asha had looked at him incredulously. Even after everything he had explained to her in the past about how people used to buy mummies to use in medication, used to grind them up and put them in tinctures to ease headaches or help them sleep, used their skulls, their bone marrow, their skin as the base of an aphrodisiac, Asha still found herself surprised. Mummia. She had never heard of it before meeting Chris. She wished she could still claim that ignorance.

"People... *painted* with them? Chris, please tell me you're not serious."

"I wish I wasn't. I wish I had time to make that kind of joke."

Asha's lips had closed into a thin line as she bit her upper lip to stop herself from crying again. Because Chris *would* have made that kind of joke if it had been a warm summer night and they were sitting at The Wharf overlooking the water. He would have said it in the most ghoulish voice he could muster just to hear her squeal. And then there would be peals of laughter and then she would slap his shoulder, tell him he was disgusting, and he would say that was true, but that she loved it. And he would have been right. But that wasn't where they were anymore... and they would never be there, under that moon and those stars, in the midst of people enjoying the music over the night breeze and the easy laughter that came from knowing each other well, ever again.

Asha spoke about the mummia then—if she didn't, she was afraid she'd lose her mind.

"They turned them into powder? Kings, queens... other human beings... they just used their bodies to make themselves feel healthy?"

Chris nodded. "It's unbelievable, I know. And some of the French pieces created with mummy brown on the palette are really famous."

Incredulous, Asha hissed, "They *ate* them! It's cannibalism! Didn't they realize they were... ingesting the flesh of someone who walked around, laughed with their friends, loved someone else?"

"I doubt thoughts like that ever entered their minds, babe. They were just thinking about themselves, what they would get out of it. If I told you about the unwrapping parties, you'd lose your mind."

Asha shook her head and took a deep breath, certain that what Chris was about to ask her to do was just as nefarious.

"I have a tube of—"

"Chris, no! Tell me you don't have any mummy brown laying around *our* house!"

She hadn't meant to raise her voice but the idea freaked her out.

"No, not the real mummy brown—not the one that was actually made of mummies. They stopped making that stuff a century ago, baby. You can't buy it now. I mean, I have some at the museum, but that's different."

Asha took a deep breath. It *was* different, but still.

"I had planned to do a comparison one day, create an exhibit around the different ways that mummies have been treated even down to us breaking into their final burial place and snatching them from their graves, but—"

Chris had stopped then; the conversation, the unavoidable reality bearing down on them took all the air out of the room and the space had suddenly felt claustrophobic.

"Anyway," he had said, starting again, the words reluctant and bitter, "I have a tube of Mummy Brown paint. I need you to get it and... baby, I'm so sorry..."

Enough.

She didn't want to remember anymore. She didn't think she could handle it.

As Asha boarded the bus that would take her to the terminal on the East Bank where she could disembark and disappear, her mind wouldn't give her the peace she so desperately needed. She thought about everything Chris had said. She had winced then at the strain in his voice and found herself wincing again as the words replayed in her head mournfully, wailing, keening like a banshee. Asha clamped her hands over her ears to shut out the sound, then removed them quickly in case someone was looking in her direction. But still the noise sounded in her head. And there was something else... something new.

Laughter.

"Almost done," she hissed under her breath and found she hated that phantom voice for pushing her, forcing her hand, baiting her. She scratched at the inside of her wrist, had nearly ripped through the skin to let blood before she wrenched her hand away and still her fingers reached for the sensitive flesh as though independent... possessed.

Asha took a deep breath, found that she was already panting, and gritted her teeth.

"Almost done."

CHAPTER 36

Chris didn't have long.

He could feel his body struggling to work, to process, to stay, even if it was only long enough to see Asha's face one more time, but he couldn't do it. His breathing was shallow and he felt out of sorts. He was sure the hospital staff knew what was happening, was sure they were secretly happy that this happened while Asha was gone—so far away that she would never make it back in time, that she might not even receive their call if they tried—even if they knew she would hate herself for having missed it. But this wasn't something she should see, wasn't something she would ever have been able to set right in her head. Because Chris wouldn't scream, wouldn't moan in pain, wouldn't call out her name or even utter a prayer with his last breath. He would simply cease to be. And Chris knew for Asha, that would have been infinitely worse.

He couldn't try to find her, show himself one more time before he left the earth because it just didn't seem to work that way. He had thought about it, tried to uncover some way to see Asha last time, to touch her cheek again, but there was no way to do it unless she were dying too, or in some altered psychosis like Autumn was. He shuddered to think of what that would mean for her considering the missions she was on. He would sacrifice himself again if it meant saving her that kind of peril.

Chris couldn't see Autumn again either, the effort to find her was so great he felt lightheaded, drained with every attempt and if he tried now he would likely die right before her eyes. She didn't need to see her big brother like that. Regardless of the time they'd spent apart, Chris knew Autumn wouldn't be able to take that. He blew a kiss to his sister and hoped it found her cheek.

Who he *could* see was his mother, ever clearer by the second, her eyes red and swollen as she sat with him through his final moments. She cried silently, keeping her eyes trained on him, afraid to look away and find him standing there next to her. Chris could see that she wanted to comfort him, console him but there was nothing she could say that would do that. His knew what was happening, knew where he would end up... understood that it meant he would never, ever see his fiancée again. There was nothing anyone could say that would make that better.

"I'm so sorry, son," Patrick said as he succumbed to a sadness that made him feel like an empty, hollow shell. Three deaths. Three members of his family forced to live in The Realm because of him and he was no closer to understanding why: no closer to changing their fate. And there were still two more people out there depending on him. Chris couldn't have known what was going on in his great-grandfather's head but he could see the pain in his eyes... the guilt.

"We're right here," Doug said, his voice solemn and low, "we'll be right here waiting for you."

"I love you, baby," Chris's mother said and he could feel his own tears stinging his eyes. He remembered the way those words sounded when he was little, the way they made him feel protected and cared for. Over the years after most of the details about his mother had faded, had been replaced by things that had also since gone away, the sound of her voice saying those words still remained. He was so grateful to be able to hear them now when he needed them most, because oh God, he needed them now, because... because it hurt... and the room was hazier than it should be at that time of day, shadows played in corners where there should be none. He was alone in that hospital room because he had sent Asha on a fool's errand, a wild goose chase, an impossible errand and now he was going to be alone when he took his last breath. He was going to die alone and it was because he sent the only person left alive who loved him away, away, halfway around the world.

He wanted to call to her, to beg Asha to come back, to hold his hand because he was afraid, so very afraid, Jesus, he was afraid...

But she was saving them.

That woman, his beautiful love who would never wear his ring or carry his name had left everything she knew behind to save them, risking herself in the process. She loved him. She loved him.

She loved him.

Chris smiled and it felt good, his muscles felt alive for the very last time.

"She loves me, Mommy," he rasped, the sound of his voice unrecognizable to his own ears but that didn't matter anymore.

He felt a hand on his forearm and the touch felt distant, like it was only the suggestion of skin on skin. But he was grateful for it.

"Aahhssssshhhhhhh-"

Chris felt rather than heard his voice cut off as he spoke her name, the syllables coming together as a sigh.

He saw Asha's mother sitting next to him, one hand on his forearm, the other covering her mouth.

He saw Nurse Bea checking his wrist, his chest, the machines, going through the motions that would confirm his departure from life.

He saw himself lying still in the hospital bed, still like he had been for months, yet there was a finality now that filled all of the spaces, colored everything like an overlay.

Nurse Bea turned the machines off.

Asha's mother patted Chris's forearm and stood beside his bed.

"-she loves me," Chris finished in the room where his family stood and let his tears fall.

CHAPTER 37

The long lead up to the first level of the mortuary temple gave her time to think about what she was doing. Time for the nerves to get to her, try to shake her resolve. Asha could imagine Hatshepsut's subjects lined up along the path that led to the terraced, colonnaded, rectangular structure, heads bowed as they mourned the passing of their Pharoah, the one who had changed the fate of their kingdom, reestablishing foreign trade to their existence, making them prosper, helping them feed their families. As she approached the series of ramps that connected the three levels and felt awed as she came as close as she could to the rockface from which the structure was cut, Asha understood the press of sadness the people must have felt to lose one they held so dear, one who showed her care for them in ways their parents and grandparents had not experienced in previous reigns—one who favored peace and prosperity over war and made it so. She felt the weight of responsibility as well, first to a man whom she would always hold dear in her heart; a man who taught her not only about the wonders of Egypt, but the importance of history and tradition; about getting it right. Chris had also taught her about love—what it felt like to both give and receive it... what it felt like to sacrifice oneself in the name of it, lose oneself in the depth of it.

Asha imagined five sister sphinxes bordering the promenade, each with the body of a lion bearing Hatshepsut's face, the *nemes* and false beard depicting her as male but the curve of her eyes and the gentle contour of her lips hinting at the truth. It must have been grand, an avenue of the sphinxes that led toward Karnak.

She imagined the twin statues of the god Horus that graced the ramp wall's entrance done in exquisite detail, feathers and distinct features that displayed in colors of gold and blue amidst the backdrop of white acacia and flowering trees from far and wide lining the ramps instead of the single likeness that existed now, weathered and alone atop barren soil.

She envisioned colossi at every pillar, each with the queen who would be king's image, each inscribed with stories of her excursions, her conquests, her reign instead of the rubble that remained, headless and broken, left to the elements by a child in a jealous rage.

Asha imagined all of those things with sadness as she realized she was about to finish what Thutmose had set out to do over three millennia ago. The urge to fall to her knees in apology was overwhelming.

But Chris had warned her about that.

Chris had told her about the things she might encounter—the wall of gnats, the unforeseen sandstorms—but none of that had happened yet and as she made her way into the Sanctuary of Amun, she was grateful for that. He had been right about how few people would be visiting Hatshepsut's mortuary temple.

Now that her mummy had been identified and she was slated as one of the pharaohs to be housed in the new museum, the crowds had died down in the Valley of the Kings as the day drew to a close. Even with the hot weather in the afternoon, most of the foot traffic happened earlier in the day, leaving just Asha and a few tourists at Deir el-Bahari so close to dusk. No one had suspected that Hatshepsut was not in the belly of the Cairo Museum, that she had been put in the mortuary temple she had never used to wait for construction of the museum to complete. Asha had read buzz about it herself; all the "Who was Hatshepsut and Where is she Now?" articles and posts had made great reading as she sat in a cybercafe just outside of New York's Penn Station waiting for her train. It had been the second leg of five that she would take to throw anyone who might be looking off her scent. Trains to nowhere, she had taken to calling them. New York. Boston. Philadelphia. Washington DC. Chicago so she could leave the States through O'Hare. All close enough to do in two days because that's when the next flight to Cairo was scheduled and she had to do something in the meantime, something that would take her mind off how crazy the whole thing was. Something other than watching Chris die before her eyes.

The setting sun and the shadows of the temple's interior gave Asha the cover she needed. But still, she had to be quick.

She passed through the chambers undetected; Asha had patterned out the guards' cycles, watching them for hours before stepping foot inside. Guard #1 was smoking around the corner out of sight of the tourists. Guard #2 had started to nod off near the front gate, but before that had not ventured inside the temple at all. If there was a third guard, she hadn't seen them.

The reliefs on the columns and walls were the kind that

Chris could have looked at forever. They detailed how Hatshepsut ascended to the throne as well as her escapades in Punt and the construction of her obelisks; they spoke of a life lived over 3,000 years ago that still had so much significance today. Asha imagined the essays he might have written, the connections he might have drawn. She mourned the lack of his voice in the world about such a formidable woman even as she stood ready to destroy her.

Asha hopped the fence blocking the doorway and melting into the darkness beyond.

The Chapel of Hathor with its rows of columns crafted to resemble goddess sistrums; the Chapel of Anubis with reliefs so vibrant they gave Asha pause, the mineral pigment painted on the ancient stone belying its age; the chamber of boats erected in tribute to the afterlife that early dynastic rulers favored left above ground in haste as, rumor had it, the builders were forced to flee Thutmose's destroyers... all of those spaces bordered by a portico that was uncharacteristic for the time—it would have been maze-like were it not for Chris's memory of the layout. She found the false wall he told her was there and the passage that stretched out beyond it, pressed herself inside, having to make herself small in some places and turn to the side in others as she traversed hidden passages that likely hadn't been used in centuries. Chris had told Asha about two routes, giving her more than one way to access Hatshepsut's funerary chamber, the place where they had likely left her mummy. She came upon the larger entryway first; that one would have been wide enough for two people to walk through side by side. It was the one that Hatshepsut's court would have used during her interment. But it was also where security could be stationed if there were any guards posted in the back of the structure. So Asha opted for the other way in, a sneaky little passage that showed itself on the rudimentary layouts sketched by Edouard Naville in the late 1800s but not on any of the more modern blueprints. She had time to wonder if the newer maps didn't have the route she was on because it had been sealed up or had collapsed, or if, in the uncovering of the site, something had shifted and now the walls were pressed together at the end. She had time to worry that that very thing might happen as soon as she got inside, her presence tripping some kind of trap or curse that caused the room to seal off, locking her in. Her breathing quickened at the thought even as her mind tried to calm her down, to remind her that there was another way out, that this was not an *Indiana Jones* movie.

It was so dark, too dark see her own hand in front of her face. Too dark to see what was at the end of the passage.

Asha inched forward, forcing herself to keep going, to get all the way through, and was treated to a sense of openness as she entered a much larger space once she reached the end. It took a minute for her eyes to adjust but when they did, Asha found herself in a vast room that was far bigger than she expected it to be. It was adorned with depictions of Hatshepsut traversing the afterworld on a boat through waters filled with sea snakes and five-headed crocodiles; Osiris greeting her to receive her incantation; the heart weighing ceremony of virtuousness, and other imagery from The Book of the Dead that Asha had read about.

She had found the right place.

Asha took another step, wishing she had learned more about what the hieroglyphics that Chris had poured over meant, awed to be in the presence of so much history. She saw imagery she recognized from books; the commonalities of funerary chambers staggering. Her eye landed on the relief of a bird, intricately detailed with green and gold wings next to the image of the pharaoh in full regalia. The image of Hatshepsut.

Asha's heart began to race.

Hatshepsut was there, right there—Asha was sure that her next step would reveal the pharaoh in front of her eyes beneath the depiction of her soul leaving her body.

That meant it was real.

It was really happening.

She was really going to unwrap the woman, claw at her dried flesh and brittle bones with her bare hands, pull the hair from her scalp, rip the skin, break the bones, grind it all into powder, as fine as she could get it, much like she would herbs using a mortar and pestle. Asha was really going to press everything, every bit of the queen, into the 70oz water bottle she had brought with her, the one she had kept pulling out of her backpack all day and making sure that people saw her drinking from because *not* drinking anything would have been more suspicious than having an oversized bottle all to oneself in the sweltering Egyptian heat. Asha drank from it, trying not to gag because she knew she had been rubbing her fingers in as far as they would go for days, spitting in it, rubbing her tongue along the mouth of it to collect bacteria because that, combined with the humidity and the very air itself would cause the homemade mummia to disintegrate, to melt into the liquid like sugar does in water. And she would shake it, dear God, she would shake it to make sure that the water got to every granule that was Hatshepsut because she had to be sure.

She wouldn't have to see the black sludge that would be left, at least not for long. She would pour it into the Nile at the foot of the Qasr El Nil bridge before she could think too hard about what she was doing... about what she had already done.

Asha was really going to do it because if she didn't, Chris's whole family line would be damned to endure an afterlife in The

Realm, a place filled with monsters and the condemned, and no future.

Asha was really going to do it because it didn't matter if Chris had all the details about his grandmother's manuscript right and in his compromised state, Asha highly doubted he had —he had figured out a way to save his sister from everything that came after. Asha worried that everything Chris had planned would help everyone but him, but she couldn't think about that for long—couldn't let herself get stuck there. Her fiancé was on his deathbed and she owed him enough respect to carry out the last thing he would ever ask of her.

And she would because without Chris she would have already been dead.

Hatshepsut was there.

Right there.

Asha felt humbled.

She covered her mouth to conceal the sob working its way up from her throat as she looked at the woman whom she had come to destroy, the woman for whom love was a poison rather than an elixir.

"I'm sorry," she whispered as she cut into the tempered glass with a sharpened scarab bearing Hatshepsut's cartouche and exposed the ancient wrappings to the open air. Asha had found the scarab among Chris's things. It was, no doubt, something a tourist could easily buy from any street corner vendor, but she filed it, fashioned it to a point, turned it into a weapon. That it bore Hatshepsut's name made her feel sick and vindicated at the same time.

Asha worked quickly, remembering the words Chris had used to explain, to substantiate, to absolve.

'The body has to exist for the *ka* to go back into it at some point," Chis had said. "It's the whole reason for mummification;

Egyptians thought they could preserve their bodies well enough that, when the time came, the pharaohs could inhabit their bodies once again. That's why food and drink, servants and riches were left in the tomb as well, so they would have access to everything they needed in the afterlife and beyond."

The sound of Hatshepsut's body bending and breaking beneath Asha's touch was one that would replay in her dreams for the rest of her life.

Chris had cautioned her, repeating this point over and over.

"Baby, you have to make sure you destroy the whole body and pick up every piece to be certain there is nothing left behind. With her mummy destroyed her *ka* will have no body to enter. It will be forever trapped in the afterlife—forever separated from the host. It's the *ka* that allowed her to take another body and use it. If the *ka* is gone…"

Chris had hesitated then, afraid to hope.

"… the curse will be broken," Asha had finished, saying the words he didn't dare hope for. As her hands broke brittle bone, Asha prayed they were true.

Her eyes fluttered open and Asha was surprised to find herself alive and seated on the bus that had carried her away from Upper Egypt. She covered her mouth to stifle the shriek rising in her throat, hoping she caught it before it spilled out. She looked around herself to see if anyone had heard her muffled scream, had noticed her surprise… to see if there were scorpions in the aisle, in the pouch in the seatback in front of her, or beneath the seat. Because there had been scorpions in her dream.

Asha had been stuck in the maze that was the mortuary temple which was suddenly more difficult to navigate a path out than it had been to find a way in. She could hear the voice of a man bellowing behind her at every turn, his language unintelligible to her, but the tone unmistakably menacing. Senenmut. Chris had cautioned her about him, warned her that if she heard his voice she should keep going, should start running to get out of the temple if she had to. He said he didn't believe the stories that claimed Senenmut haunted the temple, protecting his love in death the way that he could not in life, but that stranger things had been known to happen when it came to Hatshepsut so if Asha heard him, she'd better get out fast. Asha could tell there was more to the story, details that Chris was deliberately leaving out, but she didn't ask what they were. If Asha actually knew what Senenmut would do if he caught her, she would have been scared senseless.

Chris warned her that Senenmut had designed the temple so he knew it well. He said he had likely installed passages that no one knew about, passages that led to hidden places in the tomb where no one would ever discover her. Chris reminded her to look up at the ceiling and take note: if the celestial diagrams, the constellations and planets, seemed to be moving, she was in danger.

In her dream the ceiling was still but the voice still bellowed behind her, in front of her, all around her. Reliefs seemed to peel themselves from the wall to pursue her; giant statues of Horus, of Osiris, of Hatshepsut herself followed her escape with the turning of their massive heads, the sound like granite grinding against itself.

Her backpack was heavy, weighted down.

In the dream Asha emerged from the temple disoriented and frantic to see a pink and orange sky as the sun set behind El-Qurn. She ran down the first ramp at a sprint, unable to shake the feeling that Senenmut was on her heels, was swiping at her backpack to free his love. She ran across the platform and started down the second ramp at the same pace, trying to ignore the gnats as they flew into her eyes, up her nose, into her mouth... as they tried to gain access to her throat. She could see the bus waiting for her at the end of the ramp, a cross-country behemoth parked where the open-air tram normally would be and she ran for it, cycling her legs as if her life depended upon it. As she stepped onto the promenade she heard a disconcerting sound, something very much like burrowing, only whatever was making it was coming out rather than going in. Asha made the mistake of turning her head to look, knowing even in her dream state that she shouldn't, that seeing what was happening would only slow her down. But she looked anyway and was treated to the sight of sections of dirt the size of boulders falling from the yellow ribbed exoskeleton of a deathstalker scorpion that stood on legs that were at least 6 feet tall. Its pincers were huge; they reminded Asha of the gloves that boxer used, the hardened claws opening and closing where the thumb would have been. The ridges of its back were sectioned by deep grooves and Asha could see it expanding and contracting as the creature breathed. The deathstalker's stinger was long and curved, mounted atop a whip-like tail and sharpened to a point. Its six black eyes were trained on her.

And it wasn't alone.

They were everywhere, breaking through the ground, the stone walkway, the road leading to the mortuary temple... the same one that the bus was parked on. And they were hissing and growling as they sized her up, opening and closing their pincers as though trying to satisfy an itch, to feel her in their clutches... to snap her in half.

It felt like all of the air had been sucked out of the world and Asha stood frozen, unable to run, to move, to do anything but see. And then a woman, as tall as the bus, with skin as fine as copper stepped into view. Her headdress was of pure gold and was fashioned into the shape of a scorpion. She was nude save for the headdress, her body shimmering like heat coming off hot asphalt shadowed in the waning light. She walked toward Asha, assessing her curiously, her stride slow and steady. The scorpions pulsed with anticipation all around them, waiting for her order.

Asha knew who she was. While she was waiting for Chris to talk to her again, she had come across a book of goddesses and this one was mentioned. She was Serqet, the goddess of nature and magic and fertility. She was also the goddess who protected the dead on their journey to the afterlife. She was the apotheosis of the scorpion, which the Egyptians revered for its resilience and poisonous venom.

She was there for Hatshepsut.

Asha took a step backward and then another but Serqet kept coming. Asha could feel the presence of a scorpion behind her, her body stopping of its own volition to save her from feeling the beast's flesh against her own.

Serqet got closer, closer, so close that Asha had to look up, to rest her head on her upper back to meet her eyes.

Serqet leaned down, her eyes black and hexagonal like those of a bee, and parted her lips. A stinger reached out to bring blood to her lips.

CHAPTER 38

The girl's tears were distracting, but something else commanded Cecelia's attention. Something that, at first tickled the back of her mind, light but persistent, like a gnat flying in front of her eyes, too attracted to the sweat on her brow to fear being swatted. It irritated her, pulled her away from her thoughts— thoughts that were dancing around ways to handle Autumn. It would be easier to inhabit her than to continue to keep her in limbo. Autumn wasn't eating enough to nourish the baby inside her; she wasn't moving and that would damage her muscles over time. And now that she had gained an awareness of what was going on, Cecelia found it increasingly difficult to bend Autumn into submission. Taking control of her body would be the simple choice, but then she would cease to be. By extension, so would the baby.

She needed that baby.

The baby meant another cycle. The baby meant more time for Mal to learn his place. It had been a long time already and she craved his touch more than she was willing to admit, but Cecelia had to be sure that the next time they met, the next time she asked him to join her, the answer would be unequivocally yes.

She'd made it difficult, never let him believe there would be anything other than the purgatory she had banished him to, had even talked herself into believing that she never intended to let him out, give him another chance at the throne... another chance to be with her. Maybe some of that had been by design. Maybe she thought she'd find another to love and forget about him, leave him in the nether to rot or rule—his choice. But she had not. There were few who turned her head beyond physical pleasure, few who piqued her interest outside of the bedroom. Before him only her beloved Senenmut had intrigued her, kept her wanting everything he had to offer: his mind, his body, and his soul. Only those two, and no one since.

She wanted Mal.

Still.

Autumn had started crying in earnest and it tripped Cecelia's thoughts, disturbed them, made them jump the track and follow another course. Thoughts of Senenmut warmed her but she didn't feel like the person who had once loved him anymore. Ma'at-ka-re. Khnumt-Amun. Netjeretkhau. The names that others had given her; the required titulary to solidify her place on the throne. Joined with Amun, Foremost of Noble Ladies, Divine of Appearance. Lady of the Two Lands.

Hatshepsut.

She hardly ever thought of herself as that woman anymore.

She remembered feeling alive and in love, seen in the most intimate of ways by the one she wanted most. Their visits to the grotto at Speos Artemidos, the ones where he would kiss her breathless as she tried to survey the text on the architrave, making sure her position was properly reflected... those moments— that excitement, that honesty, that love—seemed to have happened to someone else. Stolen kisses behind Mut Temple as Hatshepsut surveyed the reconstruction work she had sanctioned there, unable to wait until they were back in the palace for the touch of skin; escapes under cover of night to sit at the water's edge at Isheru or the Nile itself, their feet touching the water while their hands found each other in the moonlight; Senenmut's loving smile as she stood nervously by the obelisk she had mounted in Karnak marking her contribution among the Kings. He knew the worry that lived in her heart, the feeling that she was not accepted for who she was, the frustration that she had to don a male countenance during ceremonial traditions. He encouraged her desire to show her true self, commissioned work from his own purse to reflect the beauty of the woman that she was. Senenmut had loved Hatshepsut. In many ways they had died together long ago.

Cecelia heard Autumn's crying and felt she might shed a tear as well. One for the woman who had been lost to the past, buried and forgotten, wiped away by those too immature to do anything else; rendered insignificant by a future that didn't care.

She almost did. But just as quickly, she righted herself.

Hatshepsut could make no impact in the world— she was dead and gone— but Cecelia could. Cecelia had built an empire that was just as vast as Hatshepsut's, one that was not inhibited by the constraints of time.

She was Cecelia.

Now.

Forever.

And she would do what she would.

The sound was muted to Hatshepsut's ears, like a wet branch that gave way underfoot—felt more than heard. It mingled with Autumn's tears as Cecelia turned toward her, watching, empathizing, commiserating in silence.

CHAPTER 39

The Qasr El Nil bridge was beautiful at night. People walked across it at a leisurely pace, the stresses of the day pushed away in favor of enjoying the night air. Asha would join them when she was done, walking from downtown Cairo to Gezira Island and back again pretending to be interested in the Egyptian skyline. She would try to purge the memories of the day, clear the feeling of dried skin beneath her palms away, erase the hiss of the gigantic scorpions that plagued her dream as she moved among living, breathing people. She would do all of that before going to the hostel she had booked for the night—her last night in Egypt. The next morning she'd be enroute to Italy; the first flight out had a seat with her name on it.

And then it would all be over.

Asha wondered if she'd ever know what happened to Autumn. She couldn't find her when it mattered most, so she doubted she ever would. Unless she came to the funeral, but Asha didn't think she would. And maybe that was just as well.

There would be money for her, keepsakes she should have. Asha would do what she could to help, would pack up her would-be father-in-law's house, sell it if she could find a way to, put everything away for Autumn on the off chance that she came looking for it one day. Maybe then Asha would be ready to talk about what happened... maybe then she could tell Autumn about how her brother had saved both of their lives.

That is, if she got away with it.

Empty fishing boats moored for the night bobbed in the Nile at the base of the bridge, far below the moderate but consistent foot traffic that balmy evening. A warm breeze tousled Asha's sweat-streaked hair as she reached behind herself to put her backpack on the ground.

It was the perfect night to set things straight.

The water bottle was heavy, its pliable sides swollen. Asha tried not to envision the mummia in its thickened state, the blood and bone of a queen blackened by age and mealy, like wet bread. She tried not to think of anything but Chris and the words she wanted to say to him, words she *would* say, uttered low as if in prayer. Asha uncapped the bottle, recoiled from the rancid smell of rot and myrrh, the medicinal notes of the latter striking Asha as obscene there, where an atrocity was being committed, under cover of night... where no healing would ever come. She kneeled at the water's edge and tilted the water bottle, using both hands to ensure that what was inside sank into the deep instead of depositing onto the shore. The mixture was heavy like oatmeal; it plopped into the water with a splash, the sound loud to Asha's ears but she was afraid to bring herself closer to the Nile to reduce the sound; she was afraid some of it would splash into her eyes.

"I hope this worked, Chris," she said in her head, afraid to even whisper now, terrified of being overheard. "I hope your family can find peace now. Maybe this will change everything and you can be released from The Realm and... well... maybe we can meet again."

Asha stopped while there was still mummia left in the water bottle. She picked up her bag and walked a few paces away, resuming her pour a distance from the first, feeling somehow that this separation was a precaution she needed to take.

"I will always love you, Chris, I hope you know that. You will always be the man who made me want forever."

The tears flowed freely now and she let them wet her face unfettered. She had something to finish and would not deviate from the task for a second, not even to wipe her face.

"I can't believe I missed you, baby. I know I did. I know it in my heart. I hope this makes up for it."

The flow from the water bottle was ebbing. She watched as the mummia dissolved in the movement of the water, let her mind relax with the realization that soon what was left of Hatshepsut would be ingested and excreted by tigerfish and crocodiles and whatever else lived in the river. Before she even left to join the people traversing the bridge above, fish will have devoured any of the thicker bits that hadn't dissolved yet.

The thought made Asha sick.

Asha moved to another spot, dipped the water bottle into the Nile to gather water, sloshed it around inside the water bottle and dumped it out. She did this several times to make sure she had gotten every bit of Hatshepsut out of the container and into the Nile. And then it was done. She would ditch the bottle somewhere in the city and then the whole ordeal would be over.

"I'll miss you, Chris. Forever."

Asha made her way to the entrance for the bridge, hoping that no one noticed her shambling emergence from the darkness. As she reached the approach, the bronze lion statue looming large in the night, Asha realized there was one more thing to do, one more thing to finish before she could feel that the loop was closed.

Asha swiped her finger over the tube of paint and scrawled a message at the foot of one of the lion statues that welcomed pedestrians and drivers alike. Pahket. The statues made Asha think of Pahket, the lion-headed goddess, and as that brought Hatshepsut's sphinx to mind, Asha felt it apropos to leave the message she had prepared there, in that very spot.

لا تدنث ... احتفل

Her hand was unsteady but that was ok. It didn't need to be perfect, shouldn't be if someone was to believe that it was scrawled there by a person who didn't speak the language natively. If anyone ever saw the message written in small print beneath the bronze platform upon which it sat, pressed into the stones, it might make them smile, maybe even nod their head in agreement.

Don't desecrate... celebrate.

It wouldn't mean anything specific to most people; just some slogan for a cause that didn't get any traction. But some people might catch on, might look at the golden parade, if it ever happened, and frown at the spectacle, remember the slogan they saw someplace but couldn't remember where, that phrase that hadn't meant much at the time but stuck with them anyhow. Only the really savvy would notice the color and connect it to the words. But few would ever realize that the words were written in not just brown, but Mummy Brown; fewer still would make the connection between that and the inconspicuous swipes of that same color that had been placed all over the city. And Asha didn't think anyone would ever connect any of that to her, a woman whose life got turned upside down one fateful day thanks to a freak accident on the other side of the world. And they would definitely never suspect that the very desecration the author of that message had denounced on the bridge had already occurred right there, beneath their feet.

CHAPTER 40

Gabby's breath caught in her throat as she heard the sound of her son's voice behind her. He was in the room with her, really there, not half in or half out and the sadness that came with that realization made her feel ill. He was there because they hadn't done enough to save him. He was there because she had wasted so much time walking around in the woods feeling sorry for herself, not realizing how quickly time passed, how utterly fleeting it truly was in The Realm, especially if you weren't watching. He was there because he was dead.

Christopher.

Her little boy.

Was dead.

She sank to her knees, unable to stand any longer and her son, that beautiful boy who had to grow up without a mother, not ever knowing how much she cherished every hair on his head, went to her, fall down in front of her, mingled his tears with hers. They held each other, felt each other's faces, cried on each other's shoulders, mourned the life they never shared.

Doug couldn't bear to watch; he knew the pain of losing his child all too well. He had watched Gabby die in front of his eyes the same way that his father had watched him. He averted his eyes instead to the space where the manifestations seemed most prevalent, looking for Autumn, praying he would like what he saw.

Patrick kneeled next to them and held them both to his chest. He wanted to apologize, to tell them he was sorry, so very sorry for whatever he had done to condemn them to that place; wanted to tell them that he would spend the rest of whatever this existence was trying to figure it out, trying to make it right so that none of the people they loved would have to go through this again. But he couldn't. His mouth wouldn't form the words, his voice cracked and rasped, unreliable under the strain. So he cried with them, uttering half-formed apologies and pleas for forgiveness, none of which could be put together to form intelligible sentences.

Doug's relieved laughter dissipated the fog of despair in the room.

"I see her," he said, laughter cutting in on his words, bringing tears of joy to wet his face. "She's fine. Autumn's just fine."

They all turned to the see what Doug was talking about, each rising and taking steps toward the place that had grabbed Doug's attention, each marveling at what they saw.

Autumn was sitting in a park. The day was sunny and bright and likely warm, considering the spaghetti strapped top she was wearing to show off her sun-kissed shoulders. Her cheeks were full and rosy; Chris felt like he understood what people meant when they said pregnant women glow. An oversized headband kept the bulk of her dark brown hair away from her face; the bangs she had allowed to stay free were flipped off from her forehead as though windswept. She wore sunglasses, but they rested on top of her head, braced by the headband, at the ready when she needed them. She was engrossed in a book but the cover was facing her legs and Chris was unable to see what it was. He imagined that it was the newest paranormal romance because she had always loved those, would have read them cover to cover without stopping if their dad hadn't made her come up for air sometimes, maybe put a little food in her stomach. Chris told her mother about it, repeated the very words his father always said, smiling in that way that belies the sadness beneath: the loss. They mourned in silence; Chris for his father and Gabby for her husband, the man she didn't get to share a life with for nearly long enough, the man who had raised their children to be wonderful human beings. When Autumn's hand rested on her ample stomach to caress it in the way that expectant mothers the world over often did, Gabby, Chris, Patrick, and Doug smiled in unison, grinning wide with genuine happiness.

It had worked.

Autumn was alive and so was the baby.

Alive.

Chris felt like he could scream, like he could jump for joy. He didn't know what would come next, whether what they had done to Hatshepsut had truly saved Autumn and the baby if not them... he didn't know anything at all, except that his sister was healthy and that the baby was growing inside her. She wasn't locked away in her own head, her body withering away in a neglected house, merely the vessel for the next generation of the damned. His sister was alive and well.

Asha.

His smile broke in the middle, cracking at the sides, and deteriorated on his lips.

Where was Asha?

Has she gotten out of Egypt? Had she been arrested? His stomach dropped at the next thought, the one he wanted to banish before it came into view but was too late.

Was she still alive?

"Where is she?" Chris started, his frightened eyes darting around the room, looking at the other walls, hoping they had a story to tell.

"Does anyone know what happened to—"

CHAPTER 41

Cecelia saw them, faces she recognized, one she would never forget. They had their backs turned to the place in the room where she manifested, surprise and anger threatening to coax a scream from her throat. Something had happened, something terrible, and for a moment she didn't know what. But as she remembered the sounds that filled her ears, cracking like kindling rising to a cacophonous pitch; as she remembered the press on her chest like the weight of three men; felt the very walls closing in on her until she could no longer see, no longer think, no longer breathe, Cecelia realized with brutal clarity, that it was over. She could not return to rule the way she had before; her *ka* had nowhere to rest. She didn't know how it had happened but she had been cast out of the cycle of life, pushed into the air to tumble and twist like a leaf on the breeze. She was no longer grounded; her roots had been dug up... destroyed.

She was homeless.

And then she was there behind them, there in some other place away from the palace of her memory, all regalia stripped from the walls in favor of peeling pedestrian design, there in a place she had never intended to be, her soul following the dead boy's as it found its way to his family. She watched them as they fawned over the girl she had intended to discard once the child was born, the child who she would set on a path alone, devoid of history and the stories that could have been used to poison his mind: the child who would keep it all going, produce descendant upon descendant until *she* said it was enough. But that wouldn't happen, not now. Autumn was safe and healthy as was the baby inside her swollen belly, Cecelia could see that much. And she was there. In The Realm.

Cecelia felt her lips curl back into a snarl as she looked at the youngest man in the room, Autumn's meddling brother. She was happy that he had met his end, had time to wonder what turn of events happened to make such a horrible thought pleasing to her, but meant it just the same. He was dressed in a casual suit, a loose linen blazer and slacks the color of sand, a casual off-white crew neck shirt. They must have been the clothes he was wearing when he had been brought into the hospital because when she saw him he was wearing a hospital gown and Cecelia was sure he hadn't gotten up and walked out of there to enjoy a day in the sun after that, not looking the way he had. He was the one who had seen the place where she was hiding Autumn, that corner of her mind that Cecelia created for the girl's benefit. He could actually identify her Egypt, knew exactly what he was looking at and for that she hated him. Because she wasn't ready to give Mal another chance yet; he hadn't suffered enough, not through his sheddings; not directly. Cecelia wasn't ready to call his cards either. She hadn't stacked the deck well enough yet. Mal's line was already dying out and without a descendant who would be ignorant of their past, who had never heard about the manuscript that Joanne had written, had never been told about vampires and immortals or of embattled lovers out in the universe, the plan she had for The Realm could slip through her fingers. Cecelia needed ignorant offspring, children who would never know from whence they came, who would die and find themselves in The Realm and fight against the hierarchy in place. If Mal was allowed to merge with the older man before her, the perfect shedding, the one she had worried about from the start, he would become all-powerful in that place. No one would challenge them: they would be indomitable. If that happened Mal might never bend to her will.

As Cecelia stood she saw their mother, the one who had unearthed the book, and her father, the deer in the headlights she had discounted years ago. It wasn't them who gave her pause, who made her stop in her tracks. It was the eldest in the room—it was always him. He had been cut from the same cloth as Mal, the one she had given her heart to in what felt like another life: the man who could change everything.

Cecelia was rendered mute as competing emotions vied for center stage. This man was the center of it all. His wife had written the book that had ultimately cost her everything. This man, who looked so much like Mal it made her eyes sting. And he was right there... vulnerable. Cecelia began to consider a new twist to their sordid tale, one that spoke of spilled blood.

"Uncanny, isn't it?" a voice asked from behind her and she knew its owner instantly; her soul could never forget, regardless of the time that had passed.

"But still, he is not me. But his desires reach for me. They lean in like a moth to a flame."

Cecelia turned around her, her face reflecting a mixture of relief and pleasure that made her feel like a girl again.

Mal had entered the room before he had time to think it through, the pull toward Cecelia as strong as it always was. She was there, right there. He realized, as he stared at her in awe, that he never expected her to come for him... thought he she would live on in his memories and nowhere else. He had made a kind of peace with it— a resignation that wasn't apparent until the scab was scratched away to reveal flesh that no longer bled. But seeing her now, there in front of him, sharing the same space instead of being out there in some nebulous universe that he couldn't fathom the magnitude of— it changed things. He wanted her again, as much as he had when they had first met, back when all he wanted was the taste of her blood on his tongue. Mal had called her and she had come to him. He smiled. She wanted him too. Good. He would use that. Mal decided he would show her what kind of ruler he had become, demonstrate the power he wielded, show her the kingdom they could rule together.

Mal's voice quivered in his throat but he pushed through.

"My queen," Mal said and closed his eyes as he dipped his head, the bow shallow but symbolic.

"Such formalities, darling. There's no such thing between old friends," Cecelia said languidly.

Gabby screamed.

Doug gasped.

They had all turned around at the sound of voices behind them, unaware that there was anyone else in the room. Gabby stood in front of her son, instinctively blocking him from harm's way. Before she even got a good look at the woman, Gabby recognized the way the air in the room changed, shifted in a way that reminded her of how the air feels just before a storm. She had felt it before and had hoped she never would again.

What did you do to Asha? The question was on Chris's lips, in his mouth, ready to come out but he never got the chance to ask it because his great-grandfather stood, his back ramrod straight and emitted the most deafening shout he had ever heard.

CHAPTER 42

The sound was loud, so loud that Tara cracked the door of the pantry to reduce its reverberation in the small space as she clapped her hands over her ears like a defiant child. It had come from Patrick and it was like nothing she had ever heard before. Almost inhuman. They were all facing where she hid now; Patrick, Doug, Gabby, and Chris had turned toward Mal and a woman she had never seen before. Tara had thought she would scream herself when Mal passed by the pantry door, his footfalls raising the hairs on her forearms to attention. She wasn't ready to fight, she had no weapon nor plan and knew that if Mal found her she would have to do exactly that, but if he detected her presence he didn't show it. And that made sense—there were more exciting things going on in the other room.

Patrick shouted when he saw Mal, issued a sound that was like an animal dying in agony, and she understood why. He must have felt like he was looking into a mirror.

Tara saw Doug reach out and grab his father's shoulder but Patrick didn't seem to feel it.

"Dad. Dad, it's ok," Doug started, "It's not y—"

"It's not what, my fault? The proof is right there!" Patrick nearly screeched. He pressed his hands to either side of his head, the heels digging into each temple while his eyes went wide, wide, so very wide. He looked as if his mind had been blown, like everything he had worried about had come true. And Tara supposed it had.

CHAPTER 43

"How? How could this be true?" Patrick asked, the questions sounding more like accusations. "Tell me! How can this be happening?"

"Patrick—"

Mal took a step toward Patrick and he took one backwards. Mal sighed; this was not the way he wanted things to go. Patrick was supposed to realize he wanted this as much as Mal did; he was supposed to come into his own as a leader and decide to take the reins, claim them for himself. This way, with anger tainting the situation, was very much like what happened to him when Cecelia bid him choose. A knot formed in his stomach at the betrayal he would have to commit. He wondered how else he embodied the dictator he had turned his back on.

"That's... that's not you, grandpa. It *can't* be," Gabby said, her voice small.

"Child," Mal said, his voice regaining its gravity as he moved further into the room, "You should not speak about that which you do not know."

"My father is a kind, loving man. He would never have hurt anyone. He died because he was trying to *help* someone. He's not a killer, like you," Doug said, wishing he sounded more like a grown man than a petulant child.

"And that is because I too was once kind and loving. Perhaps I can be again," Mal purred, his eyes landing upon Cecelia appraisingly.

"What? What do you mean?" Chris asked, his head still caught in the whirlwind of experiencing life, death, and rebirth within the span of a few minutes.

"Think upon it, boy. Think beyond the fantasy spun by your great-grandmother, clever though it was. With all of your schooling one would think the conclusion easily drawn."

"What is your plan for the shedding, my darling?" Cecelia asked and Mal heard the lie in her voice. Did she *not* know what having a shedding of this caliber meant? Did she *not* know what he would be compelled to do if left to fend for himself against those who would try to overthrow him? Surely she understood what was at stake, even if it did not factor into her plans. Was she still so hell bent on punishment that she could not see how effectively he had ruled?

He wanted her, he knew that then. Mal wanted Cecelia, but she had to see him first.

"It was all true... all of this – you created this place because you were *angry* at him?" Gabby asked Cecelia incredulously, the pieces finally falling into place for her.

"All those people outside, running for their lives the moment they wake up in this... this nothingness," Patrick added, picking up the baton. "Monsters as big as houses chasing people down and killing them, but not everyone... not me. Me they stepped aside for, didn't touch a hair on my head. Why? Because they knew that we were one and the same?"

Patrick felt sick to his stomach.

"How... how can this be? How could someone who kills when he doesn't get what he wants, someone who plays people like pieces on a chess board, who creates monsters straight out of somebody's nightmare—how can you be inside me?"

Patrick looked as if he wanted to beat the answer out of Mal.

Mal smiled, seeing the irony, the stark duality of his words in contrast with his posture.

"You can't deny you feel the rush too. The taste of power you've had went to your head right away. I know it did. We're not so different, you and me."

Patrick faltered, feeling exposed.

"There was a time when I didn't want power either, when I was happy just living as everyone else did, doing what I was told. And yes, Cecelia, our queen, sent me here because..."

Mal hazarded a glance at Cecelia and was happy to see that she was looking at him with soft eyes.

"... I was not ready for what was required. I could not give her what she wanted of me then. But I am ready now," he continued, addressing Cecelia directly. "And now that we have merged, The Realm can be your playground."

He took Cecelia's hand, found it soft to the touch.

"Merged? What do you mean 'merged'?" Patrick exclaimed. "I don't want this. I only agreed to rule so that I could figure out a way to save my family without worrying about The Hunters killing me before I could do anything."

Patrick looked down at his hands.

"A lot of good that did me."

Gabby touched her grandfather's shoulder and spoke, her voice quiet.

"You saved Autumn. At least for now. We'll come up with something before—"

Mal's attention was drawn to the woman manifesting from the living world, guided by Gabby's slight nod in reference as she spoke to Patrick, and suddenly it was like a veil was lifted. He looked at Cecelia sharply, feeling foolish. Nothing was clear, yet everything was now, finally. Cecelia's presence in The Realm, as sudden as it had been after so much time begging her to come but being ignored; the woman in the living world, pregnant with another of his descendants; even the manuscript written by Severna's shedding... Patrick had been right. There was a game of chess afoot. Mal just hadn't realized he was one of the pieces on the board.

CHAPTER 44

Tara was panting.

Everything. Every fucking thing she thought she knew had been a lie.

The Realm wasn't some place that existed between Heaven and Hell because of some divine ordination. It was there because a woman was angry at a man and she wanted to punish him.

The Hunters, those green bastards with horn-like bones sticking out of their heads and suctions on their hands... the fuckers that killed her friends – they existed because that woman—this Cecelia—thought it might be fun? Something to mix things up, keep them on their toes?

Tara didn't know if all of that was the way it went down, but she knew what she saw. Patrick and Doug and Gabby were throwing shit out there and Mal was fielding it all. And Cecelia didn't deny anything.

This was *her* fault.

All of it.

She had killed The Watchers.

No, fuck that, Tara thought through her tears, tears that felt foreign rolling down her cheeks.

She had killed Tara's *friends*.

Lydjauk.

Kincaid.

Aadi.

Qiao.

Sebastian.

She had killed Mileeha.

Tara's heart was pumping way too fast; the sound of blood that should no longer exist rushed in her ears.

She had heard enough.

She had heard everything she needed to know.

CHAPTER 45

The room had erupted, the sound like the din at a crowded sporting event in the middle of a stadium wave. Chris would wonder later how he didn't see her coming, how he could have missed the distinct movement of a person approaching from the room right in front of him but he had. And so had everyone else. They were all wrapped up in their own questions, one shouting over the other, trying to be heard. He would never know if he could have stopped her—if anyone could have. He wasn't even sure that he would have tried to if given the chance.

"How do we stop this?" Chris asked but his questions was swallowed up by accusations and incredulousness, disbelief and regret.

"How do we make sure no one else ends up here?" Chris shouted, ready to shake Mal to make him listen.

And he did, but the response was not what Chris had hoped for.

"There's no way to save her. She will end up here just like

you did, like her baby will, like her baby's babies will. That is, unless you decide to change your mind..." Mal said, turning his attention to Cecelia, "My love."

He kissed her hand but she could tell he didn't mean it. Something had changed— between the moment when they walked into the room and him kissing her hand, something had changed, flipped on its axis, and Cecelia wasn't sure she could right it. Not there, in front of everyone, now that he had a chip on his shoulder. Not when she wasn't sure he was as ready as he claimed to be.

Nothing about this masquerade could conceal that.

"Why do you need us?" Doug said. "Why can't you handle your lover's spat by yourselves and leave us out of it?"

Cecelia regarded Doug as if seeing him for the first time.

"Lover's *spat*?"

She laughed and the sound filled the room.

"I assure you this is so much more than that. Do you know to whom you are speaking?"

"Hatshepsut," Chris answered, trying to turn Cecelia's attention to him. He didn't like the way she was looking at his grandfather... as if she might rip him to shreds for his insolence.

"Pharaoh from the 18th dynasty. The most formidable woman to take the throne in all of antiquity."

This answer seemed to placate her, so Chris decided to try something.

"You were a benevolent ruler. There were no war stories, no conquests shown in your reliefs."

The room was quiet.

Cecelia was listening.

"Why change now? Can't you see what this is doing to us?"

Cecelia's eyes flashed red and Gabby understood then why her grandmother had written her as a vampire.

Mal chuckled, the sound like the roiling sea.

A mistake.

A mistake.

Chris knew it for what it was as soon as the words had left his mouth. Oh God, such a massive error... he didn't know if they would survive what came next. The books he had dedicated his life to, the ones with authors who captured what they found important and discarded the rest, made assumptions and jumped to conclusions that, once printed, became canon. Those authors who had at once vilified Hatshepsut and revered her, who had both accused her of stealing the throne from her helpless stepson and accepted the narrative that she was unimportant because someone had taken pains to deface her, to wipe her from the royal scrolls. Those authors who created a backstory for this ruler, one that was more fiction than truth in the history books that prevailed, didn't know the real Hatshepsut at all. That meant Chris didn't either. The fire in her eyes told him that this time what he didn't know *could* hurt him.

Chris touched his mother's arm and pulled her back protectively.

The smile on Cecelia's face was anything but pleasant. She opened her mouth to answer, to speak words that would most likely have deafened them with their intensity, but nothing came forth. Instead, a broomstick, slick with gore, protruded from her mouth, reaching toward Chris as his own jaw slacked.

Cecelia went limp, her legs rendered useless as the handle separated her spinal column from her skull. They watched as the broomstick jerked up sharply as though the person wielding it was trying to split Cecelia's head in two through the mouth. And she was: the look on the woman holding the broomstick's face was savage, feral as she slew the monster before her. Her eyes were wild but focused and that was the most terrifying thing of all.

The first attempt at breaking her skull in two was not successful and Tara wanted to try again but she wouldn't get the chance. With a surprised roar, Mal lunged at her, first trying to wrestle the broomstick out of her hand, and then throwing his body into her to knock her away from the woman he loved. Tara fell to the ground, felt her teeth clamp down on her tongue and her mouth fill with blood, but she held onto the broomstick. This is what had to be done. Tara had gone there for revenge and she was damn well going to get it.

Tara's scream pierced the room as she kicked at Mal all the while digging the broomstick into Cecelia's head. Gabby closed her eyes against the blood; she felt her stomach sour and turned away, certain she would vomit. Cecelia's body was limp, dead weight on the end of the stick that Tara was working in circles through her head. She was dead, Doug could see that from where he stood, but her body was animated from the movement like a grotesque marionette on a string. And she was slipping off.

Tara grunted with effort as Cecelia's body slid to the end of the stick, the weight lifting Tara up like she was on a seesaw. She marveled at the inhuman strength that adrenaline could supply and wondered if being dead had anything to do with it, but she didn't have time to think about it for long. Mal was pulling his arm back to strike her and she knew she couldn't withstand a direct hit, not from a man who seemed to have swelled to double his size as the reality of what had happened sank in. But she had done it. That bitch was dead and Tara had gotten the revenge she had been looking for. Now, maybe she could rest. Now, maybe she could die for real.

Tara felt more than heard the crack.

CHAPTER 46

The Hunters heard the scream and stood up en masse. Some had been sleeping, enjoying an unprecedented rest under the stars. But while some had been resting, channeling parts of their pasts that had been out of reach for more years than they could count, others had continued to listen. The words didn't have much meaning to them. Any comprehension of language outside of basic instruction had left them long ago, but tones still made sense, signified intent, warned them of threat.

Something was going on in the master's house.

The Hunter closest to the house approached the steps carefully. They had been told to stay where they were and obedience was paramount in their positions. But still, something was happening, something that threated the master. They could feel it. They could smell anger and fear in the air, the latter a stench they enjoyed very much. But there was more. They had felt it when the other walked by them to enter the house, electricity seeming to outline him, bring a haze to the air around him the way an impending storm rings the moon. There was a power shift happening in there. And there was death.

As the Hunter stepped forward to peer into the dirty glass, its tentacles writhed, leaning closer, trying to feel the energy. It was dark inside. The protective membrane that covered its eye retracted for clearer sight, but they were too deep in the house for it to see anything from where it stood. The pus-filled sacks that floated on its skin rippled as though bubbling. It looked back at the other Hunters that had begun to gather at the mouth of the house, and took a step inside, folding its shoulders forward, concaving its chest so that it could fit. One of its nails, as long as a talon, scratched its arm as it pressed itself inside, letting blood. The suction on its palm latched around it to suckle.

CHAPTER 47

It all happened so fast.

Patrick watched as the woman came from out of nowhere, emerging from some place in the house to attack Cecelia with such a vicious first strike that the woman had surely been dead before the broomstick had broken through her mouth, knocking teeth out to litter the floor. Before he could take a breath Mal was on her, trying to get the woman off of Cecelia as though he could save her, but it was futile. Still he swung at her, knocked her over, used his body to gain the upper hand, but she held fast. And then everything changed.

The crack was deafening but there was no time to process that before the woman had stabbed the jagged end of the broomstick into Mal's eye, Cecelia's blood mingled with Mal's as he staggered backwards. The woman moved with him, pressing the broomstick handle into his head as far as she could even though his thrashing whipped her around, pulled her off her feet. Her aim had been perfect; she had plunged the broken handle of the broom that had killed his long-lost love into his orbital socket, exploding his eyeball as it pushed into his head, into his brain. He flailed arms outstretched as he stumbled, his scream more like a startled wheeze; he was nearly dead on his feet.

Mal reached for purchase. And Patrick knew what he had to do.

Without looking at Doug or Gabby or Chris, afraid that they would read his intentions in his eyes, Patrick lunged forward, clasping Mal's hand. He shouted, with both fear and certainty in his voice,

"I merge with you, Mal. We rule The Realm together."

Because that was the way to end this; Patrick was certain. If The Realm had been opened by Cecelia to punish Mal, if he was the shedding to emerge as co-ruler, it only made sense that if they all died there would be no more curse, no more kingdom... no more Realm. Patrick hoped that meant that Doug and Gabby and Chris could leave, could meet their loved ones in the Heaven they had been taught about. He hoped it meant he had closed the loop and that Autumn and her baby would never, ever know what could have been. He hoped so. And that was all he could do.

Patrick wrapped his arms around Mal and looked at him one last time as the woman released the broomstick and fell to the floor with a thud. He found it difficult to see his own face in such ruin but knew that it had to be that way. He smiled at the dying man, hoping that what he had heard of the true death was real. In close quarters he spoke, the message for Mal's ears only,

"Now we die together."

CHAPTER 48

Gabby vomited on the floor, missing seeing her grandfather grabbing Mal's hand. She turned around in time to see him impaling himself on the blunt end of the broomstick, trying unsuccessfully to cast it into his brain. Once, twice, a ghastly three times she saw him pull back and thrust forward, pressing the handle into his eye, through his eye, to butt up against the next layer. He was exhausted and in pain... and it was unfinished.

Gabby wanted to scream, wanted to stop him from hurting himself, wanted the whole thing to be over, but she didn't have time to do any of those things. The woman who had spilled the blood of two in the room already jumped into action, pressing Patrick's head down onto the broomstick, lodging it deep in his brain.

Later Gabby would recognize it as an act of kindness, but there was no time for reflection, not then, when three bodies lay at their feet... not when the woman was being raised off hers, jerked up toward the ceiling, her body flopping in the air, alive and moving suddenly, like a ragdoll.

A beast unlike anything Gabby had ever seen before held Tara away from the bodies she had slain, regarding the scene. The muscles in its arm rippled with effort, the shape and color of it reminding Gabby of a Komodo dragon standing on two legs. That reference would haunt her forever, the randomness of it at such a time. But it was what she felt and she couldn't wipe the thought out of her head. She was considering that when two things she never would have expected to happen occurred in tandem: the woman closed her eyes, a look of unutterable peace taking over her face and her father issued the beast an order to kill.

CHAPTER 49

Chris remembered the wind.

He remembered the feeling of being sucked up, tumbling, twisting, rolling.

He called out to his mother but she didn't answer.

He looked around himself but didn't see what he expected to. Instead of the house, the bodies, the blood, he saw clouds, white and gray, like an overcast day. And he was part of those clouds, inside them, was one with them.

And then he felt the ground beneath him.

Chris opened eyes he hadn't realized were closed and saw a crowded sidewalk under a sunny sky. He took a step toward them tentatively, unsure if he was really there or just dreaming. Iridescent bodies walked by him keeping pace with each other as they roamed the sidewalk. They were naked, these people, and Chris quickly looked down at himself only to find that he too was nude.

His instinct was to cover himself, indeed called his hands

into to action to do that very thing but stopped when he felt a hand on his shoulder... a touch he would never forget.

"Christopher," Gabby said softly, unadulterated joy dancing in her voice. "He saved us, baby. It's over."

Chris turned to see his mother standing before him, her skin aglow with the same iridescence that the people on the sidewalk had. She was radiant, beautiful in ways that the living world hadn't allowed. He smiled, awestruck.

His grandfather appeared behind her, his gaze on the people on the sidewalk. His father had told him about the glimpse he'd had of this place, but Doug never thought he'd see it for himself. He still couldn't believe they were really there.

"So, this is Arcadia," Doug said, his voice tempered with all the honor the place deserved. "Heaven."

Chris felt his mouth open in surprise.

"We're... we got out?"

Gabby nodded and looped her arm in his.

"Grandpa did it. He saved us."

Gabby grabbed her father's arm as well, knowing that he was suffering. His father's sacrifice was the only reason they were there and Gabby would be forever grateful.

"Autumn? She's—"

"Not here yet. Hopefully not for a long time She's got two little ones to raise." Gabby pointed to a space on the ground that opened to show his sister with a baby strapped to her and another one running just ahead. A boy and a girl. It brought tears to Chris's eyes.

Gabby rubbed his back, knowing the emotion he was feeling all too well. She had felt the same when she found her daughter alive and well only minutes before.

"Asha... Did you see Asha?"

Gabby shook her head, wishing she could have answered

differently. Chris bit his lip and looked to the floor the same way his mother had. He thought of Asha, hoping that was the way to do it, the urgency of finding her stopping him from asking how. He concentrated on her and their house. Nothing. Then he tried thinking of DC, of the places they used to go... the places she loved.

Still nothing.

"I can't—" he whimpered, but didn't finish, still trying to find her but coming up with nothing.

Chris felt his mother's stabilizing hand on the small of his back and took a deep breath. He was afraid to look there, but he had to try.

Chris thought of Egypt.

He saw a cluttered space, people standing close, feet shuffling as they moved out of view. Amorphous shapes in the distance, tall and wide. High ceilings and vast space. Statues blocked off by velvet ropes, glass cases, information placards.

A museum.

Chris tried to scour the crowd looking from high above and homing in as closely as he could go. He was afraid she might have decided to wear a niqab, that only her eyes would be visible, so he tried to get close, close enough to look into them. But when an imam turned around, startled by a presence he couldn't see, Chris pulled back. He had surprised the man somehow, had created a surge of energy that the holy man recognized as supernatural...not of his world. Chris was afraid that the imam might fear the presence of a jinn, one who was in search of someone who could be possessed, and in a place like that, where the artifacts that had once belonged to people who had lived thousands of years before were on display, it wasn't entirely implausible.

He didn't want to scare him.

Chris pulled away, out of the museum, out of Egypt after traversing the Nile and its coastal refuges and coming up empty.

Asha was lost.

"That doesn't mean she's not out there," Doug supplied and Chris nodded, not convinced that it was true. She had desecrated the body of a pharaoh, had performed the physical act herself. What if she had ended up in Hell for it? His breathing quickened as some part of his mind considered what that might look like for the first time. Would he be able to see her if she was there? After everything they had gone through, would they still be separated forever?

Chris looked at the people walking on the sidewalk in Arcadia and realized that they too were walking now, moving among the crowd, doing as they did. He had been in his head, tortured by uncertainty, so he missed the first call.

"Christopher? Is that you, son?"

His father's voice was smooth and rich: familiar. It spoke to his soul.

Chris bounded toward him, seeing him brilliant and invigorated, pushing the memory of the last time he had laid eyes on him—the moment their eyes met as his father was pulled from the hot air balloon—out of his mind forever. They hugged and Chris was happy to feel his father's skin beneath his hands, happy to feel the strength in his embrace again.

"I waited here, hoping against hope that you'd come one day, even if that book said you wouldn't," his father said as he regarded his son, relief etched on his face.

"We made it, Dad. Great-grandpa Patrick saved us," Chris said, allowing himself to feel happiness, to be grateful.

"We?" Chris's father asked and looked beyond his son to see his wife and father-in-law.

Gabby met him on her knees and so did Chris, the line

curving away from them, giving room for the heartfelt reunion. Doug smiled as they embraced, thoughts of his father filling his mind. He wished Patrick could be there to see what he had done, could know what he really meant to them and everyone in his line who would come after. Doug thought about all the things he would say to his father to express that if he could, to make sure there was no more doubt. But he would never get that chance. So, as he watched his family reunite, he did the only thing he could.

"Thank you, Dad," Doug whispered, hoping that somehow, some way his words would find Patrick's ear.

The End

About the Author

L. Marie Wood creates immersive worlds that defy genre as they intersect horror, romance, mystery, thriller, sci-fi, and fantasy elements to weave harrowing tapestries of speculative fiction. She is the recipient of the Golden Stake Award, a MICO Award-winning screenwriter, a two-time Bram Stoker Award® Finalist, a Rhysling nominated poet, and an accomplished essayist. Wood has won over 50 national and international screenplay and film awards. Wood has penned short fiction that has been published in groundbreaking works, including the anthologies *Sycorax's Daughters* and *Slay: Stories of the Vampire Noire*. She is also part of the 2022 Bookfest Book Award winning poetry anthology, *Under Her Skin*.

Her nonfiction has been published in Nightmare Magazine and academic textbooks such as the cross-curricular, *Conjuring Worlds: An Afrofuturist* Textbook. Her papers are archived as part of University of Pittsburgh's Horror Studies Collection. Wood is the founder of the Speculative Fiction Academy, an English and Creative Writing professor, a horror scholar with a Ph.D. in Creative Writing and an MFA in Speculative Fiction, and a frequent contributor to the conversation around the evolution of genre fiction. Learn more about L. Marie Wood at www.l-mariewood.com.

THE
BLACK
HOLE
[The Black Hole] is a pulse-pounding journey into a real-life
nightmare." – Midwest Book Review
L. MARIE WOOD

About Horror:
The Study and Craft

TELECOMMUTING

L. MARIE WOOD

OPTIONED FOR FILM
THE
REALM
THE REALM TRILOGY BOOK 1
BRAM STOKER AWARD® FINALIST AND GOLDEN STAKE
AWARD-WINNING AUTHOR
L. MARIE WOOD